Champions of Time

Books in the *After Cilmeri* Series

Daughter of Time (prequel)
Footsteps in Time (Book One)
Winds of Time
Prince of Time (Book Two)
Crossroads in Time (Book Three)
Children of Time (Book Four)
Exiles in Time
Castaways in Time
Ashes of Time
Warden of Time
Guardians of Time
Masters of Time
Outpost in Time
Shades of Time
Champions of Time
Refuge in Time
Unbroken in Time

This Small Corner of Time:
The After Cilmeri Series Companion

A Novel from the *After Cilmeri* Series

Champions of Time

by

Sarah Woodbury

Champions of Time

www.sarahwoodbury.com

To my Carew

Dearest Reader:

While many of you will have a better recollection of the events of the previous books than I do, some readers might be joining us only now (note, if that's you, you might consider starting with the prequel to this series, *Daughter of Time*, which is *free* in ebook at all retailers! https://www.books2read.com/daughteroftime) or be struggling to recall some key events from the previous books. If that's you, read on!

The *After Cilmeri* series begins with Meg, a young, troubled modern American widow, who, at a moment of catastrophic danger, falls through time and into the life of Llywelyn ap Gruffydd, the last Prince of Wales. A strong and charismatic leader, he saves her, and she in turn saves him, thanks to her knowledge of future events. Although powerful forces seek to divide them, by working together, Meg and Llywelyn navigate the dangerous and shifting alliances that constantly undermine his rule and threaten the very existence of Wales.

But before they can create a future which avoids Llywelyn's predetermined death at Cilmeri, Meg is ripped from his world and returned to her own—in time to give birth to their son, David.

In *Footsteps in Time,* David and his older sister, Anna, as teenagers, return to the Middle Ages to save Llywelyn yet again. As Meg warned him they would, Norman lords have lured him into the fateful ambush at Cilmeri in eastern Wales. Without warning, David and Anna are thrown into a world they do not understand, among a people whose language and customs are totally unfamiliar. Ultimately, David is recognized as Llywelyn's true son, and he and Anna begin to make a life for themselves in the Middle Ages, culminating with David's crowning as King of England (*Children of Time).*

Over the course of fourteen books, it becomes clear that the medieval world is actually an alternate universe, and Meg, Anna, and David (and ultimately his son, Arthur) time travel when their lives are in danger. In the process, many new characters, both medieval and modern, are introduced. These include Math, a distant relation of Llywelyn, who marries Anna (*Footsteps in Time*); Ieuan, David's captain, who travels with him to the modern world, also known as *The Land of Madoc* or *Avalon* (*Prince of Time*); and Lili, Ieuan's sister, who becomes David's wife (*Crossroads in Time*).

From the modern world comes Bronwen, an anthropology graduate student who marries Ieuan; Callum, an MI-5 agent suffering from PTSD, who attempts to prevent Meg and Llywelyn from returning to their world (*Children of Time*); Cassie, a Native American woman, who was plucked from the mountains of Oregon in the wake of Meg's plane crash (*Winds of Time*) and must survive on her own in medieval Scotland (*Exiles in Time*); a busload of twenty-firsters, who make the mistake of traveling on the same bus as Meg and Anna and end up in their alternate universe (*Ashes of Time*); Meg's family, including Christopher, David's cousin (*Masters of Time* and *Shades of Time*), and three twenty-firsters, George, Andre, and Sophie, who work for David's new ally, Chad Treadman.

All the while, the combined efforts of Anna, David, and their family and friends are transforming the medieval world. Not everyone appreciates the burgeoning equality, universal education, and democracy, however, and throughout the books, the twenty-firsters face threats both from outside their inner circle and from within it.

Champions of Time picks up where *Shades of Time* and *Outpost in Time* left off.

Cast of Characters

Anna—Time traveler, Princess of Wales
Math (Mathonwy)—Lord of Dinas Bran, Anna's husband
David (Dafydd)—Time traveler, King of England, Anna's brother
Lili—David's wife, Queen of England
Llywelyn—David and Anna's father, King of Wales
Meg—Time traveler, David and Anna's mother, Queen of Wales
Christopher Shepherd–Time traveler, David and Anna's cousin
Callum—Time traveler, Earl of Shrewsbury
Bronwen—Time traveler, Ieuan's wife
Ieuan—Lili's brother, Bronwen's husband

Mark Jones—Time traveler, MI-5 agent
Livia Cross—MI-5 agent
Chad Treadman—Avalonian mogul
Andre—Time Traveler, Chad Treadman's employee
George—Time Traveler, Chad Treadman's employee
Sophie—Time Traveler, Chad Treadman's employee

Humphrey de Bohun—Earl of Hereford, Constable of England
Edmund Mortimer—Earl of the March
Roger Mortimer—Edmund's brother
John Balliol—King of Scots
Robert FitzWalter—Lord of Beeston Castle
Matha O'Reilly—Irish ambassador
Samuel—Callum's companion
Bevyn—David's companion
Venny—one of David's soldiers
Constance—Lili's bodyguard
Cador—Archer, Constance's husband
Hugh—Venny's father
Rhys—one of Math's soldiers
Mathew—Venny's friend

1

Dinas Bran
24 March 1294
David

David stepped into Dinas Bran's receiving room and immediately came to a dead halt as the various members of his family who were present looked at him. "Uh oh. This looks like trouble."

Mom patted the chair next to her. "No trouble at all—or at least, not more than you already knew about."

"So why are you all looking at me?"

Anna picked up one of the balls of yarn Bronwen was crocheting into a hat for Catrin and threw it at his chest. It bounced off and hit the floor. "Because you walked into the room, silly."

He tossed the yarn back to Bronwen, who caught it, and then sat in the chair his mother had indicated. "I don't believe you."

There was a pause as the various members of David's family—Dad, Mom, Anna, Math, Bronwen, and Ieuan—looked at each other, silently communicating in some fashion that resulted in Mom turning to speak to him again. "You're right. We were talking about you."

"Specifically, you becoming King of Scots," Anna said.

"I knew it." David slapped his hand on the table. "The answer is no. Besides, any idea of me claiming that throne is premature. While its current occupant has invaded England with an army, at the moment he still wears the crown. John Balliol was elected democratically. I don't have the power to dethrone him."

"You do, actually," Anna said.

David didn't know what it was about her latest trip to Avalon that had done it, but in the few days since she'd returned, it was as if the real Anna had been unleashed. She said what she thought more than ever without worrying about anyone's sensibilities. He was willing to bet quite a large portion of his treasury that it was she who'd called this meeting.

Mom shot her daughter a quelling look. "Regardless of what happens over the next weeks and months, Balliol incited a rebellion against you. You can't let him keep his throne."

Anna nodded. "Give us a chance to explain. We need you to listen to Mom."

David's father had been the first to push David to take England's crown, and while he'd accepted the mantle out of a sense of desperation, he wasn't sorry about being King of England now. Similarly, the High Kingship of Ireland had been thrust upon him by events that had careened out of control. And as his father's eldest son, he was the heir to the Kingdom of Wales. He would accept that crown because, if it was anyone's birthright, it was his.

Scotland was another matter entirely. It had a long tradition of choosing its own rulers, and David's claim to sovereignty there was beyond tenuous. The fact that, according to Uncle Ted, he did have a blood descent from Avalon's King Alexander was beside the point. This was Earth Two, so that connection meant nothing.

But because it was Anna who'd spoken, David held back a further retort. She was certainly right that something had to be done. Some had hoped that Balliol would fold his tents, apologize for conniving with wayward English barons, and fall back into Scotland from his current position at Barnard Castle, his family's seat in the north of England. David had not been one of those optimists. Balliol would not be able to stand the resulting loss of face.

Thus, with as studious an expression as he could muster, David prepared himself to be lectured. His mother usually knew what she was talking about.

"In the past, English kings have aspired to the thrones of all four countries: Wales, England, Ireland, and Scotland, either by force of arms or by claiming the right through a fictive or mythic past."

"Sometimes dating back to Rome," Bronwen said, "but always including King Arthur."

"Who was Welsh anyway," Anna said.

The three women were on a roll, but Mom made a gesture, asking not to be interrupted. David had no doubt they'd discussed what they were talking about at length before he'd arrived.

"In Avalon's Middle Ages, which is really the only time we care about at this point, King Edward came the closest to achieving the goal of uniting all four kingdoms. Once he conquered Wales, he allowed his barons to pursue absolute power in Ireland while he moved on to Scotland."

"The last thing I want to do is follow in King Edward's footsteps—"

His mom put out a hand to him. "We know that, David, and we're not proposing anything along the lines of what Edward attempted—or any other English king, for that matter, up to and including present-day Avalon."

"Then I really don't understand. Why the history lesson?" David narrowed his eyes at his mother. "I thought you just suggested I become King of Scots?"

Mom gave a vigorous shake of her head. "We did. We do, but not for the reasons you think or the way you think. The kings of England who had designs on ruling all four nations rooted their right to do so in the fact that each of them was the *King of England*. We're not proposing that at all."

"In fact, quite the opposite," Bronwen said.

David sat back in his chair. "You have completely lost me."

He noted that Ieuan and Math weren't looking at him—and he knew why. It wasn't because they were as confused as he was. They agreed wholeheartedly with where the women were going with their argument and saw no reason to interfere.

Anna leaned forward. "We are proposing that you do—we do—what you've always done: include people instead of exclude them. King Edward conquered Wales, Ireland, and Scotland and ruled them as the English king, from England, with the idea that English culture and laws were superior to any tradition in the barbaric north and west."

"I could never do that."

"Of course you couldn't. And we couldn't support the idea—" Bronwen was practically bouncing up and down in her seat, "—which is what is so great. This is the chance we've been waiting for. We talked about it years ago at Rhuddlan before Anna and Meg went to Avalon."

David took in a breath, and his heart actually beat a little faster. "You're talking about the United States of Britain."

"With you as High King." Before David could protest at her choice of title, Bronwen put out a hand to him like both Mom and Anna had done. "For now."

Mom took over again. "This wouldn't be a situation where Wales, Ireland, and Scotland were subordinate to the English throne, and everyone had to become English, speak English, and abide by English laws. It would be a confederation, with each country having equal say, but united out of an acknowledgment that all the countries that make up Britain share a common future."

Anna nodded vigorously. "Here's your challenge and our dream, David: to leverage your unique position into a meaningful monarchy of the whole of Britain, one that doesn't make everyone English, but makes room for everyone."

David ran both hands through his hair and dropped them. "I agree with everything you're saying. Of course I do. I want what you want. But it's overstepping. How can we create unity out of something that will so plainly cause disunity?"

"Who's to say it will?" Anna said, and then at David's baleful look, modified her question. "Yes, of course not everyone is going to like it. But seeing as how you're already King of England, High King of Ireland, and Prince of Wales, are any of the people in those countries really going to argue with what we're proposing? If the people of Scotland accept the idea, would that be convincing enough?"

David looked around at the rest of his family. "All right, gentlemen. You need to tell me what you think. Ieuan? Or you, Math? Dad? You've been awfully quiet."

Ieuan laughed. "As you'd undoubtedly guessed already, Math and I are of one mind and have been for some time. Rule Scotland as the King of England or as High King or as—" he made a dismissive gesture, "—president if you must. As long as you rule, we don't care how or why."

Bronwen patted her husband's thigh. "Some people are less concerned with theory than with practice."

"I see Bohun and Mortimer aren't here either. Nor Lili." David had left his wife bathing their sons.

"They don't care about the specifics of rule either, though for different reasons. Bohun and Mortimer are Norman and know only power and the ability and willingness to wield it." Math looked hard at David. "I have been at your side for twelve years now, and I barely comprehend what my own wife is telling me. If it weren't she saying it—and clearly of so much importance to all of you—I would probably have dismissed it out of hand as a finer point that means nothing in the end."

"But we have come to understand that it means everything in the end—not just to you but to all of us," Dad said, speaking for the first time. "When you insisted that I welcome the Jews into Wales, I agreed. But it was more to show you that I respected your ability to make decisions than because I understood your reasons. I understand them now." He looked around the table. "We all do, now."

Then he focused again on David. "Take the throne of the High King, son. Britain—and the world—will be better for it."

2

Chester Castle

1 April 1294

William de Bohun

"Bohun! Get a move on! It's nearly dawn!" The not-so-dulcet tones of his friend Christopher shouting at him from the corridor roused William from a deep sleep.

He blinked his eyes and lifted his head, disoriented about where he was, though the feeling dissipated immediately when he recognized the room in the guest house he shared with the other young men at Chester Castle.

"I'm coming! I'm coming!" He grumbled the words, annoyed at himself for waking late but also at Christopher for waking him. He'd been dreaming about Aine, a girl he'd met in Ireland. He hoped he would see her again, but right now this blasted rebellion was interfering.

The door flew open to reveal Christopher, fully dressed but not yet wearing his armor or sword.

Huw, the tallest of the three, bobbed up and down behind him. "King Dafydd has been asking for you."

That got William to his feet like nothing else could have. Excitement was building in his chest, not just at the summons from the king, but also at what today would bring. This was the morning of mornings. They were finally moving out, and he was thankful his friends wouldn't consider leaving him behind. The plan today was to begin the march across England as the latest step in showing the world that David was not only alive but willing to fight for his throne and his country. William himself was long past the point of admitting that he would follow David anywhere. If that meant more battle, then he would be right beside the king when it happened. He wasn't David's squire anymore, but a squire of the king never quite gave up the job.

"Where's the king?"

"On the wall-walk." Christopher gestured to Huw. "We've already had our talking to. We've been waiting for you."

"What kind of talking to?" William wracked his brains for some reason he might have garnered the king's displeasure, but couldn't come up with anything recent.

"You'll see." Huw sounded pretty cheerful about the coming chastisement.

And since whatever William could have done wrong had been done by his friends too, his stomach settled enough for him to realize he was hungry.

While for men like King David or William's father, the last two weeks had been a blur of preparation for war, William and his friends had been given little of importance to do. After the battle of

Tara, all three of them (four with Robbie Bruce, who'd gone with James Stewart to Scotland) were knights now, but their elevation hadn't noticeably changed their status or routine. The three of them had whiled away the hours in training, as they had most of this past year, or leading scouting parties from Chester, which was a good-sized town, refortified by King David after the death of the Earl of Chester ten years ago.

While his friends went down the stairwell, William made his way to the doorway at the end of the corridor that led to the curtain wall. The news that King David was on the wall-walk was in no way a surprise, especially on a day that had dawned clear, and they could see for miles. If the king wasn't in his quarters or the hall, he was usually to be found on the ramparts, often walking with Arthur, or Alexander when he was fussy.

David was without his sons today. He stood with bared head, though in cloak and boots, facing away from the rising sun, his hands resting on the stones of two adjacent merlons. Chester Castle stretched a hundred yards along the River Dee, taking up a dominant position in one corner of the town of Chester.

William's room was in the guest house, a large stone building built into the western curtain wall, putting the wall-walk some thirty feet above the level of the bailey. Below him on the other side of the wall was the moat with its connection to the sea, one of the many improvements that David had made since taking over the castle.

To William's right, the bailey teemed with men and horses and, on second glance, wasn't quite as chaotic as it had first appeared. Ieuan, who was in charge of the king's men, wouldn't tolerate anything but an ordered muster. Besides, most of the soldiers who'd come at David's call had been camped in the fields around the town, not inside the castle itself, and most of them had started their march at first light, under the command of their captains and minor lords from whose domains they'd come.

"You asked to see me, my lord?"

"I did." David turned to him, and William was relieved to see the benevolent expression on his face. The king was feeling good today too.

So William risked a query. "Did I do something wrong?"

David laughed. "Not unless there's something I don't know about—"

"I'll see you in hell!" The shout echoed in the still morning air, heard clearly above the movement of men and horses below them.

William turned his head towards the opposite battlement from which the shout had come and was forced to put up a hand to keep the newly risen sun's light from blinding him. He could barely make out the figure on the opposite wall-walk a hundred feet away, but the silhouette appeared to be that of a crossbowman.

The realization that the king's life was in danger came over William like someone had thrown a bucket of cold water over his head. At the same instant that the crossbowman released his bolt, William shouted, "Get down!" and launched himself towards David, his only thought to shield him from the bolt as best he could. But David was already moving too, reaching for William and trying to move *him* out of the way in order to take the missile himself.

The crossbow bolt ripped across the bailey.

Pain exploded in William's side.

And the world went dark.

One ... two ... three ...

3

1 April 1294

Sophie

The first volley of arrows came from men on Chester's highest towers. Up until that moment, these men had been facing outward, watching for an approaching enemy army. Everyone in the bailey had heard the assassin's shout, but in the single moment between his shout and when he released the bolt few were able to process what was happening.

These guards were constantly prepared for danger, however, and were the quickest on the uptake. Certainly quicker than Sophie had been, not that she could have done anything constructive by way of a response. She and Bronwen had been talking together in the shadow of the keep. They'd watched the events unfold, but so quickly there'd hardly been time for two breaths.

But in the five seconds it took, first to register that the crossbowman had actually shot a bolt at David, and then to reach for bow and arrow, the would-be assassin dropped his weapon and flung himself through the crenel behind him.

Even Morgan, David's chief archer, who was among those in the muster in the bailey, could do nothing. Nobody had noticed the assassin before he shot, and even if Morgan had marked him, his bow had been tucked into its rest alongside his saddle.

"No! No! No!" The disappearance of the crossbowman released Bronwen, and she ran for the stairway up to the wall-walk from which David had disappeared, hiking up her skirts to take the stairs two at a time.

A host of men, Morgan and Bevyn among them, ran for the wall-walk opposite, from which the crossbowman had escaped. Even as Sophie mounted the stairway after Bronwen, she glanced over her shoulder and saw Morgan pointing to other soldiers, telling them to go around the outside of the castle, something they could accomplish either by slipping through the postern gate or going through the town. Men moved to do his bidding. With so many prepared to travel this morning, they had more than enough men for any kind of pursuit.

The two women arrived at the top of the stairway a half-second before Samuel, Callum's friend, who'd come out of a nearby tower, all of them pulling up short at a spot halfway along the rampart. A crossbow bolt, bloody along its full length, lay on the stones of the wall-walk.

Samuel reached down and picked up the bolt to hold it gingerly in his fingers, which came away bloody. "How-what-what just happened?"

Callum came to a halt behind him, and Sophie was sure she'd never seen such a grim look on any man's face. Samuel may not have seen the events unfold, but Callum had been standing at the far end of the wall-walk, as was his habit, as a kind of guard for David. He held a gun loosely in his hand, but now he wordlessly reached to the small of his back and holstered the weapon unfired. He had arrived back at Chester only last night, having spent the last ten days in Shrewsbury, marshaling his portion of the army, as the Earl of Shrewsbury.

Sophie knew medieval weaponry. She'd learned something of it in the months of research about the Middle Ages she'd put in as part of the preparations Chad had made for the eventual arrival in Avalon of someone from Ted's family. When she'd told Anna on the plane that she wanted to go to the Middle Ages, that it was part of her job, and that she'd prepared for it, she had been completely serious. Neither she—nor Chad Treadman—ever did anything by halves.

So she knew a modern crossbow could fire a four-hundred-grain bolt at four hundred feet per second, achieving a kinetic energy of a hundred and twenty-four pounds at thirty yards, which was roughly the distance across the bailey. Even at half that weight and power, this crossbow bolt would have been unstoppable in the time between when the crossbowman fired it and when it hit William.

Only William, it seemed, could move faster, and Sophie thought it likely that his movement to protect David had started out of instinct before the bolt was fired, like a striker in cricket who was already swinging before the bowler released the ball.

By comparison, the crossbowman had moved much more slowly, but even he had wasted no time getting away. On the opposite wall-walk, one of the guards held up a hook and rope that had been anchored to the corner of the crenel. Morgan, meanwhile, bow in hand, was loosing arrows one after another over the other side of the wall. Sophie was pretty sure the only way out of Chester for the assailant from that part of the wall-walk was to swim the moat, which he could be doing now under fire.

Callum called across the bailey, "Don't kill him!"

Morgan didn't respond to the order, but Bevyn, who stood beside him, cupped his hands around his mouth to answer. "He has already hit him in the calf as he was coming up the bank on the other side. He's across the moat, but he won't get far."

"This is impossible." Callum took a moment to lean through a nearby crenel and then pulled out.

Sophie had already looked down to the ground on their side of the castle. While the medieval Chester Castle looked very different from the modern one she'd explored with friends several years ago, there was still nothing to see. All the vegetation on the slope had been cleared as a security measure, to prevent anyone from sneaking over the castle wall once they made it through the moat, and she could see plainly that David's body wasn't floating in the water.

She let out a breath. "How worried are we?"

It was a genuine question. Her experience with time travel and the medieval world was far less than the others'. Though she'd heard all the stories, read all the files, and time-traveled herself, she'd never experienced anything like this. Anyone could see that neither David nor William was here, which meant they'd gone to Avalon.

"Better in Avalon than dead," Callum said.

Bronwen had her arms wrapped around her waist. "I keep looking around, expecting him to appear at any moment."

"How did the assassin get inside the castle?" Samuel said. "He couldn't have climbed in the same way he escaped. Someone would have seen him!"

Ieuan arrived on the wall-walk, puffing to a halt behind Sophie. "I hate to say it, but the bowman was clever enough to have a plan he stuck to. He didn't waste time talking about what he was going to do but saw his target and shot."

"He shouldn't have shouted at all," Callum said, "but maybe he wanted to see David's face when he killed him."

Ieuan barked a laugh. "You mean he's an honorable villain, who couldn't bring himself to shoot Dafydd in the back?" He put his arm around Bronwen and pulled her to him.

His wife shook her head. "I don't understand how this could happen."

"We'll discover that too." Ieuan meant to be comforting, but unlike Callum's grimness, he looked worried. "I'm in charge of the men. That the assassin got inside Chester Castle is my fault."

"That's not what I meant." Bronwen made a despairing gesture towards the bolt in Samuel's hand. "What I really want to know is *how did this work*?"

Callum took the bolt from Samuel and fingered the deadly point. "I'm with Bronwen. Why did the bolt remain behind?"

"Dafydd's life was in danger." Ieuan seemed the most philosophical about what he'd seen. "Didn't something similar happen back at Dover when Dafydd fell off the wall with Lee? He fell, traveled to Avalon, was almost shot, and traveled back, all in the blink of an eye and was never actually injured himself?"

Callum let out a breath. "We can only hope. He hadn't yet put on his armor this morning. He was wearing his Kevlar vest, but—" he shook his head, "—unlike a bullet, a bolt has a non-deforming steel point. At this range, the Kevlar might not even have slowed it down. Maybe if the bolt hit the ceramic plate above David's heart it would have stopped it, but who's to say that's where it was aimed."

Bronwen looked to be near tears. "You mean it went right through him." She spoke dully and turned her face into Ieuan's shoulder.

"Or he traveled before it could." Ieuan put both arms around her now. "The blood may just be from William." He kissed the top of Bronwen's head. "We have no way to know. Not until Dafydd returns."

Samuel took the bolt back from Callum. "We must face the fact, however, that William is seriously wounded, if not dead."

"I don't look forward to telling that to his father," Ieuan said.

"William isn't dead." Callum's face became slightly less grim and took on a contemplative look. "It went through him without sticking, which means it pierced only tissue."

"That's not making me feel better," Bronwen said.

Somewhat tentatively, Sophie put up a hand to get everyone's attention. "Chad will be waiting for David."

She could fully admit to herself that she'd bought into David's mystique long before she'd arrived in Avalon, and the man himself had done nothing to disappoint her. He'd been wearing a crown when he'd greeted the plane in Ireland, but he appeared every inch a king without it. She remembered what Anna had said about him always being treated like a kid when he went to Avalon, but even not knowing him beyond the superficial conversations they'd had so far, she didn't think he'd find himself so much at a disadvantage this time.

For her part, the medieval world was everything and nothing like she'd imagined. Bronwen and Mark Jones had assured her that she would find her feet, but she felt so far out of her depth that the bottom was a hundred feet down with no hope of ever touching. In a way, losing David and William a moment ago was just one more mad event in a world gone mad.

Not knowing the direction Sophie's thoughts had taken, Bronwen nodded. "I'm still reluctant to trust, but I'm not sorry that David has Chad—glad of it, in fact. He'll call him as soon as he can—and get back to us as soon as he can. He knows the urgency." After a quick glance into the bailey, she made a motion with her arm and headed along the wall-walk to the guesthouse doorway from which William had arrived on the battlement hardly twenty minutes ago.

"We'd better get off the wall-walk. We're too much of a spectacle up here."

They reached the doorway at the same moment that Lili opened it. David's wife was looking stricken, sad, and determined all at the same time. Bronwen embraced her, and there was a moment when the rest stood awkwardly in a line behind them.

Lili released her sister-in-law and wiped at her cheeks with the backs of her hands. Then she gestured everyone inside. Now, instead of standing on the wall-walk so everyone could see them, they clustered together in a narrow hallway. Constance, Lili's bodyguard, stood a respectful distance away at the top of the stairwell.

Quickly Ieuan filled his sister in on what they knew so far, which admittedly wasn't much. Lili took the bolt and held it up to the light of the lantern hanging from a hook on the wall. By now, the blood was streaked and drying.

"It's from Chester's armory," Ieuan said flatly. "Englishmen employ crossbows, and it was among the stockpile intended for the garrison's use."

"That means the crossbowman blended in well enough here to get to it." Lili sighed. "Is it really someone we know? None of you recognized him?"

"I never managed a good look," Ieuan said, "but whoever it is, we'll find out soon. Morgan was shooting at him, and Bevyn said they could see the direction he was taking. He won't get away. Even had he escaped into the town, not a soul would aid him."

Lili straightened her shoulders. Between one second and the next, she transformed herself from grieving wife to Queen of England. While David had taken the throne reluctantly, Lili had been even more reluctant than her husband. But she'd accepted the mantle anyway and had lived within it for the last five years.

Standing before them now, her hands on her hips, Lili didn't spend any more time on tears. "I need your thoughts. How do we move forward? Without Dafydd, how much of our plan can survive?"

"The army is already marching, and we know how it must be used." Ieuan turned to Callum. "Have we heard from Math?"

"I spoke with him this morning. He will meet us at Beeston." Their conversation would have taken place through their telecommunications network that linked David's major castles.

"I thought he wasn't coming?" Last Sophie had heard, David and his father had decided that he and Math should remain in Wales, held in reserve in case the fighting went badly. This was an English rebellion, and including Welsh forces sent the wrong message to both the English people and the Scots. For that reason, David had also moved his command center from Dinas Bran to Chester, to highlight the fact that this was an English rebellion and he was England's king.

"Dafydd changed his mind." Lili shook her head. "He claims to have nothing of the Sight, but sometimes I wonder ..."

"Math can stand in for Dafydd better than I can," Callum said.

"Or I. I lead the men, but they all know that I'm merely the go-between." Ieuan made this comment entirely without resentment.

"I have a couple of ideas, actually." Sophie raised her hand again, like she was in school, and then dropped it when everyone looked at her.

Lili spread her hands wide. "We're listening. Just say it. Everyone outside is still in shock, but in another minute they'll start to feel lost without Dafydd to lead them. They were just getting used to having him back. I need to speak to them soon, and I need a clear idea of what to say and what we are going to do next."

"David was going to parade across England to show everyone he's alive, but it wasn't really necessary, right?" The words tumbled out of Sophie's mouth. "Everyone knows by now that the plot in Ireland failed. David went to Warenne, who surrendered. All the men have seen him, and word has spread."

John de Warenne had predicated his rebellion on the supposed fact of David's death. When David had ridden to Lyons Castle to confront him, Warenne had come out alone, with bared head, and bent a knee in the middle of his drawbridge. David had accepted his obeisance, his offer of payment, and his castle. He'd instructed Warenne to lead his army against Beeston, and that's where he now sat with Humphrey de Bohun and Edmund Mortimer, who'd insisted that if anyone was going to take down his brother, it would be he. Even now, their army of nearly five hundred men was camped around the massive plateau upon which Beeston Castle sat.

There were nods all around, so Sophie barely paused to draw breath. "That means we should divide the army now. Those who've just left Chester should be diverted to Barnard Castle and Balliol.

They aren't necessary for the taking of Beeston anyway, not with the weapons we have. Those of us who go to Beeston can simply tell everyone there that David went to Barnard, and those who go to Barnard can tell everyone that David stopped at Beeston."

"Lie, you mean," Ieuan said, though she didn't get the sense his words were an implied criticism, just a point of clarification.

Sophie shrugged. "If you like, but communication being what it is, you have no idea where David is. He could have turned around straight away and come back, and you wouldn't know it until he showed up. Once you separate the two forces, neither will know anything at all for certain."

Callum laughed. "I like it. It's clear-eyed. And with Math's forces coming to Beeston, we'll have more than enough men there to do what needs to be done."

"Would David agree?" Samuel asked.

Lili said gently, "He's not here. None of us can operate on what we *think* Dafydd might do or say in our place. Without him, it is up to us to act in his stead as we think best."

"Though I've obviously only known him for days instead of years, David isn't the same boy who arrived here to save Llywelyn, or even the man who was crowned King of England five years ago," Sophie said. "He is as capable as anyone of being clear-eyed and calculating."

Lili laughed lightly. "It's true that my husband can be quite unpredictable."

"Besides, you all realize what just happened, right?" Bronwen said. "He—and we—are part of a greater plan. The fact that we know it but don't understand it doesn't change the fact that a plan exists."

Bronwen's idea was the one part of the universe shifting with which Sophie struggled most. Still, she couldn't argue with what she'd seen with her own eyes.

Lili raised both hands and dropped them. "Regardless of the hows and whys, we are left to pick up the pieces, and it does us no good to be standing around while there's work to be done. I will speak to our people now." She headed for the door that would take her back to the wall-walk.

"Tell them all is well, and Dafydd has gone to Avalon, and that he'll be back," Ieuan called. And then, after a nod from Callum, went after her. Ieuan left the door open, so Sophie could see him raising his hands to the people below, telling them to quiet so Lili could speak.

"Right." Callum made an expansive gesture, indicating everyone who was left in the corridor should huddle closer. "Sophie is absolutely correct. There's no better way to show how unconcerned we are about David's absence then to take Beeston Castle as we planned. With or without David's physical presence, Roger Mortimer's defiance cannot be allowed to continue for even one more day."

4

1 April 2022

David

They dropped three inches, landing with hardly a thud onto thick, wet grass, but even so, William's weight caused David to stagger. He clutched his friend to him, afraid he was going to slide right out of his arms.

Once David regained his balance, he didn't waste time lamenting his arrival in Avalon but immediately laid William full length on the ground, unhooked the toggle on William's cloak so the fabric had more give to it, and wadded up a handful of the cloth so he could stanch the flow of blood from William's wound. The bolt had pierced William's underarm at something of an angle and passed through the muscle back to front.

A weightlifter would have more tissue in that area, but William was somewhat less large, even though as a knight he was very well muscled. It was a wound David had never seen before, and indicated that William had thrown up his arm and been twisting forward in an attempt to save David when the bolt had entered his flesh at the back, grazed his ribs, and come out the other side. He had blood staining the whole right side of his body from armpit to hip.

It didn't matter how it had happened, only that it had. David pressed hard on the wound, trying desperately to stem the bleeding. The only saving grace was that the hole was in about as safe a place as it was possible to be shot and not have it be fatal. William *was* losing a lot of blood, however, which if it went on much longer would be.

"Help!" David looked around. "My friend needs an ambulance!"

When they'd first come in, David had seen over William's shoulder that upwards of a hundred people were sharing the field with them, but they'd been a football field away at the time, with archery butts between them and him. While these were out of place anywhere in Avalon David had ever been, he could recognize an archery tournament when he saw one.

Thankfully, by now a dozen or more had begun to walk towards them. They appeared somewhat wary, however, and David would have waved at them to hurry if he wasn't already using both hands to staunch the flow of blood from William's wound.

Then William groaned, and David looked into his face. "Hang in there, my friend. You're going to be okay."

"I feel terrible."

"I'm not surprised, since you have a new hole in your body where there isn't supposed to be one. What were you thinking?"

"I was thinking that your life was worth more than mine."

David tsked through his teeth. “Tell that to your father.” His words came out angry, but he didn’t mean to be angry at William. It was more that he was angry at himself for being caught off-guard *again*. So he added, “Thank you, by the way. It isn’t possible to thank you enough.”

William took in a trembling breath. “You tried to push me aside and take the bolt yourself. You—you weren’t looking to die, were you?”

David could hear the horror and fear in his voice. In the past there had certainly been days when David had been overwhelmed by his responsibilities, seeing them primarily as a burden, but he’d never been so far gone as to hurt himself on purpose.

“No,” he said simply. “I knew if I was shot, I’d come here.”

“Here?”

“We’re in Avalon, William.”

But William had closed his eyes, and he made no response, which he would have done if he’d heard him. David didn’t bother to repeat his words. William didn’t need to understand just yet how unnecessary his sacrifice had been. David couldn’t die if he wanted to. The fact that they were in Avalon yet again proved it.

That wasn’t to say that David at all understood what had happened. Within the space of a single second, the crossbowman had fired his bolt, William had thrown himself at David, and David had tried to stop William from sacrificing himself by moving him out of the way. The next second, they were overcome by the darkness that heralded their arrival in Avalon.

David could get his head around that much. The problem was that he had no real sense of *how* they'd traveled. He hadn't fallen off the rampart as he had in the past. It wasn't as if he'd just wrecked a car. He looked down at his chest. The crossbow bolt should have been sticking out of it, but while he was covered in blood, all of it seemed to be William's. David could only conclude that before the bolt could hit him it had de-materialized.

Or rather, he and William had.

"I didn't see them there! I swear it!" Members of the crowd had finally arrived, and the first man to reach them was a few inches shorter than David, more stocky, and spoke English with a Welsh accent. He held a bow, wore a quiver on his back, and was otherwise dressed from head to toe in medieval gear. "Oh my God! Oh my God! I killed him!"

If the parking lot in the distance wasn't enough to tell him he was in the modern world, he would have known it by the man's choice of words. Not even hardened knights cursed as easily as modern people. Though, really, knights were the least likely to take the name of the Lord in vain since they were also some of the most superstitious men David knew.

David tried to reassure the archer. "You didn't, really."

But before he could explain, a second person, a large man in his mid-fifties, huffed up. "What in the *hell* are you doing back here! Where did you come from? We had this whole area blocked off."

"I-I—" David didn't have the wherewithal to answer, but it wasn't necessary since the question had been rhetorical, and the man didn't wait to hear his explanation. He turned exasperatedly to a young woman about David's age, who was also wearing a bow and quiver. She was gaping down at William with her hand to her mouth. "I know you still have your phone on you, despite the rules. Call an ambulance."

The woman's mouth closed with a snap, and she hastily dug into a pocket in her breeches, came up with a big screen smartphone, and started poking at the screen with one finger. David had a flash of satisfaction that he knew about phones now because of Anna and Mark, but then he returned his attention to William. Though his former squire was breathing easily, implying that the bolt hadn't gone through anything important, he'd lost a lot of blood by now, and his eyes were fluttering. David told himself that as long as William breathed, there was hope.

"An ambulance is on its way," the woman said.

Beyond the field, to the west, which David could tell by the direction of the light, sat a truncated castle that he'd noticed first thing and knew didn't exist in his world. To the south lay a parking lot full of cars, then a body of water, and beyond that were gray clouds and green hills.

With a profound sense of relief, David recognized where he was: Gray skies? Check. Wet grass? Check. Cloud-covered mountains? Check. They were on Anglesey, the body of water was the Menai Strait, and the nearby castle was Beaumaris, which lay across the Strait from his father's palace at Aber.

What's more, it was clear now that the people running towards them had been participating in a twenty-first century medieval festival. It seemed he and William had dropped into the center of nerddom in Wales. Whatever power had brought him to Avalon had made him appear at the right place at the right time, in a place where his clothing and the wound in William's side could be explained with a minimum of fuss.

William regained consciousness enough to grip David's wrist above the hand that pressed against chest. "It hurts." He closed his eyes against the pain.

"I know. Keep your eyes open."

"I can't." He paused, his eyes fluttering a bit again. "My lord, I don't want to."

For once, David wasn't sure if William was speaking to him or actually to God.

"What-what happened to the arrow?" This man was the fourth to speak and was distinguishable from the others by his jester's costume. He also had bright red hair and freckles. By now, a dozen people had gathered around David and William.

"In the woods, most likely," the burly older man said. "Billy always was a crap shot."

Billy, the first man to arrive, fell to his knees near William's head. "I'm so sorry. What can I do?"

David looked him up and down, feeling guilty about misleading everyone about the source of William's wound. While he could accept the gift of his present location, he wasn't going to let an innocent person suffer because of it. “I need to tell you straight out that it wasn’t your arrow that went through William.”

“What do you mean? Nobody else was shooting.”

“I know. I can’t explain what happened right now, but if I were you, I’d find your arrow. It will prove to anyone who asks that this isn’t your fault. It won’t be bloody and won’t match the wound.”

David didn’t know if anyone would be clever enough to try to match the arrow to William’s wound, but if he did, he would find that crossbow bolts were slightly thicker than the arrows used for longbows. At least, this was true in Earth Two. Thankfully, unlike guns, bolts didn’t make bigger holes on the way out than on the way in or the hole in William’s chest would have been a lot bigger.

“O-Okay.” Billy looked highly skeptical, but he got to his feet and set off for the woods.

David bent over William again, and to his great relief, William’s eyes opened. “It’s okay. You’re safe. We’re in Avalon. Help is coming.” As he had earlier, he spoke in French, intending his words for William’s ears alone. William spoke Welsh with some fluency, as well as medieval English, both of which the people here might understand pieces of, and David didn’t want to risk being understood.

“Did you just say we’re in Avalon, sire?” William was suddenly wide awake.

David breathed a sigh of relief at William’s newfound coherency. “Yes. We arrived where a group of people were practicing archery.”

“I thought you said they didn’t do that here?”

"Apparently some still do."

"Am I going to die?"

"Absolutely not." The more William recovered his senses, the more relieved David became. "The bolt couldn't have entered your chest at a spot less likely to kill you. I know it hurts like hell, but I'm telling you the truth when I say you're going to be fine." *Provided the ambulance gets here soon!* He didn't say that, though, just smiled reassuringly.

William gave him a tentative smile back, though it turned almost immediately into a grimace. "You better be right. My father would kill me if I died."

"You really should have thought of that sooner."

"What's that you said?" The burly man had chosen that moment to move closer and stand with his hands on his knees, overlooking William and David.

David looked up. "I'm just reassuring him."

Then someone came out of the crowd and slid to his knees beside David. "Good. He's awake. Keep him talking." Shorter than David, with floppy curly black hair, the man was dressed somewhat oddly to David's eyes in a long gray robe—though David supposed it wasn't far off from what his friend Aaron wore by preference. More importantly, the man carried a white case with a red cross on it, which in this context was the most beautiful thing David had ever seen.

William was able to turn his head to assess the newcomer, and his eyes lit on the case. "Is he a Templar?" He sounded hopeful.

"I think he's an EMT. That's a kind of healer they have here who's trained to deal with wounds like yours."

William didn't have the wherewithal to raise his head, but his eyes flicked from David to the EMT, who by now had the case open and had replaced the end of William's cloak with a wad of gauze.

David had initially responded to what he thought was an unspoken suggestion that he move aside and let the EMT do his work, but the man said, "Keep pressing down."

David obeyed, and he was feeling enough better about William to allow himself a moment of humor at the realization that the EMT hadn't called him *my lord* or *sire*. The last time he'd been anywhere where he was treated so cursorily was here, in Avalon, two Christmases ago.

"An arrow did this?" The man took out a pair of scissors and began to cut William's clothing off him. The fabric parted easily.

"Yes," David said, not bothering to make the distinction between an arrow and a crossbow bolt. "It went in at the back and came out the front."

With William's clothing pulled aside, David got a good look at the wound for the first time. If William hadn't woken late, he would have had time to put on his armor before coming to speak to David, and perhaps the wound wouldn't have been as bad. Still, a crossbow bolt fired from only thirty yards had been known to punch right through mail armor.

"I assumed as much since the arrow isn't sticking out of him. When I say so, I want you to move your hands aside." The EMT was holding a white bottle, the cap of which he'd unscrewed and set aside.

"Okay." At a count of three, David moved his hands, and the EMT squeezed a runny clear gel from the plastic bottle into and over the wound. He got David to roll William up slightly onto his side so he could more easily get to the hole in his back. Within thirty seconds, the bleeding stopped.

"What is that stuff?" David's jaw was on the ground. This was battlefield medicine unlike any he'd ever seen.

"Medigel." The EMT ripped open a different packet, this one just made of paper, and replaced the now bloody gauze with a fresh pad, which as far as David could tell wouldn't be needed since the wound was no longer bleeding, either on the front or at the back where the bolt had gone in. "I'm Michael. What's your name?"

"David. This is William. He may not understand you. He speaks French."

The EMT leaned over William to look into his face and said smoothly, "Comment allez-vous?" *How are you?*

"Bien," William said, with a wide-eyed look at David. *I'm well.*

"Don't listen to him. He won't tell you the truth," David said, back to English, not bothering with Welsh because Michael didn't have a Welsh accent. "He can't really be feeling good, but he's a tough one."

"I don't doubt it," Michael said. "Thank goodness this isn't really the Middle Ages, or he'd be a goner, yeah?"

"Yeah," David said and, for the hundredth time in the last twenty minutes, shook his head over everything else he couldn't say.

5

1 April 1294

Sophie

Once Ieuan returned to the corridor, Callum said, "We have to know what we're dealing with here. Was the bowman a lone assassin, or do we have a much larger problem within our ranks?"

"Though I want to say it can hardly get worse, once you march out, the only people left inside the castle should be those personally known to Lili or me," Bronwen said. "That will eliminate a good portion of our fears that this wasn't a lone assassin."

Ieuan put his arm around Bronwen again. "I hate to leave you."

"You have no choice," Bronwen said. "With David gone, you and Callum must lead the army. Bevyn and his men will protect us here."

Callum looked hard at Sophie. "Your idea to lie about David's whereabouts is mad, really, but I like it, and we should do it. And furthermore, I would say we need to move to plan C for the taking of Beeston."

Sophie almost laughed. "What happened to A and B?"

"The assassin just blew both to hell," Callum said. "We can't do them without David."

"Can you and the others do what needs to be done?" Bronwen asked.

Sophie took a breath. "I'll have to see the lay of the land before I can say for certain, but ... I've been to Beeston in Avalon. If it hasn't changed irretrievably in seven hundred years, the answer is yes. We can do it."

"Good." Callum put a hand on her shoulder, like she was one of his men, which she supposed she was. "Go check your gear."

Sophie left for the room in the outer bailey that had been commandeered to hold all of the modern equipment and weapons, painstakingly carted to Chester from Dinas Bran. These included guns, computer equipment, and a rocket launcher, though George had explained it was technically a MAAWS, the latest multi-role, anti-armor, anti-personnel weapon system. Sophie didn't think it mattered what they called it, only what it did.

The plane remained in the field where Andre had first parked it. George and Andre had taken to sleeping with the gear rather than in the keep, so they hadn't heard the news of David's sudden departure.

Ten days ago, Sophie would have laughed with a combination of joy and incredulity to think that she would ever find herself standing in the bailey of a fully functional medieval castle as a companion to a family of time-traveling twenty-firsters. Sophie had loved the idea of time travel her whole life, read every time travel novel out there, and she and her friends had joked about walking through a ruined archway and finding themselves in another world. It didn't matter that the very idea of time travel was absurd. The only time traveling anyone was ever going to do was straight ahead, one second at a time, into the future. She was with David—and Chad—that it couldn't be possible.

World shifting and alternate universes, however, were another thing entirely. That was science fiction, which, with the way things were going in Avalon these days, was just a hop, skip, and a jump from science fact. The science part of it, in fact, was why she'd read engineering at Cambridge instead of history, which, as she'd known before her father had told her flat-out she couldn't study it, was useless in career terms. If she took a degree in history, he wouldn't pay for it. A different daughter might have rebelled, but Sophie knew she needed a degree to get to where she was going, and she was willing to go along with something she liked rather than loved if it meant keeping the peace. Besides, if she was going to build a machine that could travel between universes, she would need knowledge of engineering to do it.

So in the end, she found herself of the same mind as her father, was content with her studies, and put aside her love of history as a nice hobby—until her employment with Chad suddenly allowed her to do both.

And boy did it. And not just her.

George stood with his hands clasped on top of his head. "He's gone? He's really gone?"

"I saw it with my own eyes."

"Bloody hell." George was a thirty-five-year-old American, but he'd lived in England long enough to curse like a native. He kicked at a loose stone that had been tracked inside the room from the bailey.

"We knew it was possible." Andre stood with his arms folded across his chest, much more subdued, as was his nature. In the last two weeks, Sophie had come to appreciate the way he wasn't fazed by anything. Maybe that was because he was fifty instead of thirty or the result of a lifetime of training. Probably both.

George spun around. "But so soon!"

"Would you have wanted to return with him?" Sophie asked.

George instantly tamped down what had appeared to be genuine dismay, anger, and disbelief. He let out a sharp burst of air and even managed a laugh. "No. I'm not ready at all. But it's awful quick. They've gone years without traveling, and now both Anna and David have done it within a few weeks."

"They go when their lives are in danger," Andre said, "and they're in the midst of a war."

"I suppose." With the toe of his boot, George nudged the leg of a chair so it angled away from the table and sat in it. "Nothing here is like we imagined it would be, is it?"

This was a conversation they'd had before—a hundred times in the last two weeks—and Sophie couldn't agree more. Everything was different: from the taste of food, to the quality of the light in the sky, to the way the air smelled. She had always known that she had a sensitive nose and was a bit picky about cleanliness, but she was finding the lack of modern soap and deodorant borderline unbearable. Initially, if David hadn't arranged for the installation of a toilet and shower at Dinas Bran for Anna, Sophie thought she might have gone over the edge. But even then, sitting on top of a mountain as the castle did, water for the shower had to be hauled and heated—by servants—and Sophie didn't feel right about asking for the shower very often. Here at Chester, she'd bathed in a tub with water hauled from the Dee instead and suffered the cold.

The one major concession Sophie hadn't had to make was in regards to her dress. When she'd climbed the steps up to the wall-walk earlier, she hadn't had to hike her skirts like Bronwen. During the first few days of her sojourn in Earth Two, she had balked entirely at conforming to the medieval female dress code, but as the days had gone by, she'd agreed that the stares she kept getting were making her and everyone around her uncomfortable. Change was happening in regards to the status and role of women, but this wasn't Avalon, and she'd decided it wasn't fair to ask it to be just yet.

Eventually, with the help of Anna and Lili—who'd been known to wear men's clothing herself—she'd settled upon a modified dress that she wore over breeches. Slightly shorter than was currently fashionable, the skirt had multiple slits in it from hem to waist, something already done occasionally so a woman could ride a horse astride. The alteration gave her legs room to run and move. And when she was still, the fabric settled into a more conventional shape. Lili liked the style so much, in fact, that she'd had several made for herself.

Andre unlocked a black case, this one containing a high-powered rifle, and took it out. "We, each of us, have to face the fact that we're not going home any time soon and shouldn't want to."

George nodded. "Oh, I got that."

"Would you not have come had you known what it was really like?" This was the first time Sophie had asked George that question outright. Like Chad, George was an American, and as such, she knew everything about his family down to his fourth cousins once removed because he never stopped talking. But what went on in his heart of hearts remained closed to her. She held her breath as she waited for him to answer, wondering if he would tell her the truth.

He let out another burst of air. "I would have. You know I would have. Maybe I'm just tired."

"We're all tired," Andre said. "We come from a place where the three of us are on the top of our game, and here, we can hardly communicate, we have few of the necessary skills for survival, and nothing is familiar. If we hadn't instantly been named as companions to the King of England we might be dead already."

"We could have survived," Sophie said, a bit of pride rearing up.

Andre laughed at her. "How would we have eaten? Poaching? Begging? Do you see yourself as a serving girl in a tavern? Some of us stick out like a sore thumb more than others. Perhaps I could have earned a few coins by displaying myself on a village green."

"Andre—" Hearing the underlying anger in his voice, Sophie spread her hands wide. "I'm sorry. That's a fair point, but thankfully not our concern today because we *are* companions of the King of England, even if he isn't here. I came to tell you that Plan C is on."

"Really," George said, his tone deadpan in a way Americans did very well. "Who decided that?"

"Callum."

"Why?"

"David's gone," Sophie said. "Callum doesn't feel like any other approach will do what he wants as well, which is return the hostages to us alive with minimal casualties on both sides. He feels it's time to show the whole of Britain what we—and by that he means David—are really capable of. Callum also doesn't want to take up so much time laying siege to Beeston that the men are hard-pressed to deal with Balliol."

Andre looked at George, his anger gone in favor of a dry wit. "Our approach does have the advantage of being risky."

George laughed. That was something Sophie had grown to appreciate about him—he was never down for long. "I'm not complaining, actually. Who's on the team?"

"The three of us, plus five others, including Ieuan, who insisted on coming along," Sophie said. "You'll have guns, they'll have swords and bows. We want this to be quick and light."

Andre returned the gun to the case. “It seems I get to make use of this far sooner than I thought.”

6

1 April 2022

David

With the bleeding miraculously stopped, William was able to lift his head, and then he made a move to sit up. At first Michael tried to stop him, but William pushed his hand away and persisted, so Michael gave way. David positioned himself to allow William to lean back against him.

Once William was sitting upright, Michael took advantage of that fact to add additional tape to the gauze that covered the holes in William's body. While Michael worked, David held William still, with his head leaned into David's shoulder.

"Don't pass out on me," David said. "You're heavier than you look."

"I won't," William said. "I promise."

At long last, an ambulance siren sounded in the distance. Among the crowd that had gathered and watched Michael's ministrations with interest, David saw relief in many faces that mirrored his own.

With more help on the way—though Michael really was going to be the man who had saved William—David looked at the woman who'd called the ambulance. She still held her phone in her hand. "May I use your mobile? It would be really great if I could call someone."

"Sure." She swiped at the phone to light up the screen and navigated to a phone setting.

Last week, Mark Jones had given David a tutorial on the smartphone, what Mark called a mobile, which was why David had used the word. *Cell phone* would have been understood in Wales, but it was what Americans said. In any case, thanks to Mark, David knew how to dial Chad's number, and he pressed the keys with feigned confidence.

He actually had Chad's card with him, slipped into a pocket of his pants, but he didn't need to take it out. David had memorized both phone numbers on the plane from Ireland, and since then, Bronwen had turned them into a nursery rhyme for Arthur and the other children to memorize. David had found it useful too.

A woman picked up after one ring. "Hello?"

Sophie had told him that the phone number was a dedicated line. While it would go to a general operator, she would be able to tell which number had been dialed and escalate the call immediately. So all he said was, "I need to speak to Chad Treadman. This is David."

Michael was crouched beside William, having finished his taping, and his head jerked as David spoke, conveying sudden interest. David shrugged and raised his eyebrows as if to say, *it is what it is*.

The extra beat of silence on the other end of the line wasn't far off from Michael's reaction, but the woman recovered professionally and said, "Are you safe?"

"It appears so for the moment."

"Please hold the line, your majesty."

"Okay." David was bemused by the honorific. Technically, she should have used it the first time she spoke, when she'd said, *Are you safe*? As promised, Chad was trying hard.

Ten seconds passed, by which time the ambulance, its sirens wailing, turned into the parking lot. The field onto which David and William had fallen was situated on the east side of Beaumaris Castle, a place David had never been. There was a reason for that: in Earth Two, Beaumaris had never been built. If David continued to have a say in the matter, it never would be. With the establishment of this castle, the contrast between the history of Avalon and the trajectory of Earth Two couldn't be more stark.

In Earth Two, Beaumaris Castle not only didn't exist, but the town it had replaced was called something else entirely. Since Celtic times, the village of Llanfaes had been on one end of the pathway across the Lavan Sands and a waypoint on the ancient road that ran from Holyhead on the tip of Anglesey, to Llanfaes, across the Menai Strait during low tide, past Aber Castle, through the pass at Bwlch y Ddeufaen and its ancient standing stones, to the ford across the Conwy River at Caerhun, and all the way east to Chester.

In Earth Two, Llanfaes was a thriving town, one of the largest in Wales because of the trade through the Menai Strait. Anglesey, with its relatively flat countryside, was the breadbasket of Gwynedd. But in response to yet another Welsh rebellion ten years after David's father's death, King Edward had forcibly removed all the Welsh from the area, razed the town to the ground, and built his castle. Princess Joan, the wife of Llywelyn Fawr (David's great-grandfather) had been interred at Llanfaes Abbey, and the English soldiers had used her coffin as a horse trough.

While David waited for the ambulance workers to arrive, a woman carrying another first aid kit and wearing medieval dress edged her way through the onlookers. "What can I do?" she said to Michael.

"Nothing here, but if you could tell the EMTs I've got a through and through, they'll know what to prepare. Tell them I've stopped the bleeding."

"I can walk." William couldn't have understood everything that Michael had said, but he'd clearly caught the gist. He bent a knee and reached for David with his left hand.

As David helped William to his feet, Michael shook his head. "He really is one tough bloke, isn't he?"

"I've always said so," David said.

While the woman ran ahead, the three men set off slowly towards the parking lot, and the crowd opened a pathway to let them through.

If they'd been on the battlefield, William would have been in a lot worse shape, but just as much would have been required of him. David had left the cataloging of the medical supplies to others, so it wasn't something he'd looked for, but he really hoped Chad Treadman had put some Medigel in the plane. Regardless, David resolved then and there to bring home cases of the stuff if he could.

Finally a voice spoke tinnily from the phone, still in David's hand, though down at his side. "David? Are you there?"

David hastily put the phone to his ear. "Yes. Is this Chad?" It was only after he'd spoken that he wondered if it would have been more polite to say *Mr. Treadman*. But then, he wanted to be treated like an adult this time around, so it was best to start as he meant to go on.

"Yes. I thought for a moment that someone among my staff was punking me. It's April Fool's Day, you know."

"I admit, that never occurred to me."

"By the fact that you called this number, I'm to take it that Anna made it? My people are safe?"

"They were an hour ago when I left."

Chad let out a burst of air. "First things first. Where are you?"

"Beaumaris ... at a medieval reenactment." David tipped down the phone to speak to Michael. "Who are you people?"

"You don't know?" Michael frowned, though whether because of David's question or over William, who continued to put one foot in front of the other, David didn't know. Now that they were crossing the field, David noticed how lumpy it was. Unless Chad had discovered gravitic reversion technology since he was last here, it would have been impossible for a stretcher to roll across the field without constantly jarring William in the process. He supposed they could have carried him on a board if they had to, like they would have done in Earth Two.

"I know it's weird, but please just tell me."

"We're the *Saethwr Cymraeg*."

"Right. Thanks." Now David spoke into the phone. "Did you get that?"

"My Welsh is poor on a good day," Chad said.

"They call themselves the *Welsh Archers*." David shrugged. "I don't know that it matters. You need to know that I brought a friend who needs medical attention. He's been shot." He made a motion with his head to indicate William, even though Chad couldn't see it. According to Mark, they could be using video as they talked, but David didn't know how to set it up.

Chad drew in a breath. "The last time that happened—"

"Thankfully, it isn't the same this time. Ieuan was gut-shot. William took a crossbow bolt through the armpit. Sort of."

"Jesus! Okay. I'm already organizing people your way, but it can't be immediate. Anna took my prototype plane. The next one isn't coming off the production line for another month, so everyone's driving to Wales. It's faster."

The ambulance had come to a halt in the last parking space in the lot adjacent to the field where the archery competition had been set up. The burly man had long since forged ahead, and he was standing in the parking lot, directing traffic. Some people liked to be involved and in charge, and David didn't begrudge his efficiency. It was one less thing David himself needed to worry about. Of course, the man had an ulterior motive in that the competition couldn't continue until William was off the field.

Two EMTs got out of the ambulance, pulled a stretcher from the back, and set it up on the blacktop. A third was immediately intercepted by the female EMT. With her talking a mile a minute, the two of them headed towards William, David, and Michael. This man was older, with gray hair, and when he arrived in front of them, David saw that his nametag said, 'Robert'. It was among the most common Anglo-Norman names in Earth Two, and David smiled to see that, in this at least, little had changed in seven hundred years.

Robert didn't at all like the fact that William was moving under his own power, but by now they were only thirty feet from the parking lot, so he and Michael exchanged a series of clipped sentences as they traveled the distance, with Michael detailed what he'd done for William so far.

William just kept putting one foot in front of the other until he reached the pavement that marked the start of the parking lot. The two other EMTs were right there to greet him with the stretcher.

David said to Robert, "I'm American. He's French. We have no ID on us. Where will you be taking him?"

"To Bangor."

"To Ysbyty Gwynedd?"

Robert nodded.

"Great." David gave way to the new EMTs, who helped William ease onto the stretcher and finally lie backwards. David had almost forgotten he had Chad Treadman on the line, but now he returned the phone to his ear. "Did you get all that?"

"Most of it, I think. My people will meet you at the hospital. Do you have a ride?"

David looked at Robert again. "I need to go with him in the ambulance."

"I'm sorry; you can't." Robert spoke over his shoulder, since he was tightening down the lap belt over William's hips. "It's against policy."

David wavered over whether to choose this moment to throw his weight around—if he had any weight to throw—or let Chad do it—when Michael nudged his shoulder. "I'll take you."

"Thanks. I really appreciate it." He gazed around at the people who surrounded them. They had remained a respectful fifteen feet away, so as not to interfere with the ambulance workers. "Thank you all for your help. I'm sorry to have disturbed your contest." It was what he would have said had he been their king.

Various people gave him relieved smiles, and even the burly man who'd taken charge looked content.

William, who was resting on the stretcher, his head elevated so he was half-sitting up, put out a hand. "What's happening, my lord?"

“They’re going to drive you to a hospital. They won’t let me ride in the ambulance with you, but I will be right behind you in Michael’s car.”

William’s brows pinched together, pain and stress combining to make him anxious, which was unusual for him.

David moved closer and took his hand. “Really. It’s going to be okay. They know what they’re doing, and they will take care of you.”

“Are you sure? This is completely mad.”

“Oh yes. Always. Try to keep your head about you.”

William laughed, as David meant him to, and relaxed against his pillow. “When I asked you to take me to Avalon, my lord, I confess this isn’t entirely what I had in mind.”

7

1 April 2022

William

Before the battle of Tara, William had spent much of his life in fear of disappointing his father. Failure had seemed far worse a fate to him than death. Since Ireland, that fear hadn't entirely left him, but in the wake of his exploits—and his father's—in uncovering the plot against David, the two of them had come to a new understanding. William had felt freer in the last fortnight than in his entire life up until now. For once, he'd felt confident of the world and his place in it.

He'd been a fool.

He'd moved in front of David to take the crossbow bolt because he could do nothing else. He could have chosen not to do it, but then he would not have been William. That his sacrifice had brought them to Avalon could not be regretted, but he could see now that the world was a whole lot bigger than he'd ever imagined—and he'd never been so afraid in his life as over the course of the last half-hour.

This was *not* how he'd imagined Avalon. Not.

He'd known at the outset that what he'd pictured Avalon to be like was going to turn out to be wholly unrealistic, but he couldn't understand why everything had to be so *loud.* There was a constant hum in the earth and in the air, occasionally growing louder as an airplane flew overhead. Motors were everywhere. People were everywhere, and they just kept *talking*. It was worse than London.

Speaking of people, they were shocking too. Those to arrive initially had been dressed in breeches and shirts in a not unfamiliar cut, though with odd designs and strange hats. Many carried bows, which, as he'd said to David, he had understood to be no longer in use in Avalon. Because of them, at first he had thought David was mistaken, and they weren't in Avalon, but rather in some far off country.

Once David had clarified again, William had, in a sense, felt even more lost. He'd been to France and knew that people dressed differently there. He'd met dark-skinned men, some of whom were members of David's court. But the people here in Avalon were an order of magnitude different, and not just in regards to their clothing or skin tones. He had never seen so many overweight people, men and women, and even those who were thinner had no muscle and were unfit. And still, many of the women were as tall as he was, and he was of above average height for a man.

He thought he knew what people from Avalon looked like, since he knew so many of them, but none of those he'd met at home had hair unnaturally colored or strangely shaved (or both), jewelry pierced through their nose or lips, or tattoos—at least not that he'd seen anyway. If anything, these people looked like Danes: big, loud, and decorated. David had never mentioned that a large number of people in Avalon were pagan. William wanted to ask him about it but decided to wait and observe further before exposing that particular ignorance.

To top it all off, it was King David's assessment of the place that was the least accurate. According to him, he was never showed respect by anyone here—either as a king or as a man. But that wasn't what William was witnessing today. He'd been distracted by the newness of it all—and the fear—but even he could tell that people were listening to the authority in David's voice and responding accordingly. As they should.

For the rest, most of the conversation and virtually all of the interactions had passed William by in a blur of anxiety and pain, including walking to the ambulance. As it turned out, it was the least unfamiliar thing here, since it bore more than a passing resemblance to the vehicles in the barn in Llangollen. He tried to deconstruct the origin of the word, which if he had to guess came from *ambulare,* Latin for *to walk*. If riding in the vehicle would somehow get him walking—and riding, and fighting—again, he was all for it.

While a big part of him wanted to turn around and go home right now, another part that wasn't keeping quiet told him not to be an idiot. Two weeks ago, William had fought in a battle for his life, for David, and for Ireland. In some ways, a crossbow bolt wound and a trip to Avalon paled in comparison to what he'd gone through there. That day at Tara, he'd found a courage within himself he hadn't known he had. Although Avalon was nothing like he'd imagined, he did appreciate that everybody around him was maintaining a calm demeanor, as if a bolt through the armpit was something they encountered every day. Maybe they did. Maybe literally everything that he'd been told and thought he knew about Avalon was wrong.

The only thing that did seem familiar about Avalon—and it gave William some comfort to see it—was the landscape. It was covered with buildings and stones and people, but the Menai Strait was still there, along with the mountains and the air and the grass beneath his feet. For all the strange wonders that were to be found here, they hadn't changed the contours of the earth.

And when drops of rain started to plop-plop on the black stone that covered the ground under the ambulance, William found himself grinning.

"Okay," David said, speaking to someone else. He'd used the word many times since they'd arrived. Back home, people from Avalon used the word often, and William did too, but he hadn't realized how commonly it was said until it was one of the few words he could pick out amidst the mishmash of Avalonian English.

"No, no." Now David was shaking his head at someone dressed all in black except for a vest of a yellow color William had never encountered before. David turned to William, switching to French. "Just tell him no."

"No," William said, obeying instinctively and trusting David implicitly.

David nodded, and the man went off.

"What was that about?"

David leaned into the back of the ambulance, his feet still on the ground outside and his hands deep in his pockets. "He asked if you wanted to press charges against the man who shot you."

"I don't understand what you mean by that."

"Press charges means *to pursue the law against another person*." David pulled out one hand and flicked his fingers dismissively. "You may not have realized, but one of the archers missed a target just as we arrived. He thinks that your wound is his fault. I told him straight out that it wasn't. He didn't believe me, and since I can hardly say that we materialized out of thin air, I have no counter-argument right now. Regardless, you have just informed an officer of the law that you don't want the poor archer arrested."

"Who was the crossbowman, my lord?"

"At home, you mean? The one who really shot you? I have no idea. We have plenty of people there who will find that out."

"The crossbowman who shot at *you*, you mean."

David ran a hand down his front. "The blood on me is all yours."

"The bolt didn't touch you at all?"

"Nope."

William paused a moment. "How is that possible?"

"That, my friend, is Avalon."

William stared at David. He had spent the last ten years serving him but only now was he seeing him as he really was: a miracle. He didn't understand how the people outside could be walking around, talking to each other and David, and not realize it. Truthfully, Avalon was a miracle too. More than ever, everything here was impossible.

David narrowed his eyes. "Don't look at me like that. I don't understand why it happens or how, only that it does. I don't control it."

William glanced away, trying to get a grip on his emotions. The pain from his wound had eased, thanks to whatever they'd done to stop the bleeding, which was a miracle in and of itself. At David's urging, he'd accepted a *pain killer* too. David had assured William that the EMT had assured *him* that it was a mild one and wouldn't make him insensible. It might be a relief to fall asleep, but at the same time he didn't want to miss anything. He'd *dreamed* of this day.

He also didn't want to be asleep if some new danger threatened. "What about our plan?" This was the first moment William remembered what effect David being in Avalon would have on their world. "What are they going to do?"

David raised one shoulder in a half-shrug. "What they must. As will we."

"No, my lord!" William tried to sit up, though the EMT who squeezed past David to climb into the ambulance put a gentle hand on his good shoulder, and he subsided. "You must return immediately."

David laughed outright. "And leave you here alone? I don't think so." He leaned forward. "We didn't die, William, neither of us. We have work to do here."

"You have work to do, my lord."

David canted his head. "Oh no. You don't get off that easy. You wanted to come to Avalon, and here you are. It may be that the lesson for you to learn is only to be careful what you wish for, but now that you're here, we have to play it out."

That was the kind of statement that was a daily lesson back when William had been David's squire. Half the time, the king's comments left William grinding his teeth, even if he had to acknowledge that David wasn't wrong.

"If you could step away, sir. We need to go now." Robert, the gray-haired ambulance man, also climbed into the back with William. His French—or what appeared to pass for French in Avalon—was as good as Michael's.

"Are you sure I can't come with him?" David tipped his chin to indicate the front of the ambulance. "You have an extra seat."

Robert shook his head regretfully, which was a clear answer to William, but the words that followed were nothing if not murky. In fact, they made no sense whatsoever. "Liability issues, sir. These Americans ruin everything—" he paused a beat, "—no offense intended."

"None taken." David let out a breath and stepped back. "I'll be right behind you. I promise."

William gritted his teeth and spoke around them. "I know you don't make promises you can't keep." But before David could make a reply or William could ask what *liability issues* were, the last EMT, the driver, closed the ambulance doors.

Then he opened the front door behind William's head, and the ambulance's motor rumbled to life. Before William knew it, they'd started moving, though the motion was so smooth William could tell it had happened only because the archery field, which he could see out the two small back windows, grew more distant. Then he turned to look at the healer to his left, who wore blue gloves and a label on his shirt that said 'Dan'. The man was tapping on the inside of William's elbow with one finger. He seemed to be about to poke William with a needle. William's eyes widened, and he made to pull away.

But Robert, also with blue-gloved hands, leaned in and said, "No need to be alarmed. Your costume is really well done. Did you make it yourself?"

William saw every reason to be alarmed, and the rest of Robert's words were nonsensical in light of the fact that no knight would ever manufacture his own gear—and he couldn't believe that knights did in this world either. But the man seemed sincere, and William could only conclude that the signs of a man's station were different here.

At home, whether a man was Welsh, Saxon, Norman, or Scot—or even Irish—one could tell at a single glance and before he opened his mouth whether or not he was a nobleman by the weave of his clothing. This man's clothing was unlike any William had ever seen, so perhaps William was dressed poorly by their standards, and they thought he was a peasant.

He drew himself up as best he could. "No. Someone else did." Then he expelled a breath because Dan had inserted the needle in his arm. Robert had been talking to him to distract him.

"As I said, no need to worry. You need antibiotics, and this is the best way to administer them. If we set the IV here, it makes everything easier once we get to the hospital."

Again, William heard the man's words, but with little comprehension. He was speaking 'French' but William had a passing thought that maybe he ought to try a different language on the chance the meaning would be more clear. Maybe Welsh, though the little he'd heard since he arrived was even more difficult than English.

His confusion must have showed on his face, because Robert smiled and patted his thigh in an attempt to be reassuring. "For a while, my son was really into these reenactments. I suppose you will be less so from now on."

William attempted a smile too. He recognized the manner of someone trying to put a very ill man at ease, and he had a moment of panic that David had lied to him. "Am I going to die?"

The other attendant, Dan, genuinely scoffed. "Not a chance."

Robert glared at him, and the man replied with a contrite, "Sorry, sir."

"What-what do you mean? Why is he apologizing?" The hodgepodge of French and English was making William's head spin. Still, when they spoke English, both of these men sounded very much like the Avalonians who'd come on the bus, and *sorry* had been something they'd said all the time.

"It is against policy to promise anything," Robert said shortly, with another glare at the other healer.

William really was starting to feel light-headed. He hadn't understood the implications of that sentence either. "If the wound suppurates—"

"We have antibiotics that are designed to root out infection. Though a wound from an arrow is new to me, I've seen men impaled on splinters and poles many times."

"Mine is from a crossbow bolt," William said before he considered that maybe David wouldn't want him talking about exactly how he'd been wounded.

"I'm sure it was, lad." Robert's tone, more than his words, since William was used to being agreed with, again implied appeasement. William's head was starting to feel woozy, and he worried now that the needle had put something into him that was making him ill. He looked up at the clear bag on the pole above his head. Water was dripping every heartbeat into the tube attached to his arm. He didn't like it one bit.

But William reminded himself that David had condoned what was happening here, and before he made the decision to actively protest his treatment, the ambulance slowed and stopped. Someone shouted outside, words William didn't catch, and then the doors opened.

To William's great relief, David stood a few paces away from the ambulance, next to an enormous building with floor-to-ceiling glass windows. Such a display of wealth and skill was almost more than William could believe existed in all the world. And here it was at a place of healing. It was one more overwhelming and unfamiliar thing in a world of overwhelming and unfamiliar things. William's mind took a moment to note the absurdity of it, accepted what he couldn't change, and moved on.

With David in tow (since William was facing backwards, he could see him following the cart), William was wheeled to a little room with a curtain around it. The sign at the door to the building had said *accident unit,* and he had paid enough attention to Anna's description of her experience in Avalon to understand that this place was what she'd been talking about. But like everything else about the last hour, the reality was far different from what he'd imagined. When she—or Ieuan at one time—described white floors and ceilings, with machines and men and women talking and constantly moving, and these *tablets* Mark Jones had showed him, William had nodded and acted like he was a confident witness to their knowledge.

He hadn't had any idea. *Bewildered* was the best word he knew to describe himself, and he didn't like the feeling at all. This world was a blur of machines and sound. And odd smells that he couldn't place but closed his throat. Earlier, one of the smells had been from 'gasoline', the fuel that ran the vehicles. The wet grass and fresh earth had reminded him of home, but the black stony ground had a burned essence to it, and the interior of the hospital smelled both sweet and sickly. None of the doctors smelled of anything at all, which was so unusual he was tempted to touch their skins to see if they were flesh and bone.

He wasn't displeased at the rushing of people around him, but it was making his heart race, and someone beside him mentioned that he was bleeding again. Then a man wearing a blue gown and more blue gloves approached with another clear bag, which he hooked next to the one currently dripping fluid into William. He bore another needle, the point of which he stuck into the tube attached to William's arm.

"I want you to count backwards from ten to one for me."

David, who was standing in the corner where a curtain met the wall, translated into French, though William had understood the simple English well enough. It was only when people started talking fast or in long sentences that he found himself in trouble.

He started counting, "Ten, nine, eight—" and then he remembered nothing more.

8

1 April 1294

Christopher

"What do you want us to do?" Christopher and Huw planted themselves in front of Callum. Between the two of them, they had deliberated briefly but heatedly as to which of the commanders would be least likely to dismiss them, and by extension most likely to do what they wanted. "David told us he was sending us north, but that was when he was sending us with William."

Christopher was really glad his mom and dad were back in Wales with Aunt Meg and Uncle Llywelyn. They'd had a lively debate about that too, but Christopher had argued successfully that if he'd been in Avalon, he wouldn't have lived at home anymore either. Earth Two wasn't exactly college, but they couldn't argue that he wasn't learning a lot—and that it was his job to serve David. Just because his parents were here now too didn't mean that he was going to change who he was and who he was becoming.

For sure, Sir Christopher had a really nice ring to it, and the longer he stayed here, the more reasons he had to stay, and the more he understood why David did too. Whatever happened in the future, Christopher was determined not to go back to being a twenty-first century kid. In Avalon, men his age had three more years of sitting around in classrooms all day to look forward to, and he didn't know a single person—the smart ones included—who wouldn't have done something different if they'd had another real way other than going to college to get ahead in life.

In prior arguments, Callum had usually supported Christopher's quest for independence, if quietly, and now he looked unseeingly towards the battlement from which David and William had disappeared.

"It's what the king wanted," Huw said helpfully.

"I know what David wanted better than you two, I think." He gave them the beady eye. "But you're in luck in that we already resolved not to second guess David's plans nor try to imagine what he would do if he were in our shoes and faced with new information. As it is, in your case we know what he had planned because he'd already told you about it. So I'm not going to change it."

"Yes!" Christopher went to punch the air, but Callum's hard look arrested the movement, and he lowered his hand. "Sorry."

Callum bobbed his head. "You don't have to be sorry. I'm glad you're excited about this commission David has given you. Though—" the stern look was back, "—would it make you feel better or worse if you knew how important it was? David was hoping to hear back by now from the scouts we sent north ten days ago, but they have not returned. We can't wait another day for information."

"I know," Christopher said. "Plus, we *need* the Stewarts and the Bruces, and they need to know what we're doing—and what has happened to David."

James Stewart had been needed as one of the few elder statesmen of his adopted Irish clan who'd survived the carnage in Ireland, but his Scottish estates had always been the most important. He'd resolved to sail for Scotland within a day or two of David's own departure for Wales. Robbie himself was a Bruce and had felt an urgent need to warn his grandfather of Balliol's treachery, if he didn't already know of it—and to stand at his side when he faced it. Even now, the Stewarts and the Bruces were supposed to be riding out of Carlisle Castle, a royal stronghold, to hem in Balliol's forces from the north.

"I'd go myself if I wasn't needed with the main army. I'd love to send Cassie, but Gareth is too young to travel into a war zone, or to be without his mother, were she to go alone for as long as this might take."

"We'll manage," Christopher said staunchly.

Callum rolled his eyes. "Like you did in Ireland." He laughed. "You must have something of your cousin in you to pull off a stunt like that."

Christopher tried ineffectively to look modest.

Undoubtedly Callum wasn't fooled. He had the ability to see through everyone. "For that reason, I think I'll send Matha O'Reilly with you too. He's recovered, for the most part, from the airplane ride, and with David gone, he's going to be a bit at loose ends. It will give him something to do."

Christopher nodded. He understood all too well the need to have something to do. And he liked Matha well enough. "His English is improving. He ought to do fine."

Huw looked somewhat more askance. "I haven't forgiven him for forcing William and me to run across Ireland."

"He was doing the job his father set him with admirable single-mindedness," Callum said.

Huw still looked sullen, which prompted Callum to openly laugh. "Don't let David hear about this. We're friends with the Irish now, remember?" He put a hand on Christopher's shoulder. "This doesn't mean you have permission to take unnecessary risks."

"No, sir. Only necessary ones."

"Pshaw." Callum scoffed. "Off with you. I've chosen three other men to go with you to keep you honest."

Huw and Christopher hastened away before Callum could change his mind. Christopher was glad to be going on the road, even if he was missing William's company. Motion was better than no motion, as David often said.

Thus, an hour later, fully armored and armed, he, Matha, and Huw rode out the castle gate, along with Jacob, John, and Cedric, each a seasoned English soldier. None had been at the Battle of Tara, but they'd heard about it. For that reason, Christopher thought that the eyes that looked back at him were more respectful than they might have been a month ago.

It was a relief to have fought in a real battle and comported himself well. Up until now, it had been an awkward thing being the king's cousin. Because of his blood, Christopher had been accorded a respect that he and everyone else had known he didn't deserve. Not that it wasn't still awkward sometimes, but maybe he deserved it now.

And that was an awkward thing too. Ever since he was seven years old and David had come to Avalon, Christopher had dreamed of being a knight. Now he was a knight, and while he had no regrets on that score, in reality, it wasn't as magnificent as he'd imagined. He didn't dream of being a knight anymore—he dreamed of fighting and blood. His dreams drowned in it. It was worse than the times back home when his friends and he had stayed up late watching horror movies. At Tara, he'd *lived* a horror movie. It felt like the blood had soaked into his skin. And while it had washed off, the memory of it never would. Just because saying so was a meme didn't mean it wasn't true.

He turned in the saddle, his eyes traveling over the faces of the men who rode behind him. "We ready for this?"

To a man, they snorted their derision that he could even ask such a thing, and Jacob, their captain, said, "More than ready."

Jacob was Jewish, no surprise given the name, and something of a friend to Christopher. Ten years ago, Jacob would never have been allowed to join the army, much less command men, but this was the world David had created, and Christopher was glad to have him. Even if Avalon was more foreign than the moon to a medieval person, Jacob understood what it meant to be different, and Christopher appreciated the resulting camaraderie between them.

Now, Jacob urged his horse a little closer. They were almost through the town, at which point they would head northeast as directly as possible. They would change horses at Warrington, Rochdale, and Skipton Castle, before circling to the west around the Pennines. The only check on the distance they could travel was their own endurance. Barnard Castle, where John Balliol's army was gathering, wasn't in Scotland, but quite a ways south into what Christopher felt to be England.

"My lord," Jacob said, "I must ask why we are traveling so far east? Skipton is miles out of our way. Surely riding through Liverpool would make a faster journey to Carlisle. And if our intent is to go to Barnard, we should be riding more east around the Pennines."

"You are right on both counts," Christopher said. "But Earl Callum wants to know who is moving in the north, and if any lord we don't know about is allied with Balliol and Mortimer. Our men have to march past Skipton to get to Barnard. Better to know something of the journey before they get there. At each castle we pass through, we'll have the castellan send a rider south, first to the main army, which will be following, if slowly, on our heels, and then to Earl Callum to tell him about the conditions."

Jacob thought about that for a moment. "That's really why the king decided to send you, isn't it?" He nodded thoughtfully. "You would be wasted at Beeston."

Christopher glanced at him, surprised by the idea, since he *had* just successfully navigated a battlefield at Tara. "Why is that?"

"Anybody can wield a sword, but if reports are true—and I have been listening closely, so I believe them—you singlehandedly won over two great lords of Ireland. If not for your embassage to them, Ireland would have been lost."

"That's right. Where William de Bohun and I managed almost instantly to get ourselves captured—"

"By me," Matha added with equanimity.

Huw guffawed. "Christopher saved the kingdom. Dafydd said so." He had taken up the Irish habit of referring to David when he wasn't there only by his first name. Everyone did it now and again, but with the Irish, David's name was like a title in and of itself.

Jacob nodded sagely. "I heard him say that too." Then he fell back to align his horse again with Cedric's.

That gave Christopher a chance to say in an undertone to Huw. "Do you really think Callum and David are expecting that much?"

Huw shot him a surprised look. "Yes. Did you really not think so?"

More than Callum's words had done, Huw and Jacob's certainty had Christopher reconsidering the tameness of this assignment. When David had explained what he wanted, he'd been pretty casual about it. Christopher had assumed that David was sending them because 1) Christopher was his cousin, which would garner the delegation instant respect from everyone they encountered on the journey; and 2) he wanted to keep Christopher out of harm's way.

Christopher would never forget the look on David's face when he found him after the Battle of Tara. There had been genuine fear in his eyes—followed by utter relief when he'd seen Christopher sitting in the field, alive and uninjured. Now that Christopher's mom was here, David would have her voice constantly in his ear, warning him not to let anything happen to her son. In the nine months they'd been apart, she may have mellowed in some respects, but not by that much.

Christopher led his friends in Ireland because leadership had been forced upon him. Now, it had been given to him, and for the first time, he was seeing this journey far less as an adventure for him and Huw—and a way to get them out of Callum's hair—and much more as something that really was necessary. Truthfully, it was an added pressure he didn't need right now. But they'd started, so he could hardly turn back and tell Callum that he wasn't ready for this kind of responsibility.

Christopher really wished William had been able to come along because he would have said exactly what Christopher was thinking: *You've got to be kidding me!*

9

1 April 2022

David

David stood in the corridor of the hospital, the door to William's room open behind him, and looked right and left. Though he could see nothing untoward, the back of his neck was telling him that all was not entirely well. Or maybe it was that he'd been on edge for so long, he didn't know how not to be.

"What are you afraid of?"

"What do you mean?"

David focused on Michael, who leaned against the wall opposite, his arms folded across his chest. As promised, he'd driven David to the hospital, but then afterwards, he'd stayed with him in the emergency room and come with him to William's room. Back when they'd first arrived, David had told him he could go at any time, just say the word, but Michael had said William was his patient, and he wanted to see his treatment through.

David hadn't argued then. But now he was concerned about what had to come next, and how to protect Michael from it.

"I'm not blind. I served, and I recognize the signs. You're jumpy. It's like you think a firefight is just over the next hill."

David had put on the best face possible to William, because there was no point in railing against what couldn't immediately be changed. He saw no reason to give William something more to worry about, but to say David was concerned about their situation was to woefully understate the case. Though William was recovering somewhat woozily in his private room, David's concern had little to do with William himself. The doctors said he was doing well enough that, if things continued, he could be discharged tomorrow. Michael's miracle gel had done its job, and a surgeon had cleaned out the damaged tissue and sewn him up front and back. Other than taking antibiotics and pain killers as needed, William would soon be good to go.

It was the rest of everything that was the problem. David didn't *want* to be in Avalon right now, not with so many people back home depending on him. It was just somehow typical that right at the point where he was going to be able to put down these constant rebellions—hopefully forever—he'd been transported away. Though the Ireland insurrection had been a long time coming, David was starting to think that it was a failure of leadership on his part that was at the root of Roger Mortimer's and John Balliol's plans. Somehow, despite everything he'd accomplished, he was still seen in certain quarters as weak.

It was a condition that could not continue, not if he hoped to keep changing Earth Two for the better. Certainly, that was why Roger Mortimer had rejected his terms of surrender, declaring that if

David wanted Beeston, he needed to ride there personally, hat in hand, to ask for it. David would have accepted a little humiliation for the sake of peace, but it would have diminished him in Roger's eyes. That might have been an acceptable trade if this were just about David. But this was about England, and as the King of England, David wasn't going to come running when anyone—particularly Roger Mortimer—called.

Maybe at one time he could have walked away from the kingship, but he couldn't anymore. Too much was riding on his leadership and too many people depended on him—not so much for their livelihood, though there was that, but for their way of life. Without him, without all the twenty-firsters, Earth Two could easily sink back into the bad old days of prejudice and brutality. If that was going to happen, it was going to happen only over David's dead body.

None of that could he say to Michael, however. But he didn't want to shut him out either. He felt he owed him more than silence. "It feels like a fight really might be."

Michael jerked his chin to point south, which from Bangor was the direction of the mountains. "How long and where?" He was asking about David's military service.

David studied Michael while deliberating how to answer. He had rehearsed in his head possible scenarios for the next time he came to Avalon, but outright lies still didn't come easily to his tongue. In the rush of dealing with William, he hadn't done more than a cursory assessment of who Michael was, but more was needed now.

He stood about 5' 10" and had an athletic physique that in Earth Two would have meant he was used to hard labor—whether in the fields or with a sword—but here probably meant his workout included lifting weights. He had dark hair, eyes, and skin, but David couldn't guess his ethnicity and was kind of pleased about that fact. England was becoming more diverse every year in a way that made him feel better about the way this world was going.

More important than what Michael looked like, he appeared to take in the world with an accepting expression that implied he had seen it all and could no longer be surprised. But he wasn't angry about his past either.

Michael misread his silence. "Dude, you look like you're going to eat me. You were special forces, weren't you? That's why you won't talk about it."

"I'm sorry, Michael. You're right. I can't."

An elevator dinged in the distance. On instinct, David's hand went to his waist, but he had no sword there. His calculations about what to be concerned about had been mostly focused on what was happening back home, but his jumpiness had to be attributed to the fact that the firefight in question would be in response to the arrival of MI-5, who were probably just around the corner waiting to pounce. David couldn't understand why nobody had yet arrived. Chad Treadman was also a force to be reckoned with. And David had no doubt that there *would be* a reckoning. Anna had done her deal with Chad only two weeks ago. David's sudden arrival in Avalon had left him a lot less time than he'd hoped to figure out what could be, and should be, expected of him.

And still, Michael deserved answers. David just didn't have any to give him.

Three people, each tall, dark, and wearing earpieces, two men and one woman, came around the corner at the far end of the hall. They were MI-5 for sure, and David squared his shoulders. He couldn't leave William alone, so he had to take what was coming as best he could.

Out of the corner of his eye, David saw Michael move into a similar stance. "What's going on, David?"

"I don't know. I guess we'll find out in a second."

"Is this the firefight walking towards us?"

"I hope not, but I've learned not to rely on hope."

By now, the man in the lead was within conversational distance.

"Stop right there." David put out a hand to confirm the order, in case the trio missed the wariness in both him and Michael.

The man put up his own hand. "I'm Reg. This is Mali and Joe." He indicated his two companions. "Chad Treadman sent us." He held out a phone. "He wants to speak to you."

Beside him in an undertone, Michael said, "Dude, Chad Treadman again? Who *are* you?"

David didn't answer Michael and simply accepted the phone, though he didn't take his eyes off the three people before him. "Hi."

Chad's voice came loudly in his ear. "Thank God. Everything okay?"

"Yes." Back at Beaumaris, David had returned the woman's phone to her once the ambulance had come, and it honestly hadn't occurred to him to ask to borrow another to call Chad again. David had told Chad where he was, and he had assumed that Chad was doing something on his end about it. David had been right about that, but the panic in Chad's voice indicated that he'd been stressed out. Anna was right that the ease of communication in Avalon had made everyone impatient with silence.

"Okay, good. I gather you've met the triplets?"

David had to laugh at the characterization, which was right on, and some of the tension in his shoulders eased. "In a manner of speaking."

"Any sign of MI-5?"

Out of the corner of his eye, David could see Michael startle again. David put out a hand to him, trying again to be reassuring. He supposed he had the volume up too loud on the phone, but he didn't know how to turn it down. "No, and I don't understand why not. They were quick enough to go after Anna. They have to have someone up here in Gwynedd, don't they?"

Now it was Chad's turn to laugh. "It's Wales. For a long time they didn't even have an office in Cardiff. That's where the only Special Branch office is too. I think the folks from Manchester are more likely to get to you first. I have eyes on them, and it's obvious they're scrambling. They know you're here. They just don't know what to do about it." He paused. "Things aren't quite the same as when Anna left."

David detected a note of pride and even pleasure in Chad's voice. "Why would that be? It was only two weeks ago."

"Well—" Chad cleared his throat, "that may be down to me."

David didn't know whether to cheer or groan. "What did you do?"

"Not long before Anna arrived, my purchase of WMC went through." Chad said this as if what WMC was and what it might mean that he'd bought it should be obvious, though it surely wasn't to David.

He said so. "I don't know what that is."

"World Media Conglomerate. It's the boringest name ever, I know. I thought about changing it, but it's nice and neutral, and tells you nothing. Basically, I now own fifteen percent of the world's media outlets. And I've been—" He paused again. David had never met the man, but he could picture him waggling his head, "—directing content recently."

David found himself staring at Michael, who had stepped back a few feet so he couldn't hear what Chad was saying, but his expression mirrored David's concern.

Chad continued, now laughing openly. "There's no reason you should know what I'm talking about, so I'll just tell you. Two weeks ago, it was the spring equinox. Two thousand people had gathered in a valley below Mt. Snowdon, and just as the sun rose, every single one of them saw my plane fly into the mountain and disappear. It was a genuine miracle."

David answered automatically because the rest of his brain was working on the problem. "Miracles are only convincing to the people who see them, and with the ability to manipulate images that I know you have these days—"

Chad cut him off. "That isn't what happened. It's a new world you're in, David. Do you mind if I call you David? *Sire* is awkward here."

"David is fine." He was impatient with the question, though if he'd had the wherewithal to think properly beyond what Chad had just told him, he would have appreciated the courtesy of asking what he preferred. It was a far cry from the dismissal and disrespect he usually encountered in Avalon. "What do you mean *it's a new world?"*

"Every one of those two thousand people on that mountain had a phone, and a third of them were filming the rising sun. A BBC film crew was there to mark the occasion—they were intending to make a documentary on modern pagans and apparently a ley line goes through Snowdon—and one of them had already heard from his superiors before the plane passed into Wales that the RAF had scrambled fighter jets to go after it. The entire world has seen the video of the plane disappearing. Your time of anonymity is over."

David took in a breath, a thousand questions circulating in his head at once. He knew that a ley line was a path on the landscape believed to have spiritual significance only from extensive reading of fantasy fiction, so he could picture in his mind's eye the scene Chad described. He also had some idea of what these phones could do, and a live TV crew certainly gave credibility to anything that was filmed. But— "I don't understand why MI-5 would care what anyone thought. They never have before."

"They never have had the attention on them that arresting you would bring. Remember I mentioned that I had been influencing content? I have spent the last two weeks broadcasting not only the videos of the plane disappearing, but also a documentary of your life."

"What does that mean exactly?" David had a definite chill in his belly overlaying the dismay.

"I've documented all the incidents of time travel, starting with your mother's disappearance in 1996 before you were born."

David found himself unable to breathe. "You've told people my name? All of our names?"

"I've told them *everything*. Last night's show was an interview with Shane and his parents. That was a good thing you did there. The bus passengers couldn't wait to tell their stories. It makes compelling television. Ratings have been astronomical."

David would have hung up. He wanted to snap the phone in half he was so angry, but he didn't, just gripped it more tightly and instead of saying *how dare you!* he merely asked, in as calm a voice as he could manage, "Have you included my picture?"

"Of course. And before you bite my head off, if I hadn't done this, someone else would have. That plane disappearing was the last straw. A journalist has been working on the story since Rupert Jones left, starting from his notes, which he found in Rupert's desk. He hadn't come forward earlier because he would have been branded a lunatic, and he doesn't write for *The Sun*. I have to say that his research and presence has given the story added weight."

The phone in David's hand dinged, as did Michael's and those belonging to Chad's other people.

"There you go." Chad sounded inordinately pleased. "I just got my new update on your story. I must say, you're looking every inch a king."

Michael had pulled out his phone and was staring at it. "You've got to be kidding me." He brought up his gaze to meet David's eyes.

David grimaced and put up one finger to Michael. "Hold on a second. Just ... just wait." Then into his phone he said, "What just happened? What is everyone looking at?"

Down at the nurse's station, a man exclaimed, "Wasn't this bloke just here?"

"Look at the screen on your phone, David," Chad said, patience for the technically challenged evident in his voice.

David did as he asked and saw a message on the screen with the headline, *Time Travel is Real!* followed by text that had his stomach sinking through the floor. "Chad—"

"CCTV footage of your arrival at the hospital has gone planet-wide. Plus, at least a dozen people had their cameras trained on the archer's target when he missed and hit your friend, who clearly appears out of nowhere with you. Cameras have always picked up the flash as you come in, you know." He paused. "I suppose you've never seen it, but you can now. It's unreal. Just click *play,* and you can see the post."

David didn't want to click play. He didn't want to stay in Avalon another second. "Why did you do this?"

"To protect you, of course. MI-5 can't touch you now."

David had a horrible feeling that what Chad had done was going to end up worse than being chased by MI-5. Michael was looking at him like he'd murdered a baby seal. Heads were poking out of doorways all along the corridor behind Chad's security force. Then three people moved around the nurse's station to gawk. Since David was the King of England, he was used to turning heads as he went by. Heck, people *bowed* to him. But that was in Earth Two. If Michael and the people at the nurse's station were any kind of example, everyone here was just going to stare. One nurse had his phone up, and he was talking into it. After a moment, David realized that he might be taking a video.

Chad had made David into a freak.

He started to take a step back, more hesitant than he had ever felt in his life—and that was saying something. The urge to run was almost overwhelming. He understood now what Anna had meant about feeling like the world had accelerated into the future and left her more behind than the twelve years they'd lived in Earth Two should have done.

But then Michael, rather than the triplets, put out his hand to the man taking the video and took several steps towards him. "Don't do this. He has a right to privacy in a hospital."

Immediately, the man dropped his arm. "Right, man. Sorry." He peered around Michael to look at David. "Sorry. I got carried away."

David lifted a hand, astonished and a little humbled by the apology, enough so that he swallowed his dismay and was gracious. "It's okay."

In a lowered voice, the nurse said to Michael, "That's really him?"

"It is," Michael answered, seemingly sure, though how he could be, David didn't know.

Because in that moment, David was sure of nothing. He'd fallen down a rabbit hole unlike any he'd entered before, and he knew, as surely as he knew his own name, that it was going to be a long drop to the bottom.

10

1 April 1294

Bevyn

Bevyn ripped the sacking off his prisoner's head. "Tell me your name!"

Perhaps if Dafydd had been here, he wouldn't have condoned the sacking and rough treatment meted out to the assassin, but then again, the man *had* tried to kill him. Maybe he wouldn't have been as forgiving as all that.

The man was dressed in faded breeches and an aged cloak that had been torn around the hem even before he'd tried to escape down the wall of the castle, swim a moat, and been shot with arrows. His buttocks and calf, where Morgan's arrows had hit him, had been bandaged, but he wasn't sitting very comfortably.

He did not appear, however, to be in any way subdued.

Lili stood a few feet behind Bevyn. She was dressed in her new skirt and breeches, with her bow and quiver on her back. Needless to say, the residents of Chester were on high alert, and that included the Queen of England. She'd denied herself inclusion in the war party that had left the castle for Beeston and sent Constance in her stead, but that didn't make her any less determined to keep her family and her people safe.

The prisoner lifted his chin. "My name doesn't matter. The king is dead. I am avenged." His Welsh was southern and fluent, though it had a lilt of something else that Bevyn couldn't place. His facial structure spoke of Norman antecedents, but there'd been so much inbreeding among the Normans and Welsh in the south that it was hard to tell the difference between them anymore.

"Do you recognize him?" he asked Lili.

"No." Her arms folded across her chest, Lili tipped her head to one side as she studied the prisoner. "His accent is noble, though, so I think he intended his garments to be a disguise.

"I know who he is." Rupert, the Avalonian journalist, crossed the threshold of the guardroom that fronted the prisoner's cell.

Bevyn guffawed. The journalist was quite literally the last person he had expected to remain behind. "Why aren't you with the army?"

"Beeston will fall with or without me. There was a story here, perhaps the more important one. I'll catch up."

Lili laughed. "Rupert hates waiting. It's only twelve miles to Beeston. If he leaves by noon, he'd make it walking by three."

Rupert scowled. "It is a known fact that you will send someone to Callum once you get out of this fellow what can be got. I sent others ahead, and they'll catch me up once I reconnect with them. In the meantime ..." He brandished a foot-long piece of paper and held it facing outward so others could read what was written on it. Bevyn's written English wasn't great, but even he could make out the *Wanted* at the top. Below were two sketches labeled *Thomas de Clare* and *Aymer de Valence*. "See for yourself."

Lili gasped and took the paper in order to look at the images more closely. "Where did you get this?"

"I had it made," Rupert said. "I was intending to have many more printed than just this one. We were going to paper all of Britain and Ireland with them."

Bevyn looked from the paper to his prisoner, whom he now knew to be Thomas de Clare. "Who drew these, and how did he know what these men looked like?"

"I met Aymer when we came through on the bus, remember? We all did. And plenty of people in Ireland knew what both men looked like. Thomas is married to a Fitzgerald after all. Then, in the aftermath of Tara, I suggested to David we cover the country with their pictures, to leave them no place to hide. I thought to print the poster on the press in Dublin once we returned there and get an artist to duplicate the images on every one." He shrugged. "I'll do a new one now without Thomas's picture, and maybe we'll get Aymer too."

Bevyn felt a rumble of satisfaction welling up in his chest. Handing the paper back to Rupert, he moved to stand again in front of his prisoner and spoke in Welsh. Thomas's family had held the Lordship of Glamorgan, in addition to the Earldom of Gloucester, which was how he'd learned the language. Gilbert de Clare had spoken it too. From all appearances, however, Thomas was a pale copy of his elder brother. He didn't have an outsized ambition or as sharp an intelligence. All he'd wanted was to be left alone in his little region of Ireland. Even his hair was a shade or two less red than the vibrant color Gilbert had grown.

And seemingly, with this latest attempt on Dafydd's life, Thomas had become all rage and no brain, though Bevyn perceived a mind to be in there, somewhere, if he ever managed to put the anger aside.

"Where's Aymer?"

Thomas sneered. "I wouldn't know. Skulking in a cave, no doubt."

"You were allies," Lili said.

"He's weak. A coward. He wouldn't come with me here to finish the job. He didn't have the stomach for a real fight."

"The real fight being shooting the King of England with a crossbow from thirty yards away?" Bevyn said. "Today wasn't exactly a battle. King Dafydd was unarmed. Who's the real coward?"

Thomas's jaw clenched tight, and he didn't answer.

Bevyn folded his arms across his chest. "How did you get into the castle?" Now that they knew the identity of the prisoner, his questioning had taken on a new urgency. Bevyn needed to know if they had another traitor in their midst, one within the staff, perhaps, or among the garrison, who'd conspired with Thomas. He'd penetrated the castle's defenses, and Bevyn wanted to know how he'd managed not only to get inside but to acquire a crossbow from the armory.

"Why would I possibly tell you?" Thomas was genuinely incredulous.

Bevyn made an expansive gesture. "Where are your friends now? It seems to me they convinced you to sacrifice your life for a cause from which you will gain nothing. You owe Roger Mortimer that much, do you?"

Thomas spat on the ground. "I didn't do it for him."

"Then it's Balliol who holds your allegiance?" Lili spoke softly from behind Bevyn. "Why? What did he ever do for you?"

Thomas focused his attention on her. "He gave me a chance to regain my honor. David took everything from me."

Bevyn scoffed. "King Dafydd had nothing to do with your inability to hold onto Thomond. You decided before he ever set foot in Ireland, before you'd even met him, that you were going to betray him—out of fear of what he *might* do rather than waiting to hear what he proposed and giving him a chance to earn your trust."

"He killed my brother." Thomas looked like he might spit again.

"That wasn't Dafydd." Bevyn moved to catch Thomas's chin in his gloved hand. "Don't disrespect your king."

Thomas grimaced around Bevyn's pinching fingers. His lip was bleeding, and he had blood on his teeth. Somewhere along the way, someone had hit him in the mouth. "He was never my king, and he can't ever be mine now that he's dead."

"But he isn't dead. Hadn't you gathered that yet? You should have waited a moment longer to make sure you achieved your goal before you fled." Bevyn laughed. "King Dafydd went to Avalon. He'll be back before you know it."

Lili's eyes glittered. "There's nowhere you can run to now where he isn't your liege lord: Ireland, Wales, and England are all his. And Scotland soon will be."

"And, of course, a Clare can have no land on the continent either," Rupert said in an aside, as if he didn't know Thomas could hear him. "France will be no more willing to harbor him than any other lord, since King Philip of France will hardly hold one such as he in high esteem." He looked hard at their prisoner. "Your brother saw to that."

"I guess it's Germany for you. Or maybe the Danes will take you in." Bevyn laughed again. "Oh wait, what exactly do you have to barter with?"

"And that's only if he gets out of here." Lili had her arms folded across her chest and was studying Thomas's face. "Which he won't."

Bevyn released Thomas and stepped back. Despite the easy mockery of his captors, Thomas wasn't nearly as subdued as Bevyn thought he should be, and he was searching for something to say that would wipe that superior expression off the traitor's face. "Now that he's failed *again*, how well is that first conversation with Balliol going to go?"

Gratifyingly, Thomas appeared to gnash his teeth. "King David has proved to be everything we thought him. He will take all Britain for himself, just as she said." He lifted his chin to point to Lili, and then returned his gaze to Bevyn. "How can you remain loyal, knowing what he is? Knowing what he will do?"

"Because I approve entirely of what he is. If he had the whole world at his beck and call, I could not be more content." Bevyn had perhaps never stated his position as clearly as that, and he was disconcerted that Thomas had pulled the admission from him. It made him question who was interviewing whom. Still, upon reflection, Bevyn was unafraid to speak from the heart. He believed in Dafydd so completely it scared even him sometimes.

He was well into middle age, and he knew enough of men by now to understand that someone like Dafydd came along once in a hundred years, if not longer. King Llywelyn was a remarkable leader, as had been his grandfather, Llywelyn Fawr. But Dafydd was the result of a special kind of alchemy, where the universe—and God—had conspired to produce someone so suited to his time and place that it was impossible to imagine the world without him. While he'd been born in Avalon, in that country called *America*, he belonged to Britain. To place him anywhere else would be to completely misunderstand who he was.

Of course, Thomas sneered at Bevyn's faith. Bevyn contemplated back-handing him across the face, which would be a mild reproof compared to what he would like to do to him. Thomas was an example of a man who'd formed a clear opinion, unreasonable as it was, that he could not be shaken out of, no matter the provocation. Thomas had never met Dafydd, so his prejudices were based on hearsay and others' understandings.

And because of it, he could not be persuaded by anything Bevyn said or did. Thomas's anger dated back to a time long before

Dafydd's crowning as King of England or the death of Thomas's brother, beloved or not. His anger was rooted in his struggle for control of his lands in Thomond. Bevyn could understand how Thomas had come to the conclusions he had. He just wished they hadn't resulted in yet another attempt on Dafydd's life.

"Bevyn, may I have a moment with you?" Lili tugged lightly on the sleeve of his coat.

He followed Lili out of the tower and up the stairs to the rampart, as always the best place for a moment of privacy in a crowded castle. Dafydd had almost died on the wall-walk, but it nonetheless drew his wife.

When she reached the third merlon along the battlement, Lili turned to face him. "Thomas knows he has all the power and isn't going to talk unless he wants to. He has the air of a man who has already decided that he has nothing left to lose except his life—and has convinced himself that he is willing to part with that too."

Bevyn let out a sharp breath. "I know it. I've known it from the moment we realized who he was. Maybe we should give him what he wants and hang him. Whatever his plan, it's dead now."

But Lili shook her head. "I don't think we're ready for that step quite yet—nor do I think he really has lost everything. Revenge alone didn't bring him here, else he wouldn't have so carefully arranged his escape. If all he cared for was triumph, why escape at all? Why not stay and gloat over Dafydd's corpse?"

Bevyn tapped a finger to his lips. "Because when it comes to it, few men are actually ready to die."

Lili shook her head again. "When he shot that crossbow this morning, Thomas wanted to live and had hope for the future, even if a faint one. We need to know where that hope came from and what piece of a larger puzzle Dafydd's assassination fits into."

Bevyn pursed his lips. "That takes us back to Mortimer and Balliol. Thomas was doing it for them. If Dafydd had died, they could still have won."

"But Thomas's life was, by his lights, already over," Lili said. "He'd already lost Ireland for good, and Dafydd had confiscated all of the Clare lands in Wales, England, and Aquitaine. What was Thomas hoping for?"

"He can't think his wife has the resources to ransom him either," Bevyn said. "Juliana FitzGerald has four small children, no husband, father, or brother, and is in no position to bargain."

Lili canted her head. "On top of which, the head of the Fitzgerald clan is dead on the floor of Trim's great hall—at the hand of Thomas's co-conspirators." Her tone was more than a little bitter, not surprising since her husband was supposed to have been numbered among the dead.

Bevyn snorted. "His Irish wife aside, he didn't come here to regain what he lost there. He must know by now that the only reason Balliol and Mortimer included Irish barons in their plans was because they believed Dafydd was more vulnerable at Trim—with his self-imposed terms of engagement—than he ever would be in Wales or England. Roger Mortimer doesn't care about Ireland at all, except as a means to power. Balliol might care slightly more, but again, only as an extension of his own influence. They must have promised Thomas something else."

"Land in Britain somewhere, most likely," Lili said. "But that is still only an incentive if Thomas escapes, and even a hot-headed fool like Thomas should have seen in advance that the chance of escape was slight. What does he gain if he's dead or captured?"

"Oh, I see." Bevyn frowned as he thought, finding nothing insightful coming to him.

Just then, her expression pensive, Bronwen came out of the keep and mounted the stairs to the wall-walk. "I hear we have Thomas de Clare in custody, and he isn't talking."

"He is not." Bevyn related the gist of their conversation, and what he'd been discussing with Lili.

"I think you might be right that Thomas could have been operating under the assumption that he would be ransomed if caught," Bronwen said, "just not by his wife."

Bevyn grunted. "You mean Balliol would pay for him? He might negotiate for Red Comyn because he loves his sister, but I can't see him caring that much for Thomas."

Lili's expression cleared as if a light had just dawned. "If Dafydd had been killed, we would have been desperate and grateful to have a man of Thomas's standing to ransom for our own freedom." She paused. "Could this plot be that intricate?"

"It's already absurdly intricate and based upon assumptions that have clearly proved to be false." Bronwen chewed on her lower lip. "Maybe Balliol promised to take care of Thomas's children."

"I suppose." Bevyn was dubious. "But Thomas would have no way of knowing if Balliol followed through on his promise. On the other hand, I can believe that a desire to see his family again would be enough for him to do his best to escape, even if he had little hope of it."

Lili gave a sardonic laugh. "How's this for ironic? He may have believed that even were he caught, Dafydd would keep him alive because he is weak and loath to do what must be done."

"Namely, hang him," Bevyn said. "After all, Red Comyn molders in a cell in Dublin Castle."

"If that's the case," Bronwen spoke slowly as she chose her words, "maybe he can still be persuaded that all is not lost. He has a young wife and four children whom he wants to see again. We are not desperate like he hoped, but he still has something we want."

"We could use his family's welfare as leverage," Lili said, "but you didn't see him in there. He is nothing if not defiant."

"I am friends with Margaret, his sister," Bronwen said.

"Who's married to the Earl of Cornwall?" Bevyn started chewing on his lip too.

Edmund de Almain, the Earl of Cornwall, had been a powerful magnate under King Edward and, in addition to the Jews and the Italians, one of his principal moneylenders. Upon Edward's death, Almain had been shut out of the regency by more conniving men like Humphrey de Bohun. On the whole, Bevyn assumed Almain had been caught on the hop by Edward's death and the speed at which his rivals had moved to install themselves as regents, but he hadn't balked at Dafydd's ascension to the throne either.

To Bevyn's mind, Almain was a prime example of a man, like John de Warenne, who'd found favor under Edward but had been slighted under Dafydd—not intentionally, but simply because Dafydd was a different man with his own favorites.

Upon Dafydd's return to Wales two weeks ago, Almain had been among the first men Dafydd had contacted to acquaint him with his resurrection. Even now, he was supposed to be marching north with a host of men to join with Dafydd's forces—now Callum's—at Beeston Castle. Bevyn had met him and found him arrogant, not to say haughty. He insisted on being called Almain because his father had been one of the claimants to the kingship of Germany.

But if Margaret was Bronwen's friend, Bevyn wasn't going to argue. "Where is she?"

"At the holy well of Saint Gwenffrewi." It was eighteen miles away.

Bevyn brow furrowed. "Almain has put her aside?" Loveless marriages were more the norm than not, and Margaret had not given her husband any children. In her forties now, ten years older than Bronwen, she was unlikely ever to do so, but if it was to happen, then the healing well was a place to start.

"She was raised in Wales like her brother. The Welsh are not so foreign to her. I think that was why she sought me out after David was crowned and Ieuan and I stayed at his side, to be a friend when I needed one—because she needed one too."

Bevyn nodded. “I will send a rider for her at once.”

Bronwen made a sour face. “Meanwhile, I suggest we allow Thomas time to contemplate his sins.”

11

1 April 2022

Livia

Two weeks ago, Livia had been minding her own business, keeping her head down, and trying to stay off the radar of anyone in authority. She'd been roundly set down at her previous position within Five and had been determined not to do anything that would make waves or cause her actions to be called into question again and jeopardize her career.

Perhaps it was absurd to care so much about her job. When an actor in a television programme speculated out loud about how some action—one that was the right action—might result in losing her job, Livia generally scoffed. Someone with her skills could find a new job. But there was only one MI-5, and Livia would like to keep working for her country as long as it would have her.

And yet, she just couldn't seem to help getting herself into trouble. She was a curious person, and when her mind started ticking over a problem, she couldn't let it go until it was solved. It had been what had made her so successful throughout her schooling. Unfortunately, that curiosity fit less well in a system where orders were given and expected to be obeyed. She'd never been very good at taking orders she didn't believe in.

Which was why, leading up to her discovery of what Mark was up to, she'd read every file and gone through every piece of equipment in her refuse pile of an office, and why she'd gone to see Mark to tell him that she knew about the Time Travel Initiative. Even as she'd been heading for the elevator that would take her upstairs to his office, she'd told herself to leave it be. But she'd pressed the button that said 'up' anyway, and now she was paying the price for her persistence.

God help her, she still wasn't sorry—though she might reach that point if she actually ended up in prison.

"Director-General Philips will see you now." The D-G's secretary motioned towards the door behind her.

Livia smoothed her skirt and walked sedately to the door, which opened a moment before she arrived, held by her boss—Mark's boss too—Jack Stine. "Come in, Ms. Cross."

Absurdly, even in this day and age, she was one of only three women in the room, and the only woman under forty. Twenty heads turned towards her as she moved to one of the two empty chairs around the large table. Before she could sit, however, Amanda Crichton, the head of internal affairs, motioned that she should move to an empty spot a few seats down. The seat she'd been about to take was Jack Stine's.

Nobody introduced her, and Livia wondered if they thought she was a secretary. Or maybe they just didn't care who she was. She had never attended such a high-level meeting before and was unfamiliar with the protocols. She assumed, however, that whatever the reason she'd been asked to attend, until she was spoken to, she should be seen but not heard.

Projecting a confidence that was the last thing she was feeling, Livia pulled out the chair and sank three inches into its plush softness. They really did things right on the top floor of Thames House. Because of her lowly status, her back was to the bank of windows, but the view of the River Thames, from what she'd seen briefly as she'd entered the room, was lovely.

"You have all seen this by now, of course, but as it's why we're here, we'll watch it again." The D-G was running the meeting himself, which revealed its importance like nothing else could have done. He tapped the screen on the tablet before him, and the wall-sized monitor to Livia's left sprang to life, playing a cleaned-up version of what Livia herself had been watching compulsively for the last half-hour before she'd been summoned to the meeting.

One moment they were looking at the somewhat inept stance of an archer dressed in faux-medieval clothing, and the next second his arrow had missed the target at which he was ostensibly aiming. The camera tried to follow the arrow and thus caught perfectly the flash that whited out the camera, followed by the arrival of two men, also in medieval dress, one holding the other. They all knew by now that the taller man was David himself, King of England in his alternate universe.

"This is all over the internet, no doubt." The tall, spare, gray-haired director of internal security, Grant Dempsey, spun slowly back and forth in his chair as he spoke. He behaved always as if he'd seen it all before, whatever *it* was. Livia found herself both irritated and amused that he continued to affect that attitude even though he'd never seen *this* before.

"It is," the D-G said.

"I don't suppose we can get away with it being an April Fool's Day prank?" Dempsey asked John Roswell, head of media relations.

"Maybe at one time, but with everything else that's out there, and the events of two weeks ago? Unlikely."

"Do we know the identity of the injured man?" Amanda Crichton asked.

"He's known as William," John said. "No further report yet as to his last name."

"He might not have one, if he's medieval," Livia said, the words leaving her mouth before she could stop them.

Everyone looked at her, and Jack Stine gave a tsk. "This is Livia Cross. Two weeks ago, she drove Mark Jones, also known as Gabe Evans, our former head of satellite software development, to connect with the sister of David, the uninjured man you see there. The brief before each of you has their bios."

Nobody looked at their folders, and Livia, who hadn't yet opened the folder in front of her, presumed they'd been pored over before she arrived. She opened it now. It contained perhaps a half-dozen pieces of paper—far fewer than what the Time Travel Initiative had accumulated, which she knew because she'd read all those files herself. They were still in her office, each folder secreted among other files. Someone would have to go through each filing cabinet file by file to find them.

Even Chad Treadman had more information than this. She'd tried to stay out of the investigation that followed the disappearance of the plane, and she realized now how little her bosses really knew. She couldn't decide, now that it came to it, if that was good or bad.

"At the time, Livia was cleared of all involvement in Jones's activities," Amanda said. "Are we to understand differently now?"

"Nothing has changed," Jack said. "She's here because Jones trusted her enough to ask her to drive him, and she had contact with him up until the plane disappeared."

There was a little stir around the room at the revelation, which most appeared not to know. In the aftermath of Mark's disappearance, Livia had decided to confess it, thinking that bit of information could do neither of them harm and telling the truth in this instance might distract her questioners from all the truths she was hiding.

She looked up from the folder. "I had nothing to do with anything Mark did or knew prior to the day Anna arrived. He asked me to drive him to the hospital, and I did. I've learned a great deal more since that morning."

"Haven't we all," Amanda said dryly. "What can you tell us?"

Livia gestured towards the screen. "I don't know anything about why David is here now. He certainly hasn't contacted me, not that he would have any way of doing so."

"We know that David has arrived." Grant Dempsey's tone was all patience. "The question is what to do about it."

"Why do we have to do anything about it?" Livia said. "He's broken no laws, and he can't help what he is."

"Which is what, exactly?" Grant said.

Livia cast a glance around the room, wondering what the reaction to the words she was about to say would be. They had to already know them. "David is the King of England in an alternate universe, a place Mark called 'Earth Two'. We cannot take that status lightly."

"So he's insane." Grant slapped a hand on the table and made to rise. "I don't know why we're wasting our time discussing this. Pick him up. Lock him up. End of story."

"Sit, Grant." The D-G's words were a clear order, and Grant obeyed, though the speed at which he lowered himself back down to his seat was just short of insubordinate. The D-G gave a grunt that might have been of disgust and swept his eyes around the room to encompass everyone else, just as Livia had done a moment ago. "Chad Treadman has forced our hand, quite deliberately, I imagine. However it came about, this David has allied with him, and Treadman's purchase of GCW, which some of you may recall I opposed, has given him a platform. David has shown a resourcefulness—and an ability to acquire allies—that makes him unpredictable." Most everyone in the room wasn't looking at the D-G directly, finding the folder in front of him suddenly fascinating.

Livia wasn't afraid to meet the D-G's eyes. "From what I understand, he doesn't mean to be."

"How do I approach him?"

Livia allowed herself an indrawn breath. "It has to be with respect, sir. From the little Mark said, David is still a companion of Alexander Callum, who I think everyone in this room would agree was one of the best agents Five ever employed. Callum serves *him*. I think we would be wise not to forget that."

Grant seemed to have recovered from his run-in with the D-G's glaring eyes, and now he sat back in his seat with a sigh. "I agree. Reluctantly, but I agree. I hadn't considered the issue quite in that light."

"On top of which, Mark Jones, if he's alive," Livia said, "will have told David everything about the current workings of MI-5. We pursued David's sister, to the point of scrambling the RAF to force down Chad Treadman's plane—"

"—and look where that got us," Jack Stine said mockingly into his folder, though his words were loud enough that more than a few lips twitched. "He will not be disposed to view us with anything less than total distrust."

"Will Mark have gone so far as to give him security codes? Passwords?" Amanda said.

"I can't imagine why he would, and Mark would know that we would have changed everything the day he left." Livia made a dismissive gesture. "Again, to see David as an adversary is to look at the situation incorrectly. He doesn't want to destabilize Britain. He, of all people, as the King of England, understands what we do here and why we do it. Again, from the little Mark said, usually David has no choice about the circumstances by which he arrives here." She made another gesture towards the paused video. "That certainly appears to be the case today."

"What does he want?" The D-G's expression was intent but also curious. Livia felt a genuineness that she hadn't expected emanating from him.

"At worst, to be left alone. At best, to help *us*. Callum was the director of the Time Travel Initiative, a project that had David's full support." She paused. "Naturally, we killed it."

"Help *us*?" Jack Stine was also looking interested. "How might he help us?"

"Mark didn't tell me much, but Chad Treadman wanted contact with David because David, whether he likes it or not, is living at the cutting edge of all knowledge. *He travels back and forth to an alternate universe*." She emphasized the words in hopes they would finally get through to her audience. "How could we not want him on our side? Knowing what we know about him, why was he ever put in an interrogation room?"

"Mistakes were made." The D-G tapped his fingers on the table, and nobody interrupted his thoughts. He was a political appointment, as many senior officials now were, but that didn't mean he wasn't intelligent or competent. Livia had never met him before today, but the longer this meeting went on, the more inclined she was to think he was both.

"I was caught on the hop by what went on two weeks ago when Anna arrived." The D-G lifted his chin to point to Amanda Crichton. "You advised me to pursue her with the full force of the law, and I agreed."

"Sir, I—"

"That was the wrong approach, made all the more so because of Five's history with this family, about which I didn't know fully until afterwards. Because I was kept in the dark, because I was making decisions with incomplete information, we lost her and set ourselves back possibly years with these people."

It was rare, not to say unprecedented, for the D-G to call out a senior official in front of his or her peers, no matter how grievous the error. Only now did Livia realize that the D-G was absolutely furious.

"If anyone knows anything else about the circumstances we face, now is the time to speak up, because if I discover that you know more than you're telling me right now, it won't be just your job you'll lose."

The room was so quiet Livia literally could have heard a pin drop.

"I have no desire to enter that hospital guns blazing, nor do I think we should. If nothing else, the optics are terrible. That might have been the old Five, but it isn't who we are today. It should not have been who we were two weeks ago. The advice I received that day was bad. I knew it at the time, but I followed it anyway. So this is not really on you, Amanda." He rocked back in his chair. "Since then, I've been briefed on the moth-balled Time Travel Initiative, along with its goals and accomplishments, which, despite two years of effort, I regret to say weren't much." He focused on Livia. "You know of it, I assume."

It wasn't a question, so Livia just nodded and wondered if the direction to *speak now or forever hold your peace* applied to her too.

Amanda had been looking down at her hands as they rested on the table, but now she looked up. "In the aftermath of Callum's departure, it became clear that he'd been compromised—"

The D-G's response was swift. "You and I both know the project was on the way out before Callum's departure."

Amanda's head dropped again, miming a submissive pose, but Livia wasn't fooled. She was close enough to Amanda to see how tightly she was clenching her jaw.

It was Jack Stine who came to Amanda's rescue. "Though most of us were here at that time, no one in this room was responsible for that decision, sir. Director Tate could tell us more, but so far he has been unwilling to cooperate."

"I have spoken to him," Livia said softly.

All heads turned towards her.

She grimaced at their astonished looks, straightened her shoulders, and focused directly on the D-G. "This probably falls into the *tell me now* category, so I'm sorry if I didn't speak up earlier. He rang to offer his support. Apparently Mark contacted him before he left and gave him my name as someone to be trusted."

The phone call had been unexpected—and somewhat unwelcome. At that point, Livia had been trying to remain under the radar, and a call from a former head of MI-5 and the current ambassador to Finland threatened to upend her carefully cultivated aura of innocence. The call had made her realize, however, how fine a line between right and wrong she was walking.

It was time to let go of her fear. If she was destined for a cell, so be it.

"It's probably time to tell you too that I know a great deal—if not everything—about the Time Travel Initiative."

The D-G stared at her. She'd surprised even him. "Mark told you?"

"I have read the files."

"More than this?" He held up the manila folder. "This is all we have left."

Livia's eyes went to Amanda, who was looking down at her hands. "You really have no copies left? Mark thought that the initiative had been reconstituted in the inner reaches of Five. That's how you got up to speed so quickly two weeks ago."

"That was Amanda liaising with her counterpart at the CIA," the D-G said.

"And this is all they gave you?" She pushed the folder into the center of the table. "This file is woefully incomplete. I learned more by watching the telly."

"You're saying you have more?" The D-G said.

If possible, the silence was more complete than before. Even Grant had stopped rocking his chair.

"A record, complete or not, I don't know, was left in the filing cabinets in my office." And for the benefit of these higher-ups, Livia added, "It's in the basement, where all old machines, files, and furniture go to die."

The D-G turned away, tapped on the screen in front of him, and spoke to the person who answered. "Seal off Livia Cross's office immediately. Nobody is to enter until I myself have done so. Is that clear?"

An affirmative noise came from the tablet, and he looked up again. "Fill in the blanks."

Livia swallowed. "As I assume you know, the Initiative was begun because chasing David and his family all over Britain had proved to be a losing strategy." She then related everything she could remember from the files while being constantly interrupted and peppered with questions, not all of which she could answer.

After a half hour of that, the D-G leaned back in his chair, indicating this particular phase of the meeting was over. He was back to tapping his fingers on the table. "So what do we do now? How do we salvage the situation?"

Whether or not the question was meant for Livia, she answered it, "I don't know that we can." She canted her head, about to add that if the D-G allowed Livia herself to talk to David, all might not, in fact, be lost.

But Amanda slapped her hand on the table.

"We pursued David and his family because we are obligated to protect our nation from all threats, and what he can do is a threat if I ever saw one. How can you not see that?"

Livia turned to her and opened her mouth, but the D-G put up a hand to stop her from speaking and spoke himself instead, "Explain your reasoning."

"I can't be the only one who reads." Amanda stuck out her arm, pointing a finger towards the windows behind them and gesturing expansively. "The changes to themselves or our history aside—which I'm not putting aside but I submit that we might not be able to track those changes—what are they doing to space and time when they travel? *Are* they ripping a hole in the fabric of reality?"

Interestingly, it was Grant Dempsey who laughed. "You've been watching Dr. Who."

Amanda glared at him. "We *have* to know what effect what they do is having on our world. And as far as I can see, David leaves only destruction in his wake."

Jack had his fingers steepled before his lips. "How do you figure?"

"Exhibit A: Caernarfon Castle," Amanda said. "Exhibit B: the destabilization of the intelligence services, to which even our American friends haven't been immune."

The other woman in the room, Kavya Collins, the liaison from Special Branch, spoke for the first time. MI-5 had many operatives but no police force of their own. It would be she who designated the men in black that accompanied agents on their missions. "Even if what you say wasn't absurd, Amanda, there are nations in the world today that are hostile to Britain. Is threatening them always the best way to get them to do what we want?" She shook her head, looking away from Amanda to the D-G. "The reason we went after Anna the way we did was because we thought she was a soft target. An easy target. We did it because we thought we could get away with it."

Grant scoffed. "It is not your place to—"

"It is her place. That's why she was included in this meeting." The soft voice of the D-G interrupted Grant. "Amanda, I want your resignation on my desk within the hour. Grant, are you on board? Are you able to follow my lead in this?"

Grant's skin was pale to begin with, but it became a little whiter. He cleared his throat. "Of course, sir. Always."

"Good."

Amanda rose to her feet. "I have only ever had the safety and best interests of my country at heart." She stalked from the room. The D-G nodded to a man who'd been standing unobtrusively with his back to the wall. He opened the door for Amanda and then followed her from the room. He would shadow her to her office, stand over her while she collected her personal belongings, and escort her to the exit.

"Will she go to the press?" Jack said.

"She signed the Official Secrets Act, just like everyone here," Grant said.

Kavya was studying Livia. "I have been listening carefully to everything that's been said here, and even with the background Livia just gave us, there's more we don't know." As Livia had done, she pushed her dossier on David towards the center of the table. "You know more than you've said, Livia. It isn't just the Time Travel Initiative. I think you even spoke to Anna. I can see it in your eyes. You know *them*. Who *are* these people? It's time you filled us in on what we're missing."

So Livia threw caution to the winds and did.

12

1 April 1294

Ieuan

By early afternoon, Ieuan found himself standing in a field not far from where his company had hidden themselves two weeks ago, binoculars to his face, studying the terrain around Beeston Castle. Cadwaladr and his men had long since left off watching the place. With the army surrounding the castle on all sides, it wasn't as if they needed to hide in the barn anymore, and Cadwaladr had resumed his duties as captain of Llywelyn's teulu.

This time it was Callum, rather than Math, beside Ieuan. Roger Mortimer remained where they'd left him, penned inside his high walls. He hadn't hanged anyone from the battlements yet, which he could have done in retaliation for the arrival of the army. David had decided to take that risk, and had gone to Constance with bowed head to tell her that he wouldn't be trading England's safety to save her husband.

At the same time, Roger had to know that the hostages he held were the only thing keeping David from assaulting the castle with all the power at his disposal. Until a friendly force—namely the army of King Balliol—marched to Mortimer's aid, or David's army finished constructing its siege engines, they were at a stalemate.

Humphrey de Bohun appeared at his right shoulder with Edmund Mortimer in tow. "Is it true what they're saying?"

Ieuan dropped the binoculars from his eyes. He could not mistake the combination of fear, anger, and worry in Humphrey's voice. "I don't know what they're saying, but if they are telling you that the king has taken your son to Avalon, then yes, it's true."

Humphrey's hands clenched into fists. "You should have come to me yourself and told me. I shouldn't have had to find this out from your men."

Ieuan didn't think he should have to justify his actions to Bohun, but the man had lost his son and deserved a gentle reply. "I went to your tent, and you weren't there. I asked that you come to me, so that when I told you, you wouldn't have an audience."

Bohun glared at him for a moment, and then subsided, closing his eyes briefly, maybe even to hold back tears.

Ieuan stepped a little closer. "This happened to me, remember? You've been to the hospital at Dinas Bran. Believe me when I say that what we can do here is a fraction of what can be done for William there."

Bohun swept a trembling hand across his brow. "It's my son. My only son."

Edmund Mortimer put a hand on Humphrey's shoulder and squeezed. The two men were similar in age, both in their forties, cousins as well as lifelong friends.

Callum nudged Humphrey's elbow. "It is regrettable that this happened, Humphrey, but Avalon is the best place for him if he was wounded by the assassin's bolt."

"And where is this assassin?" Humphrey spoke through clenched teeth. "I will kill him with my bare hands!"

"He was in custody and not talking when we left," Ieuan said. "His identity was not yet known."

"I would have made him talk."

"So will Bevyn," Ieuan said.

Angry as he was, even Humphrey couldn't disagree with that assessment.

"He had two arrows in him," Callum added. "Nobody is taking this lightly, believe me."

"William saved the king's life," Ieuan said. "Maybe that's of no comfort, but he was doing his duty as he saw it."

"They were both moving when the bolt hit William's back," Callum said. "William was trying to protect David, and David was trying to move William out of the way in order to take the bolt himself."

"Where was William hit?" Edmund said.

"We don't know." Callum grimaced. "Somewhere on his right side. He was alive when he went to Avalon, I can assure you of that. I can also assure you that with treatment in Avalon, with exercise and patience, a year from now he should hardly be able to tell that it happened."

Ieuan didn't meet Callum's eyes. He was talking through his hat, as Ieuan's wife liked to say, because really they had no idea how bad the wound was. Instead, Ieuan looked at Bohun. "You still with us?"

"God help me." Bohun let out a groan. "But yes, I'm with you. William fights better with his left hand than with his right anyway."

Ieuan had noticed that, actually, but had chosen not to say anything in case it sounded like an excuse for why William's loss was less serious than Humphrey felt it to be.

Callum nodded. "What's the situation with Roger Mortimer?"

"No change," Edmund said shortly. "My brother hides behind his walls. Honestly, at this point, I have no idea what he's thinking."

"If he knew what was good for him, once he knew that David was alive, he would have retreated to France," Callum said. "A fortnight is a long time to wait for retribution—or rescue."

Edmund shook his head. "If he flees, he knows David will come after him. There's no place he can run. His lands are in Aquitaine, which David rules, and the King of France remains an ally of England. He will have no interest in harboring someone who arranged for the murder of an ally, especially David, who saved Philip's life."

"Roger bet everything on a single throw of the dice." Humphrey de Bohun shook himself, as if trying to reorient his mind to the task at hand rather than what it had been stuck on, which was William's welfare. "Scotland is his only hope."

Ieuan gestured to the mountain before them. "It must be as we guessed. Mortimer is waiting for Balliol to come to his rescue." He pinned Humphrey and Edmund with his gaze. "He still hasn't left Barnard Castle?"

"No," Edmund said.

"Why not?" Ieuan folded his arms across his chest. "What is *he* waiting for?"

"David's death?" Edmund said. "Perhaps the assassin was given a fortnight to accomplish his deed, on the chance that it would be all they needed, and they'd be back to where they'd hoped to be after Ireland: David gone and them in control of all Britain."

"David's quick arrival in the plane undoubtedly caught Balliol on the hop as well," Callum pointed out. "He was hoping he had weeks, and he's had only days."

"All the more reason to leave Mortimer to stew in his own juices," Humphrey said. "We can starve him, and he will eventually surrender."

"Not before we succumb to dysentery," Ieuan said.

"This was Plan A, which has not worked," Callum added. "Besides, Balliol will eventually get off his duff and march to his rescue."

Ieuan looked to the castle. "David isn't here, but we must remember his reasoning: Roger has hostages, and he *will* hang them from the battlement before he surrenders."

"So what are we going to do?" Humphrey asked.

Ieuan explained about the elimination of not only Plan A but Plan B as well, since that had involved David's personal appearance at Beeston—not to beg, but to put forth an ultimatum. When he finished, Humphrey looked disgruntled. "I don't see how this *Plan C* can ever work. You're relying on a woman."

Ieuan laughed. "Haven't you noticed by now that these women from Avalon are cut from a different cloth than most women of your acquaintance?"

Bohun's frown deepened. "They seem the same to me. Headstrong. Willful."

"And courageous," Edmund added lightly.

Bohun relented. "I'll give you that. But they're newcomers. Inexperienced. Because she's a woman, Sophie would never have fought, but George is green too."

"Why do you say that?" Callum said.

"I asked if he'd ever wielded a sword in battle. He told me no."

Callum gave a low laugh. "You phrased the question in such a way that he could not answer yes."

Ieuan himself didn't understand what exactly being a *cop in Chicago* meant, but Callum had said the words with respect and with the implication that George knew how to handle himself under difficult circumstances. Chad Treadman might not be a man to trust, but according to Ted, Meg's brother-in-law, he sought out the best and the most competent to work for him. That would be David's saving grace in Avalon as well as theirs here.

Leaving the binoculars with the man who'd taken up the post of watching the castle, they made their way to the large pavilion Ieuan's men had set up some distance from the main army. Roger Mortimer couldn't mistake the army around his castle. He even knew that it was his brother who led it. Their plan, however, was predicated on the fact that he would be distracted by this sibling rivalry and so focused on the enemy at his front gate that he would not be paying attention to the one at his back.

That was where Sophie, George, and a handful of warriors, Constance, Ieuan, and Samuel among them, came in. Bohun wasn't wrong to worry that so much was riding on the newcomer twenty-firsters, but in a way that was their strength too. Ieuan could think of a hundred things that could go wrong with their plan, but Sophie didn't know about any of them firsthand. That was why she would have people with her who *did* know.

Ieuan pulled aside the tent flap and gestured Humphrey and Edmund inside. Most of the Avalonian equipment was displayed openly in the back of a cart, around which the tent had been put up, and she, George, and Mark were bent over what Mark called 'an electronic tablet'. The presence of the equipment was the reason for the pavilion's more distant location and its closed flaps. The fewer people who knew about the strange devices, the better.

Ieuan knew what electricity was by now, though he wasn't so comfortable with what he was seeing that he could take it for granted like these twenty-firsters did. Still, he tried to be nonchalant and asked as he approached the trio, "Do you have what you need?"

Sophie made room for Ieuan, while Callum peered over Mark's shoulder. The image on the screen in front of him showed

Beeston Castle, and Mark was alternating between a picture of what it looked like now with what it looked like in Avalon, where it was a ruin of its proper self. The perspective was unique and startling, in that they were looking at it from somewhere above. With a swipe of his finger, Mark could spin the image to view it from all sides, like a cook walking around a tiered cake.

Ieuan looked away before the spinning image made him queasy.

"We're just confirming the best path to take. If there are differences between what's out there now and Avalon's version, we want to know about them." Sophie looked over at Humphrey. "What we do here can't be accomplished without your part of the plan."

Humphrey had barely glanced at the screen. Perhaps from his angle, it had been distorted or too dark to make anything out. Ieuan had noticed that many of his peers simply didn't want to know what the twenty-firsters were up to. Warenne, in his refusal to accept a radio, had been that way. Bohun had adapted to the sophisticated communication equipment well enough, but electronic tablets were apparently a bridge too far.

Instead, Humphrey turned entirely away in order to clap Ieuan on the shoulder. "Edmund and I will leave you to it. We must get back to the lines and prepare the men for what we do tonight."

Sophie took a step away from the table and engaged Humphrey again. "I am very sorry about William, but I truly believe he will be fine. He's in the best of hands where he's gone."

Humphrey paused a pace from the door and turned back. "I appreciate your sympathy and your confidence." He bent his head in a slight bow. "Godspeed."

"To you as well." Sophie's curtsey was somewhat stilted, but in the last two weeks she'd learned to accomplish it with little fuss.

Mark and George bowed as well, though the blank expressions on their faces were a clear sign that they didn't *believe* in bowing.

Ieuan, who didn't have to bow to Humphrey, walked him to the door. His ten men were waiting by their horses.

"Can they really do it?" Humphrey said.

"You saw them, Humphrey." Edmund's tone was dry as he hauled himself into his saddle.

Ieuan nodded. "I gather you are ready too?"

"Of course. We've been ready." Humphrey paused, as if debating whether or not to say what he was really thinking. Most of the time Humphrey was as forthright as any man, and this time turned out to be no different. "You do realize that nobody has ever entered Beeston except through the main gate."

"We do." Ieuan opted not to tell him that Beeston *had* been taken by this method, just not for another four hundred years and during another civil war against a different king. Humphrey knew about Avalon, but they still didn't talk about time travel in his presence. That really might be a bridge too far. Ieuan didn't think William had known the truth either before today.

Bohun shook his head. "You are mad, all of you." He was still shaking his head as he rode away, but Ieuan saw also that he was grinning.

13

1 April 2022

David

David's arms were folded across his chest as he stared at the crowd of reporters. It was a mob, really. He was standing with Michael on the top floor of the hospital at a corner window above the main entrance. The reporters had gathered on the sidewalk, spilling onto the adjacent grassy area and into the road. A hospital administrator was trying to talk to them, but they were shouting questions that he appeared not to be able to answer. David feared it was only a matter of time before the man threw David himself to the wolves.

"You should step back before they see you, sir," Michael said.

"They can't tell who I am from here." Then he looked at his new companion. "Please call me David."

"You have to assume they have someone scanning each and every window and running any person they see through facial rec."

David had never heard of 'facial rec', but he could guess what it meant and stepped back. Without his asking for it or in any way conveying that he wanted that kind of relationship with Michael, his new friend had fallen into a pattern of behavior very much like the way Callum was with David, acting, along with the triplets, like a security detail. Michael appeared to see it as his job to run interference for David and repeatedly made suggestions that fell just short of telling him what to do. David was listening, for the very good reason that Michael was making sense, pretty much from the first moment he realized who David was.

And *believed* it, crazy as that sounded to David.

In the car on the way to the hospital, David and Michael had chatted casually, with David managing to defer Michael's probing questions by asking some of his own. The last of five children, which was an unusual number of children to have in Britain in this day and age, Michael had laughed to say he'd been horribly spoiled by his four older sisters. After his mother died of lung cancer ten years ago, he'd joined the army out of grief and sheer stubbornness, to prove something to himself and those around him. He'd stayed ten years, rising to sergeant, and left six months ago, during another drawdown that gave him a small pension.

He was now a medical reservist and otherwise unemployed. He picked up part time work here and there, which was why he'd been at the archery contest. The drive hadn't been long enough to find out anything else about him, though David had learned enough in that short time to suggest that Michael wasn't someone to avoid.

"I'm glad you were there," David said. "You saved my friend's life."

"It's what a bloke like me lives for."

That was about as honest a statement as David could have asked for. Michael had been remarkably open for an Englishman. He made a note to mention to Chad, if he had a chance, that he would do well to find a place for Michael in his organization. Though on second thought, David didn't know if the request would put both men in an uncomfortable position: Chad because David would basically be asking him to hire Michael, and Michael for feeling like the job offer was coerced. Would Chad view suggestions from David as commands—and more to the point, obey them?

These kinds of issues were meat and drink to David back on Earth Two, but they'd never been relevant here before because David's interactions with people in Avalon had been limited. Every time but the first time, when David had met Bronwen, Callum had run interference for him. There had been no reason not to let him do that, and every reason to do exactly what he said. According to Darren Jeffries, Callum was renowned throughout the Security Service for being the kind of agent anyone would want to have beside him in a tight place. David had been in many tight places with Callum over the years, and he couldn't agree more.

But he was on his own this time, and whether because he was on his own, or simply because he was older now, he was willing to project himself a bit more than he ever had before. At home he did it all the time, to the point that it was a way of life. He was the King of England there! But here he was an American twenty-something with no ID, no money, and no perceivable status.

If it had been just him alone, maybe he wouldn't even have called Chad Treadman, but William was depending on him, and that made David's decision to act instead of react an obvious one. If an army of reporters was waiting to hear from him, then hear from him they would. He wasn't going to play the kid anymore, or hide, or pretend to be anything other than he was. He couldn't now, anyway, since Chad had blown his cover wide open.

He set off for the elevator.

Michael hustled after him. "Where are you going?"

"Out front. I'm going to take control of the narrative, as my mother might say."

Michael scoffed. "I didn't go to Cambridge. I have no idea what that means."

"Is that a dig at me?" He stopped abruptly to look at Michael.

Michael's eyes widened. "No! I just meant—" he broke off and took a moment before gathering his thoughts and explaining: "In the army, there's a clear division between enlisted men and those who come in as officers. For those of us who were enlisted, it was something we used to say among ourselves. I'm sorry. It just slipped out."

David laughed. "I barely went to high school, so don't worry. I have nothing on you."

They reached the elevator. The security triplets had been patrolling the halls, but at David's sudden change of direction, they'd followed him and now crowded into the elevator too. Two more of their compatriots were standing outside William's door one floor below.

So far, none of Chad's people had said anything beyond conveying words from Chad Treadman, as if they were his puppets. At this point, David wouldn't have been surprised to learn Chad was in the process of buying the hospital—or, since it was part of the National Health Service, donating a wing. What he wasn't doing was coming to the hospital himself, having decided—with David's agreement—that his arrival would only serve to create even more of a media circus. As long as William needed hospitalization, they were in a holding pattern.

"What exactly are we doing?" Reg said as the doors opened onto the ground floor.

David set off towards the main door to the hospital. "I believe it's called *a press conference.*"

Reg, still the triplet in charge, immediately hustled around David to fill the corridor and block his way. "You can't."

"I think I can." David made to cut around him, but now the other security guards planted themselves between him and the front door. Through the tall glass windows, he could see the administrator still appealing to the press, but David couldn't get past the security detail without making a scene.

"Mr. Treadman wouldn't like it," Reg continued. "Please talk to him before you do anything rash."

David pressed two fingers to his forehead, taking a breath and trying to put his thoughts in order. He still felt in his gut that being upfront with the press was the right and sensible thing to do, but in the face of a wall of people telling him it was a dumb move, he was reconsidering.

Mali had been speaking urgently into her phone, and now she held it out to David, who put it reluctantly to his ear.

"Don't," was Chad's first word.

"Why not? You yourself told everyone who I am, so you can hardly be surprised that the press is here. I'd rather talk openly to them than have them digging around for dirt themselves."

"They're doing that anyway." Chad laughed somewhat mockingly. "It isn't as if they're alone in that. What do you think I've been doing for the last six months?"

David's jaw clenched. "What's the worst thing that could happen if I talk to them?"

"You really have no idea how bad it could be," Chad said with equanimity. "I have a different idea, one that will serve you, them, and us much better. Why don't I arrange for a sit-down with someone who will be respectful, who will listen to what you have to say in a place that can be controlled. You'll be able to consider questions and answers without being thrown into the deep end with no prep." Then more faintly, he said, "Amelia, how far out are you?"

"Two minutes."

"Who's Amelia?" David said, realizing that Chad wasn't talking to him but had interrupted their conversation to speak to someone else.

"Amelia is my press secretary, in charge of media relations, and I've asked her to personally take charge of your situation. *She* will talk to the press, and tomorrow or the next day, you can have that interview."

Michael had been standing close enough so that he could hear the conversation and said, "Tell him you want someone Welsh."

David narrowed his eyes at Michael, but repeated what he'd said to Chad.

"Done. I've also arranged for you to stay in a house not far from the hospital. It's gated. My people are already there setting it up."

"I can't leave William."

"You need to sleep," Chad said in a flat voice that was hard to argue with.

David did anyway. "William is not Ieuan. He's a kid from the Middle Ages. He doesn't even know this is the future. I can't leave him alone. Bad enough I'm wandering the corridors while he sleeps."

Chad paused, and his next words showed that he wasn't irritated by the pushback but had genuinely listened. "Let me arrange for someone to sit with him tonight. Someone his own age."

David managed to laugh. "If it's a she, and she's smart and pretty, I'll guarantee he'll like her. She has to speak French."

"I'm on it. She'll be there by eight tonight."

So far, Chad had given David no reason to doubt how far his reach could extend, so he didn't inquire further. Either Chad had someone on staff already who fit the bill, or he was going to call in a girl from Cambridge he'd had an eye on already who was majoring in medieval studies and fly her over.

"What about Peter, Paul, and Mary?" David said, referring to Reg, Mali, and Joe.

"Their relief will come at the same time."

David took in a breath through his nose. "This is crazy."

"Tell me about it." But then Chad's tone went up a notch. "I'm going to figure out how to get there—or get you here. Give me some time to work out the kinks."

The staccato sound of heels on the tile floor behind him told David someone was coming before he turned to see a woman with dark brown hair and brown eyes, wearing a deep red pantsuit, heading towards him. She reached David and stuck out her hand. "Amelia Hopkins." She glanced towards the front door. "I'm here to deal with them." She paused. "Your majesty."

Before David could respond, she walked away from him, heading for the front doors. The one-way glass was the only reason the press corps hadn't spotted David already. By now, the administrator had succeeded in his job enough to convince the press corps to move farther from the hospital, across the median. Mali went with Amelia to the first set of doors, and remained between the outer and inner doors, keeping both sets open by standing at parade rest in the middle of the rug over the sensor pad.

One of the press corps recognized Amelia too, because as soon as she appeared, she shouted, "What does Chad Treadman have to do with King David?"

The wording set David back a pace. The journalist had said, *King David*, in a tone that was straightforward and not mocking.

"Why is King David here?"

"Is King David really from an alternate universe?"

"Excuse me." Amelia put a hand on the administrator's arm, and he willingly gave way, stepping back two paces. Amelia must have had a portable microphone because her words were clear all the way to where David stood in the hospital lobby.

Without Amelia having to do anything but stand before them, at long last, the press corps quieted.

Amelia chose to answer the last question first. "Yes, King David has arrived from an alternate universe, the same one to which the plane went two weeks ago. You all have seen the images. If you're anything like me, you've watched them dozens of times." She laughed, gently mocking herself, and the press corps responded with smiles and laughter of their own.

Michael whispered low in David's ear. "She's good. This is going better than it would have done if you'd been out there."

He knew it was true. "Yeah, you're right."

The words could have come out sour, but while he didn't like knowing that his instincts had been wrong, he was grateful to have been stopped before he did serious damage to himself. David might not like what was happening, but he wasn't in a cell at MI-5 either, so he could go along until such a time as it made sense not to.

Amelia paused and put her hand to her ear, the universal stance of someone who was listening through an earpiece. The press corps knew it, because they remained respectfully quiet, and then Amelia said, "King David has arranged for an interview with Owain

Williams. It will be broadcast at eight pm Sunday night, live on BBC One."

David's heart beat a little faster. That was in two days' time. "He pulled that off quickly."

"He's Chad Treadman," Reg said. And really, what more needed to be said?

What David thought, but decided not to say, was that he wouldn't have been surprised if Chad Treadman had arranged for some kind of interview in advance of David's arrival, ready to be pulled out at a moment's notice. He was pretty sure that his appearance, only two weeks after Anna had left, had only sped up whatever timeline Chad had been crafting. Chad could have already had a plan in place to reveal him to the world in person. David could be mad about being manipulated, but he could also admire competence.

Amelia was continuing to speak, "Until then, please respect the privacy of the patients here, as well as of King David. The hospital has asked that you keep to the public spaces beyond the grounds."

"What can you tell us about his current condition?" The shout came from the back of the press corps. "Was he himself wounded?"

"No, he was not."

"Who is the other man?"

"All will be discussed Sunday night." Amelia nodded. "Thank you for your cooperation." She turned smartly on one heel and marched back to the double doors.

Mali stepped inside with her so the main exterior door closed, followed by the second set of doors into the lobby.

When Amelia reached David, she gave him a hard look. "We are committed. You are committed. We have a lot to talk about, your majesty."

14

1 April 1294

Sophie

"Is this as utterly mad as I think it is?" Sophie said in an undertone to George.

"Does it feel like it to you?"

"Honestly, no more than the fact that we're here at all. As in—I'm in the Middle Ages. Could anything be more insane?"

"Scaling the outside of a mountain to sneak into a castle that up until now has never been assaulted, much less taken, free the captives, and live to tell the tale. What could be crazy about that?" George laughed lightly.

Ieuan appeared beside Sophie, dressed in the gear she'd chosen for him. In defiance of her expectations about medieval people, Ieuan was absurdly handsome and would in no way have looked out of place in a modern setting. She'd expected rotted teeth and pockmarked faces, and while ill people certainly existed, most of the people who surrounded her were the epitome of health. Dr. Abraham had explained his working theory that the immune systems of people who survived to adulthood in the Middle Ages were stronger than the average modern person, whose survival depended on modern medicine. He was studying their blood in hopes of showing it scientifically. Sophie had assured him that, if he ever chose to return to the modern world, Chad would have a place for him too.

He'd laughed, however, and said, "I've caught the bug. My home is here."

It irked Sophie a little bit that only one modern person *didn't* really want to stay: Mark. Chad had talked about how Avalon could learn from Earth Two, but so far she'd learned mostly that she could function without washing her hair every day. And then she laughed under her breath, because that was entirely the point. And she had to admit that David had taken care of the people who'd wanted to return to the modern world by driving them home to Britain in a Cardiff bus. Which he hadn't had to do.

"Second thoughts?" Ieuan said.

"Second, third, and fourth, I'm afraid," she said, "but as this was my idea, I'm hardly going to back out now."

"Cold feet is one thing," Ieuan said. "I need to know if you think we can do this."

"Yes, we can." George's words were firm.

But Ieuan's eyes were on Sophie.

"Yes," she said. "This can work. George and I have scouted the ground. We know where to go in and where everyone is being kept—or were being kept two weeks ago. If this could be done in 1643, we can do it now."

"No mission plan survives the first ten minutes, though," George warned. "Things could go to hell in a heartbeat."

"I know. We have a plan for that event too," Ieuan said. "Callum and I deem it worth it to try."

"Not all your commanders agree with letting us do this," George said, referring most likely to Humphrey de Bohun and his ilk.

"Not all our commanders have the goal to get out of this war with minimal loss of life." Ieuan glanced at him. "Shall I count you among them?"

George swallowed. "No, sir."

"Do you think Avalon's record in caring for human life is better?" Ieuan asked.

George wet his lips, clearly somewhat discomfited by Ieuan's continuing directness. "Avalon's understanding of this world is ... incomplete." He'd chosen the last word carefully.

"I have been married to a twenty-firster for nine years," Ieuan said. "I know of your wars and rebellions. Didn't your Second World War result in seventy million dead?"

George was looking stricken.

Ieuan continued without waiting for George to answer, since the question had been rhetorical anyway, "We who know him are well aware that Dafydd is the best of you and, by coming here, has brought out the best in us. But we are at war, and there comes a time when every commander has to choose among evils and endeavor to pick the least. That's what we're doing here."

"Yes, sir." George nodded. "I apologize if I implied any criticism. I'm used to speaking my mind."

"A habit to which I do not object." Ieuan looked from Sophie to George. "Don't make the mistake of confusing knowledge for intelligence, and I will attempt to do the same. We all have much to learn from each other."

Sophie nodded, understanding that it was easy, among the three of them, to feel superior to medieval people. Technology alone put them at an insurmountable advantage—or so it appeared at first. It had been David, in fact, at the very start, who'd confronted them openly about their intentions. With enough planning and the weaponry they'd brought in the plane, it might be possible for the three of them to take over Britain for themselves—or at least carve out a large piece of it. They'd assured him they meant to use their knowledge and gear for good. Tonight, successfully navigating this slope could save the lives of dozens of people on both sides, depending upon what they found on the other side of those walls.

"Gear check." Andre approached. He had to have overheard that conversation, but he was acting as if he hadn't, adjusting first the straps on Sophie's chest and then George's and Ieuan's.

Sophie and George would go up the mountain first with Ieuan and Andre following. While Andre had declared himself too old for climbing mountains, he was coming anyway because it was he who would situate himself on the top of the wall with his high-powered rifle in order to pick off anyone who attempted to stop them. Constance, one of the four other participants in this crazy endeavor, would do the same with her bow. She, however, wasn't wearing climbing gear. The only scaling of Beeston she would be doing was by rope ladder.

"Ready?" Sophie went to stand in the entryway beside Andre, who was studying the sky. The lantern light reflected off the gray at his temples. They were leaving now, hours before their intended climb, in order to get themselves situated. If they were detected by those watching from Beeston's battlement, despite the darkness, those few hours of waiting could lull the watchers into complacency.

Andre looked down at her. "You're going to need to trust your instincts. You've never been in a firefight before, and your job is not to fight. Don't get pulled into thinking it is. You're leading us up and down that mountain. Leave the shooting to those of us who've trained for it."

Sophie wasn't one to take offense when someone spoke the truth. Andre wasn't being patronizing or asking her to stay safe because she was a woman. He was right that she'd never been in battle. Though she knew how to shoot, she'd never aimed her gun at anything but a target. George hadn't fought in a war either, but he'd been a cop, and he'd hunted deer in upstate Minnesota, where he was from.

Before coming to Earth Two, Sophie herself had been borderline vegan. That had gone out the window pretty quickly after they arrived, and Andre had encouraged her to see that most of her objections to eating animal products had been due to the presence of hormones and chemicals and the lack of ethical husbandry in modern food production. None of which was a problem here. To turn up her nose at what was offered, especially when it was meat, would also be perceived as not only foolish, but an insult. Food here wasn't equivalent to a religion or about control. Dieting wasn't a thing. Food was fuel for life.

"I'll be your spotter, like we agreed," she said.

He grinned. "These eyes are too old for this. This body too."

"So you've said." She snickered. Andre commented often in a disparaging way about his age, but he was fitter than she was.

Ieuan stopped beside her. "Just say the word."

"I'm ready."

Ieuan nodded and made a forward motion with his hand. They set off in single file, Ieuan in the lead with Sophie following next.

The pavilion was hardly more than a half-mile from Beeston's west slope, so they were going to walk it. And it wasn't just the eight of them. They were saving their strength for the ordeal ahead, so other men were coming too, carrying gear, weapons, food, and water. A significant difference between now and four hundred years from now—or seven hundred for that matter—was the absence of a thick woods that surrounded the castle on all sides. No medieval castellan would allow vegetation to grow on the slopes surrounding his castle because it could hide attackers. In 1643 when Beeston had been conquered, the castle had been in disrepair and only fortified again because of the English Civil War. That was the age of cannon, and the vegetation on the slopes had been thought to make no difference.

On one hand, if it had been allowed to exist today, the undergrowth would have been hard to get through. On the other, it would have hidden them during their journey to the top. As it was, they were relying on a cloud cover and a waxing moon that was less than twenty percent full.

Small stands of trees had been left in the fields that surrounded the castle. They'd found one a hundred yards from the point where they would start their ascent, and their companions would wait there.

Sophie found herself breathing shallowly—too shallowly—and she forced even breaths in and out of her lungs. She emptied her mind of everything but where she was putting her feet along the path they were following. She, George, and Ieuan had come this way earlier in the day when they'd scouted the mountain, and she'd had her first view of what Beeston looked like in Earth Two.

Truthfully, with the gear they had, this climb should be easy enough, if they hadn't been in the midst of a war and she wasn't leading men who'd never climbed in their lives. She'd been climbing since she was eight years old, and she repeated to herself Ieuan's warning about not mistaking knowledge for intelligence. Ieuan was right that she had plenty to learn in Earth Two. It might even be that they were walking tonight because neither she, George, nor Andre knew how to ride a horse, and Ieuan didn't want to risk something untoward happening at a crucial moment as a result of their ignorance.

Twenty minutes later, they set up camp amongst the trees. Sophie took a sip of water through the straw on her hydration pack.

The cool water and the familiarity of the action helped to settle her. Andre's hand came down on her shoulder. "Better get some rest. It will be a few hours before the fireworks start and we can move."

Sophie nodded and settled her back against a tree. Around midnight, Humphrey de Bohun and Edmund Mortimer were going to begin their assault on the front gate, located on the east side of the castle. They were going to knock on the door, loudly and with fervor, while Sophie led her team in the back.

15

1 April 2022

David

"For starters, Amelia, please don't call me *your majesty*."

"I apologize. Is *your royal highness* better? You're a king."

"I'm not a king here, and it isn't what we say in the Middle Ages anyway."

Amelia was shaking her head before he was halfway through saying his very short sentence. "You need to stop thinking that way right now. You are not the king of *this* England, but you are the king of *an* England. It's like you're a—" she paused to look out the window, checking, he was sure, for stragglers from the dispersed press corps, "—visiting dignitary, come to England as part of an embassage. As such, you need to be treated with respect, as we would the King of Saudi Arabia, for example. Thus *your majesty* or *your royal highness* is what you should be called, and what I am calling you."

They were sitting in a lounge across the hall from William's room. He was asleep again, having devoured a mostly liquid meal. He was doing far better than David might have expected for someone with a hole punched through him, but David also remembered watching television shows where people with bullet holes in the shoulder were sent home the same day. He supposed it depended upon where the hole was, and a crossbow bolt had the benefit of not exploding on impact. It made the same-sized hole going out as coming in, and the damage was restricted to the area of the hole.

David had asked the doctor if everything was going okay and been assured that it was. But even the doctor had appeared a little wide-eyed about David's existence and had spoken with deference and a demeanor that made David wonder if he was telling him what he wanted to hear rather than the truth.

He said as much to Amelia, who replied. "You're the King of England." It had become her mantra.

"We're in Wales, though, in Gwynedd, even."

"So you're a prince of Wales, one who really is Welsh, for all that you're also American. England has an American princess now. Surely Wales can have an American prince."

Chad's army of employees had been streaming in and out of the hospital all day, adding weight to the idea that David might really be who he said he was. By now, everybody on the planet had seen the new video of his and William's arrival, and though David had overheard a general agreement that it could have been faked, the existence of the video plus the reality of David standing at a nurse's station in their hospital was hard to deny.

Chad's infusion of staff hadn't all been, like Amelia, about the press corps. The promised young woman, a dark-haired, blue-eyed third year university student, had arrived to sit with William. If he leaned forward, David could see her now. She had a laptop open on her lap and was typing away at a paper on Alfred the Great. Though she spoke no Welsh at all, her medieval French and English were pretty good.

For the others, David had the distinct impression that Chad was afraid he was going to disappear again—for good reason—and he wanted to gather as much information as he could while he had David in his clutches. Suffice to say, both David's and William's blood had been drawn, and scientists in labs all over the UK were rejoicing—and hard at work—tonight.

David eased back into his chair. Amelia was making a certain kind of sense, but if the pomp of being king in Earth Two had always made him uncomfortable, here in Avalon, it struck him as completely archaic. He was an American, from a country in which every person was the king of his own castle, and even the poorest person could view himself, as John Steinbeck once said, as a temporarily down-on-his-luck millionaire—though why the first semester of his high school American lit class was coming back to him after twelve years, David didn't know.

Worse, part of him wouldn't mind at all being treated with the respect *your royal highness* would afford him, and he distrusted the emotion enough to prefer erring on the side of caution.

He did know, however, as much as he hated to admit it, that he was as out of his depth in Avalon as Anna had warned him he would be. "My relationship to my people is just so much more personal."

"What do you mean?"

"It's weird the way *your majesty* or *your royal highness* changes the pronoun around. At home, while I have been called *your grace,* the honorific is usually reserved for churchmen. To my face, everyone says *my lord.* Do you see the difference?"

"You want me to call you *my lord*?" Even Amelia, the embodiment of the serene spokesperson, was aghast.

He laughed. "You can't do it, can you? That's because it *means* something. You can say *your majesty* with detachment." He sobered. "Call me David. Please."

Amelia pressed her lips together, and David had a feeling she wasn't going to call him anything at all—or he was stuck with *HRH.* When he got back home, he was going to make a point of asking his mother when the change had occurred. He guessed that some pompous European prince during the Renaissance or the French Revolution had thought it sounded better or put him above his otherwise peers.

"All right." Amelia picked up her tablet and swiped through several screens. "To get back to my main point, you *are* a king, and regardless of what you want to be called, you need to think of yourself as one here."

David took in a breath through his nose and let it out. "Okay. I will take what you've said under advisement."

"How long have you been king?"

"Five years."

"Do people still question your right to rule?"

He laughed. "I'm in the midst of a civil war right now, didn't you know?" He tipped his head. "Though admittedly, that war was predicated on the idea that I'd been assassinated in Ireland, so the people usurping the throne were taking it from my three-year-old son rather than from me."

Amelia was genuinely gaping at him. "I-I didn't know."

"I hadn't said before now. Anna only knew about the attack on her outside of Llangollen."

"You're keeping the throne, though, right? You're fighting back?"

"Oh yes." He nodded. "I didn't seek the crown and the power that goes with it, but it is mine, and I would be doing my people a disservice not to use what they have given me to better the world."

Amelia pressed her lips together in something that looked almost like a smile and glanced from him to her tablet and back up again. "Did you read my notes?"

David looked at her warily. "What notes?"

"What you just said was my next talking point." Now she genuinely smiled. "You're good. Maybe this won't require a total makeover."

He folded his arms across his chest and studied her. "You are doing what they all do, every time."

"What is that?" She was flipping through screens on her tablet, not paying complete attention.

"Treating me like a kid."

Her head came up, and her face paled. "No, I wasn't."

He raised his eyebrows. "Why do I need a makeover?"

Amelia put out a hand to him. "That's not what I meant. Really, it isn't. I was being flip when perhaps I shouldn't have been."

"You are correct that I don't have experience with talk shows or interviews. We don't have cameras in the Middle Ages, but I can be coherent when I choose to be."

"I know that." She took in a breath. "But really, you're misunderstanding me. What you wear, how you stand or sit, and everything you say is going to be dissected by the entire world. It is so easy for any of that to be misinterpreted. My job is to try to manage that process. I'm not trying to manipulate *you*. I'm trying to manipulate *them*." She threw out a hand to indicate the world at large.

David nodded slowly. "I get that. And again, I am well aware that I am out of my depth here. The world has changed, and I'm not a part of it anymore." He spread his arms wide. "I am in your hands."

Amelia nodded vigorously. "Thank you. Chad has suggested, and I agree, that we need you to look the part, to project an aura of a king. Saying you are one isn't enough." She gestured up and down with her hand to indicate his appearance. "First thing tomorrow morning, Chad is flying in a tailor."

David looked down at himself. Even before coming to Earth Two, he had cared very little about his clothing. He'd lived in jeans, t-shirts, and sweatshirts. At the moment, he was wearing his medieval pants, shirt, and boots, which he'd had on when he'd arrived. He'd removed his overtunic, cloak, and belt knife, all of which were stashed in a locked closet in William's room.

"Will you want me to wear a suit?"

"Suits are what the royal family wears to events, but if members of the younger set were going on the Owain Williams show, they might wear something more casual. Chad has people studying the issue."

"You mean he has focus groups telling him what would make me most appealing?" David laughed again.

Amelia didn't. "Yes."

David instantly sobered. "My valet would love this. The chamberlain and his varied assistants as well. He and my wife are capable of discussing the various merits of my clothing long past the point where I have any interest."

"About five seconds, I imagine?"

David grinned. "Exactly. If Lili were here, she would have understood all this immediately. We manage my image there too. It's just that the conversation revolves around the wearing of robes and scepters and crowns."

Amelia leaned forward. "You don't have to be interested, but you need to let me stand in for your wife. If you were dealing with one of those rebellious barons—or that Scot king, Balliol—you would be focused, wouldn't you?"

"Of course."

"The entire world—and I mean that quite literally—will be watching. You need to treat this with commensurate seriousness."

David eased back a little into the softness of his chair. Early on in his kingship, his natural inclination had been to think that speaking the truth was enough when it came to public relations. At the time, he hadn't understood how everything he said fell under diplomacy, but he did now, even if he might mock the need for political calculation. Lili was a master at it, and he felt she had a natural charm that put everyone at ease. He had a harder time with it, coming across as either arrogant or too earnest. He also still found himself embarrassed by the attention given him.

Over the years, however, he'd learned the folly in making light of what others cared about, so he gazed steadily back at Amelia and promised, "I will. Tell me what to do, and I'll do it."

16

1 April 2022

Amelia

That was more like it.

Amelia rose to her feet and headed for the door, leaving David contemplating the new phone she'd left with him. A glance over his shoulder as she walked away revealed him to be googling the phrase *your royal highness*.

She'd been Chad Treadman's public relations head for three years now, which was a lifetime in this business. Ideas needed to be fresh, and it was easy to screw up and find yourself out the door. Amelia had actually met David's aunt, Elisa Shepherd, at a conference several years before Ted had come to work for Chad. Elisa had been well-respected within her field, and the work she'd done for the U.S. embassy had been stellar.

It was actually Elisa's sudden absence more than anyone else's that had made Amelia provisionally believe in the whole time travel/alternate universe scenario. David's existence aside, an entire family had disappeared into thin air, along with the plane they were traveling in.

When Amelia had asked David about how his family was doing in the Middle Ages, he'd made a rueful face and said they were as well as could be expected. It was the perfect response, utterly convincing. She was faced with a stark choice: either David was a consummate actor, hired by Chad as a publicity stunt, or time travel was real. Or everyone around her was mad. Given how the world was going these days, the last option wasn't as far-fetched as it should have been.

"Is there anything I need to know?" Michael was standing with his back to the wall to the right of the lounge area door. He'd been guarding the entrance. With a dozen other security men in the hospital, it was an unnecessary precaution, but it made Amelia feel better to know that everything that could be done to protect David was being done.

As soon as Reg had scanned Michael's ID, Chad's people had, of course, run a complete background check. He was clean, exactly what he said he was: an apparently innocent bystander who had the skill to save William—and the desire and temperament to stick around once the danger was over. He didn't appear to be either an attention-seeker—quite the opposite, actually—or someone who stalked celebrities.

"I think I've convinced him of the importance of this interview and his interactions with the press," Amelia said. "Up until now he's been dangerously naïve about them."

"Can you blame him? They don't have a press corps in the Middle Ages." Michael paused. "I can't believe I just said that."

"And with such authority too!" She laughed and stuck out her hand. "We haven't formally met. I'm Amelia Hopkins."

Michael smiled as he shook her hand. "Michael Dawar."

She narrowed her eyes at him. "Pakistani?"

"By way of Manchester, but yes."

"My grandmother was from India."

"So we shouldn't be friends?"

She laughed again. "Peace begins at home." Then she drew in a breath prepared to ask him something a bit more personal. Maybe David's honesty was rubbing off on her. "Why are you here? What's in it for you? You don't strike me as someone who follows the limelight."

"Treadman's people have probably interviewed nearly everyone I know by now, checking up on me, so you know I'm not." He shrugged. "I was onsite to treat William. That's really all there is to it. Then David needed someone to drive him to the hospital, and because William didn't speak English, I was worried that he might get into the emergency area and find nobody understood him." He gestured to the walls to indicate the hospital. "I don't have anyone waiting for me at my flat, so I thought I'd see this through for a bit."

"David asked that you be given a room at the house if you want it."

Michael looked towards the open doorway. David had risen to his feet and, his hands deep in his pockets, was staring out the window at the car park. "I'll wait for him."

Amelia studied Michael another moment before reaching into her bag for her phone. "I don't want to insult you by offering you something you don't want, or implying you're here for the money, but Chad would like to hire you, for your sake as well as his."

"*His* being David's, or *his* being Chad Treadman's?"

"Either. Both. Liability is a huge issue, as you must be aware. As our employee, you would be protected under the auspices of Treadman Global. We can make the hiring retroactive to yesterday, so nobody can go after you as a private citizen. Whatever you've done in the last twelve hours, you've done for us."

Michael looked at her a bit sideways. "And what is it I've done? I'm not sure why I need this."

Amelia took a step closer and lowered her voice. "We have two concerns. The first is MI-5."

Michael swallowed hard. "I have heard bits and pieces regarding them. MI-5 sent the fighters after Anna's plane two weeks ago, yeah?"

"Yes. Five years ago, right after David became king, he returned to our world with Alexander Callum, a former MI-5 agent. Against Callum's recommendation, agents locked David up, among other things."

"So you're saying that as an employee of Treadman Global, I will be treated differently than if I were merely a private citizen."

"Exactly. In addition, as soon as the press realizes that you have been at David's side today, people are going to want your story, and they're going to tear apart your life to get it. Let us help you." She eased back. "Besides, I can attest that the pay and benefits are excellent. Chad believes in finding the right people and paying them well for what they do. People are not fungible in his world."

Michael studied her and then looked to where David still stood, deep in thought. "Is he for real?"

"Who? David ... or Chad?"

"Either. Both." Michael laughed at the way his response mimicked hers.

"Chad is a great boss. I wouldn't work for him if he wasn't, and he has never asked me to do anything I considered unethical."

Another laugh. "That would be a first, after Afghanistan." He paused. "I would be working for David, though, as long as he's here."

"Yes."

"Okay, I can do that." He hesitated. "Speaking of David, you didn't answer the other half of my question."

Amelia raised her eyebrows. "You've seen the videos and the documentation as much as I have. You were the one who was in that field today. What do you think happened?"

"I don't know. David and William appeared out of nowhere, wearing medieval gear. William's wound was all wrong for a gun, and the archer who shot in his direction eventually collected his arrow, which wasn't bloody. It isn't as if I have another explanation for how they could have appeared in that field where a second before there was nobody. You have to remember, though, that I didn't actually see it happen. Someone ran to get me, and I just dealt with the aftermath."

"What other explanation do you have?"

He shook his head, his lips pressed together.

Amelia gave him a rueful smile. "*When you have eliminated the impossible, whatever remains, however improbable, must be the truth.*"

"It's a nice thought, but I would have said that time travel was the impossible thing that had to be eliminated."

"Except for the part where they appear out of nowhere, just as David has done on and off for the last twelve years." She tsked through her teeth. "Look at me, defending the idea where five minutes ago I was doubting it too."

"If it isn't time travel—or universe hopping—the real question to ask is what else it could be? Where is the plane? Were all those people on the bus hypnotized? Where did they go for nine months? Is abducted by aliens really a better answer?"

"I wouldn't say so," Amelia said matter-of-factly. "And really, conspiracies are considerably harder to maintain than it looks on the telly. Two thousand people plus a BBC crew saw that plane disappear. How do you explain that?"

Suddenly, the communicator in Michael's ear barked loudly enough for Amelia to hear it. She had taken hers out while she'd been speaking with David. Employee or not, Michael had remained at David's side, and that meant he had been included, because to do otherwise would have been stupid.

"What's happening?" In two strides, David, who had heard the sound too, filled the doorway.

Michael hastily turned down the sound on his earbud. His head was bent, listening. "MI-5 is here."

"Not again." David's face was ashen, but there was a set to his jaw and a glint in his blue eyes that told Amelia he was prepared to fight.

She put out a hand to him. "Chad planned for this. We're going to face this head on."

"With cameras rolling." Michael pulled out his phone.

Two of Chad's security men came trotting down the hallway from the nurse's station, heading towards the elevator doors at the far end. Two more halted in front of David. Given the tight gun security in Britain, none of the agents on this floor carried a gun, but Amelia saw the way Michael's hand had reflexively reached for his hip before his hand clenched around his phone instead.

Then the elevator doors opened. Instead of a host of Special Branch officers with automatic weapons, the only person who stepped out was a lone woman wearing a trim navy suit dress and heels. She wore her blonde hair piled on top of her head and walked out of the elevator with a steady grace. Beside Amelia, Michael sucked in a breath of air. As a media person, Amelia devoted more time than she thought reasonable to what she looked like, but she couldn't hold a candle to this woman. And yet, oddly, the woman's sheer magnificence made her completely nonthreatening. And as a fellow professional, Amelia could appreciate how much harder the woman would have had to work to gain her co-workers' respect. For now, Amelia herself could give her the benefit of the doubt.

Nobody said a word until the woman was six feet away. Then the two guards in front of David moved aside. In her three inch heels, she was at most two inches shorter than he was, and Amelia felt a twist of sympathy since her feet had to be killing her.

Then she smiled and stuck out her hand. “Hi. I’m Livia. I’m hoping that you can tell me how Mark is doing.”

17

1 April 2022

Livia

David shook Livia's hand, having introduced everyone else to her and explained that she had helped Mark escape from MI-5's clutches. Those were his exact words, in fact, and Livia was glad she had insisted on going into the hospital un-miked.

The expression on David's face as he'd spoken was one of bemusement. Livia herself was struggling not to go all fan-girl on him. At least he wasn't wearing a crown, just a blue linen shirt in a color that matched his eyes. Strangely, without his cloak he seemed bigger—taller with broader shoulders—than when he'd been wearing it in the video. He filled the hallway.

To cover her uncertainty, she gestured to the lounge behind them. "Could we talk in private?" She stuck her arms out at her sides. "Check me for weapons if you must."

The female security officer did so, patting her down with no-nonsense movements. Then she stepped back. "She's clean."

David looked at his companions, none of whom appeared very happy. "I'll be okay."

Amelia glowered at him. "You had better be."

David gave Amelia a thoughtful look, but then he gestured that Livia should precede him into the room. Once inside, she made to sit, but he flipped off the light switch before gesturing that she could come with him to the window to look out. Now that the light was off, she could see down into the car park. A phalanx of reporters had set up at the far end, waiting, apparently, for something to happen. Fortunately, they hadn't known who she was and hadn't stopped her as she'd crossed the car park. Because of what she looked like, they probably wouldn't have believed she was working for MI-5 if she'd told them outright.

"I saw them when I came in," she said. "They seem to have accepted that you aren't coming out any time soon."

"We were just about to head out, actually. Chad has set up a house for me."

Livia pressed her lips together. That was something Five would have wanted to know about sooner. "Where?"

He glanced at her, a smile playing around his lips. "Close by." Then he turned to look at her directly. "What do you have to say to me? To tell you the truth, I expected you—or your agency—hours ago. Where are the men in black?"

"They are not coming." She turned away from the window and walked to one of the sofas, which when she sat down turned out to be softer than she'd expected. She supposed that people who weren't David might have to sleep in them from time to time.

David left the window too, but instead of turning on the lights, he pulled a matching chair closer to the sofa and sat as well. "Why not?"

"Director-General Philips regrets the recent events with your sister and wishes to apologize."

David laughed out loud. "Really."

"Yes, really."

His eyes narrowed. "Though I appreciate the olive branch, does he actually think an apology is sufficient? You guys chased her into a mountain."

"We know."

David gave a low grunt and leaned back in his chair. "I'm listening."

"We want you to come in—"

He scoffed. "Not a chance."

"Please give me the opportunity to explain."

"I have no interest in a windowless room."

Livia cleared her throat. "That is not in the cards. What I was going to say is that we want you to come in on your own terms, to talk to us at a place of your choosing."

"You do realize that we've done that before too? We tried to meet once on a motorway. You didn't keep your word." He rubbed his chin as he studied her. "Why should I trust you to keep it now?"

Livia had expected some resistance, but she had hoped that using her as the emissary would soften David's combative attitude a bit more quickly. Truthfully, she'd hoped her appearance would divert him. As it hadn't, she opted for more honesty. "That's why the D-G sent me. Mark trusted me, and he's hoping that you can too."

"It isn't you I don't trust." David had one arm across his chest and the fingers of his other hand to his lips studying her. "Last I heard you were a lowly tech in Mark's division. Are you telling me you've suddenly been promoted? That you have the ear of the D-G? I imagine there's a great deal he isn't telling you."

Livia nodded. "I'm sure there is, but I believe him on this."

"I don't."

"You have the D-G's word." She held out her phone to him. "He would like to speak to you to tell you himself."

David scoffed. "What exactly are you looking for, here?"

"The same thing everyone wants. Answers."

"To life, the universe, and everything?" At Livia's serious nod, though David had been joking, he added, "And you think I have them? I'm as much a pawn in this as anyone."

Livia found the way his eyes remained on her face disconcerting. She had a feeling that the mind behind those eyes was constantly assessing her and his situation. He was a coiled spring.

She urged the phone on him again. "Please. Just talk to Director Philips."

With obvious reluctance, David took the phone and pressed the green button. The D-G picked up on the second ring. She'd set it to speakerphone already, and his voice boomed out. "Hello?"

Livia leaned forward. "Director? This is Livia. I'm with ... King David." Inwardly, she cursed at the hesitation.

At first, she hoped he hadn't noticed, but the smile on his lips told her he was fully aware of exactly what she was thinking and feeling. David tipped his head. "This is David."

"Thank you for speaking with me. I'll get right to the point. We're hoping that you will meet with us in a more formal setting."

"Why?" All of a sudden, David was sitting perfectly still, as if he didn't want to give anything away by an inadvertent motion. Whatever nervous energy he'd displayed before was gone, replaced by a calmness that Livia didn't necessarily believe.

"We are seeking knowledge, that's all. We have no intention of detaining you."

"Under Callum, we had a similar deal. It was you who went back on it, not me."

"Mistakes were made."

David gave a little tsk. "But not by you?"

Livia imagined it had been a long time since the D-G had been confronted so openly, but he didn't rise to David's bait. "I know Livia has extended my personal apologies for what happened with your sister."

"Apologies are nice, but words are cheap. I have no reason to trust you."

"We have not entered the hospital in force."

David was silent a moment. "Is that a threat?"

"No. No. I'm just saying that we could have."

"I'm supposed to thank you for that, am I?"

On the other end of the line, the D-G took in an audible breath. "What has Chad Treadman offered you?"

"With him, I have a bed not in a prison cell, among other things."

"In exchange for—" The D-G left the question hanging.

"For giving him a front seat in whatever is going on with us." Even though the D-G couldn't see it, David pushed up his sleeve to show Livia the bandage across his vein from which blood had been drawn. "So far I am not unhappy with the exchange."

"He plastered your picture all over the planet."

David laughed under his breath. "Yeah, he did."

She leaned forward again. "Do you really trust him?"

"No," David said immediately, speaking both to her and the mobile phone, "but you must see my problem, right? I trusted MI-5 once and look where it got me."

"That's fair," the D-G said, "and again, I'm sorry for what happened in the past and for the role I played in it. But this time it's different."

"You have yet to explain how or why."

The D-G paused. "I'll let Livia do that." He hung up.

"Wow." David's eyes crinkled in the corners. "I must have offended him."

"He isn't used to being distrusted or ignored." Livia too was surprised that the D-G had disconnected the call so suddenly, but she had trusted him this far and thought he had a plan. It could be that he realized he wasn't getting anywhere and decided to quit before he made things worse.

"If he has a problem with me, all he has to do is send his men in here to get me. I'm not going anywhere."

"That's exactly what he doesn't intend to do, David. He just told you that."

"Can you blame me for thinking that this is all a ploy to get me to cooperate, to trick me into meeting and get me out of the public eye, after which you can do whatever you want with me?"

"Do you really think that's what this is about? That I would be a party to something like that?" Livia was offended for not only herself but for Five.

David laughter held derision. "Why *wouldn't* I think that? And this is an interesting argument coming from you, seeing as how you helped Mark and my sister in defiance of your employers. Why do you believe them now?"

"Because—" She looked up at the ceiling for a second, understanding how it might seem crazy to him. "I sat in the meeting with all the department heads. The D-G fired the head of internal security right in front of me and had her escorted from the room. He really does want to correct the mistakes of the past."

"And that wasn't all just a show for your benefit?"

Livia hesitated. "I don't see how it could be."

"Exactly my point. You have faith. Even after being screwed over by MI-5 more than once, you still believe they have your best interests at heart?"

Livia flushed. "I—"

David put up a hand. "It's okay. Mark does too, despite everything that's happened to him and what they've done to him. It's one of the things I like about him." He gazed contemplatively at her for another few seconds. "But trusting you and believing the D-G are two very different things."

"He does want to turn a page on the way we've treated you."

"So you've said, but what would be happening right now if Chad hadn't spent the last two weeks broadcasting my story? The D-G didn't send you to the wilds of Wales out of the goodness of his heart. Chad was right, as it turns out, and I will tell him so when I see him. Philips doesn't want the publicity of taking me down while cameras are rolling."

David got abruptly to his feet and went again to the window. He cupped his hands around his eyes and stared out. "Where are they hiding?"

"Who?" She joined him at the window.

"Your men."

"I have a driver, but there's nobody else. I swear it."

"Uh huh."

"You don't believe me about that either." It was a realization, not a question. She was a little stunned at how badly she and the D-G had handled David. And maybe that was the problem. They'd gone into this focusing on handling him—managing him. For all that every word she'd said to him was true as far as she knew it, the impetus behind it wasn't so things were better for *him*. It was so things were better for *them*.

"I believe that you believe there's nobody out there. I'm just not sure why I should believe it." He pointed to a SUV backing into a space in the car park. The vehicle stopped, but nobody got out of it. "That one of yours?"

She chewed on her thumbnail, a habit she'd trained herself out of years ago. "I don't know, but I will find out."

David studied the vehicle for another minute. "Call your boss. Tell him Chad will call *him* with the details of a future meeting. I want it to be with Philips, personally, or nobody. We can do it tomorrow afternoon, if he likes."

"Okay."

"Meanwhile, you can hang with us."

She paused with her phone halfway to her ear, uncertain if she'd understood him. "Really?"

He shrugged. "That's what he wants, isn't it? Access? He can have it, if it's you." With a nod, David headed for the door. "I'll let you talk to him in private."

He shut the door behind him, leaving Livia alone in the dark. Her finger hovered a moment and then pressed the green call button.

A man answered. "Yeah."

"Are you in the car park in the corner under the light?"

There was a pause. "Yeah."

"David made you."

There was more hesitation on the line. "That's not possible."

"He stood beside me and pointed out your vehicle. I swore there was nobody else, and then there you were. I told you not to arrive at the hospital until after I left. Instead, you made me look like a liar."

The man on the other end of the line swore.

Livia gave a tsk of disgust. "Patch me through to the D-G. He wanted to hear the outcome as soon as I had one."

Grumbling to himself, the man obeyed. Livia waited through a few more beats and then Philips came on the line. "How did it go?"

"He doesn't trust us."

"For good reason, I admit."

"David says he'll meet with you and you alone at a place of Chad Treadman's choosing."

Philips let out his own burst of air. "Treadman." The word had weight.

"We blew it a long time ago, sir. It's going to take time to rebuild trust."

"I know. That's why you're there."

"Is it?" The sick feeling in Livia's stomach worsened. "You promised to let me do this."

"I have let you handle it, and I will continue to do so," Philips said firmly, "but I believe strongly in tying my camel too."

She wouldn't have put the director among those who routinely referenced Arab philosophy, the more complete quote being, *trust in God but tie your camel,* but she could appreciate his point nonetheless. In other words, Philips wanted to do everything he could to control the situation.

"He made our men the moment they parked in the car park."

"Did he? Good for him." To her surprise, Philips barked a laugh. "Idiots."

"They need a different vehicle. One less noticeable."

"A black SUV is noticeable?"

"It is to David, who's been chased by them."

"Point taken." He grunted. "Good work. Stay with him if he lets you."

"He invited me to his house, so yes, I will stay with him."

"That lets us know where he's staying." The D-G's satisfaction was palpable. Then he paused. "Does he realize this?"

"I wouldn't underestimate him, sir."

There was another pause on the line. "Is that your professional assessment?"

Livia answered without hesitation. "Yes, sir. He pretty much lives up to the hype."

18

After Midnight

2 April 1294

Callum

"I never intended to come here again."

"I know." Callum stopped beside Mark as he hovered over his equipment. Since they could do no more good for Sophie and the others, who even now should be making their way up the cliff on the west side of the castle, Callum had moved closer to where the bulk of their forces were camped on the east side, in preparation for the assault on the main gate.

Mark glanced at him. "I'm not okay, if that's what you're wondering." He gestured generally. "Not with any of this. I honestly thought I could do this again, and it could be like it was before, but it can't. And I can't. I have to go home. My need for it is driving me just a little bit mad." All the while Mark was talking, in between swiping at his tablet, he was fussing with his other electronics, checking connectors and screens. He was in charge of the timing of the various aspects of this plan. This was the Middle Ages, so nothing would normally be timed to the minute, but Mark was trying anyway.

"We need you."

"I *know*." He emphasized the last word. "And it's clear to me that MI-5 doesn't. Nobody does back in Avalon. I've frittered away my life there, thinking I could make a difference, and I can't."

Callum knew he needed to tread carefully. He had come to check on how things were going, more out of due diligence than because he thought anything might be wrong. This really wasn't the time for this conversation, but it seemed they were having it anyway. "Is it the war?"

"Of course it's the war." Mark let out a burst of air.

"David—"

Mark cut Callum off with a gesture. "I know it isn't his fault. It isn't as if he's going to roll over for these people." He glanced over at Callum. "You know why I'm angry?" The question was rhetorical so Callum didn't even try to answer. "There are wars in Avalon too. The world is going to hell in a freaking handbasket, and there's nothing I can do about it. Half the world tries to insulate itself from thinking about how the other half is suffering, and I sit in my office and push paper around. I bloody well know I'm needed here and not there, and as you can probably tell I'm pissed off about it!"

During the tirade, Callum had eased slightly away. He *was* well aware that there was nothing he could say to Mark that would be right. Mark was going to have to come to terms with his current circumstances one way or another.

But he tried anyway. "You can make a difference here."

"Shut up." Mark pressed a button on his tablet. Then he glanced at Callum. "Sorry."

"Oh no." Callum put up his hands. Mark had never in his life spoken to him that way. "I got you into this."

Mark scoffed. "I got me into this. That'll teach me to do what I think is right." Then he laughed, and it actually sounded genuine. "Give me another few seconds here, and we'll be ready for this latest crazy idea."

"You're the one who suggested it."

Mark shook his head. "David was the one who suggested it. I just took the idea and ran with it."

"It has the benefit of not starting with killing people."

"I'm good with that. I have no problem with that. I'm worried about sending our friends into danger. Sophie's all confidence, but she has no idea what she's really up against. She's been here two weeks." He gave another laugh, this one mocking. "The shine hasn't worn off her new toy yet."

Callum drew in a long breath through his nose. "I'm worried about that too."

"But you let her go anyway."

"We had nobody else who could do the job. Sophie and Constance have seven men with them, Ieuan among them. They are well-protected."

"Unless they're caught. Unless they're outnumbered. There isn't exactly a Geneva Convention here. We both know what Mortimer's men will to do to them before they kill them."

From the start, this had been Callum's problem with including women in the army. It wasn't at all that they couldn't be capable soldiers, and he wasn't particularly concerned about harassment within the ranks. Few enough women were involved such that the commanders could keep a sharp eye on any misbehavior. It was what would happen were a woman taken captive by enemy forces. They wouldn't simply be killed. They'd be given to the men for their amusement first.

Mark picked up the earphone by which he was maintaining communication with Sophie's band. Poor communication had been the bane of David's existence since he'd started leading men in Earth Two, but more reliable electronics had come on the plane, including the earpieces that Sophie, George, and Andre wore, allowing them to talk to one another. Ieuan and Callum also each had a walkie-talkie, though the mountain blocked reception, so Ieuan might be able to use his only once he was at the top.

Math stood a little way away. He'd been in constant motion since he'd arrived with his army, somewhat after Ieuan and Callum. Now that David was gone, it was good Math was here, because the line of authority from David to him was clearer than from David to Callum. If Callum had known that David was going to go missing, he would have called in Nicholas de Carew, who was holding the fort in

London—and probably gnashing his teeth about being left behind again.

God help him, it was times like these that Callum actually missed Gilbert de Clare. He'd been witty and clever and too arrogant by half. David missed him too, but he was still masking that grief with anger. It was an open question how to properly mourn a friend who'd tried to kill you.

Math raised a hand and dropped it. "Light 'em up."

Not everyone was as fluent in American English as Math, but it wouldn't have mattered what he'd said because the men knew what they were doing. They may have thought the entire endeavor completely mad, but they were obeying because most understood the consequences of following the more conventional path. The men supporting Mortimer were just that—men like them, tied to a liege lord who'd led them astray. On another day, and but for the grace of God, their places could have been exchanged.

There was a spark as the tail of the first firework was lit and then a *whoosh* as it shot into the air. The red, green, and gold lights showered down above the castle, which was Callum's cue to put a microphone to his mouth and say in three languages, just to be safe: *"Surrender and you will be allowed to return to your homes and families. Fight and you will certainly die."*

David had recorded himself saying much the same thing, but with his absence, Callum felt uncomfortable using the recording, especially because that would ruin the deception that he was marching north with the bulk of the army.

Callum put his binoculars to his eyes, waiting with the others for something to happen and wondering if he ought to speak again. This was the same message Roger Mortimer had rejected earlier when David had sent emissaries under a white flag.

"David is alive, and Roger is on his own. Balliol has abandoned these men," Mark said, his own binoculars to his eyes. "They have to know it—don't they?"

"From all appearances, Roger still believes Balliol is coming to save him." Callum grimaced. "He hasn't surrendered, and that's the only thing that matters."

"He must know something we don't or thinks he does." Mark brought down the binoculars and looked at Callum. "He can't win."

"He has hostages."

"Then why not trade them for safe passage to France?"

Callum laughed. "France is hardly safe for him, is it? No place is safe. He may be holding out hope that David wants peace so badly he comes to the gate personally."

"And allows one of Roger's men to put an arrow in him? Not likely." Mark guffawed. "He is going to regret that choice." Then he grinned as more fireworks lit the night sky. "This part of Plan C I'm liking, though I don't see a white flag."

Callum scoffed. "He won't put one up himself. The question is whether or not his men will do it for him." Then his amusement faded. "David really didn't want men to die for Roger's stupidity."

"David can't always get what he wants."

Callum decided not to rise to that obvious bait. David had wanted Mark to come home to Earth Two, and events had conspired to ensure that Mark did, so Mark's tone in this instance was understandably a little sour.

So instead, Callum said gently, "David would probably be the first to agree." He glanced again to Mark, who was looking determinedly through his binoculars. "Everyone else is glad you're here."

"And I appreciate it." He made a rueful face. "I confess the tears in Bronwen's eyes when she realized, thanks to your money, that I'd brought her every out of print or free book available and a thousand dollars' worth of children's ebooks—" he eyed Callum, "—made me feel a whole lot better."

Humphrey de Bohun and Edmund Mortimer made their way to where Callum, Math, and Mark were standing.

"Roger will not surrender," Edmund said matter-of-factly, "and that means his men won't either."

Math sighed, much as Callum had, at Roger's obstinacy. "Any movement from any gate?"

They had watchers all around the castle, with walkie-talkies to radio back if anyone had decided to take them up on their offer.

Mark spoke into a microphone, waited a beat, and then shook his head.

Math's next glance took in everyone. "We'll send the fire arrows. That will be signal enough to Sophie and the others. Hopefully they've reached the ditch by now, though it would be great if you could get through to Ieuan. If at all possible I want them out of the castle before we take down the front gate. Once that happens, there's no telling how this will go."

"Yeah, there is." Mark appeared to have left any willingness to show deference in Avalon. "With the weapons we have, this is already over."

His eyes met Callum's, just for a moment. Humphrey moved away again, but Edmund Mortimer stayed behind, his left arm pressed across his chest and his right fist to his lips. "I don't want to see my brother die, Callum."

"I know." Callum gripped Edmund's shoulder. "I'm sorry if David's absence means our timeline for this stage has been moved up."

Edmund sighed and dropped his arms, visibly trying to ease the tension in his back. "Roger is a traitor. It would have been wrong for the king to negotiate directly with him. David should have let the hostages die before he made that move."

"He wouldn't have," Callum said.

Edmund nodded, knowing as well as the rest of them that mercy was David's first instinct. "Perhaps, then, that's the reason he isn't here."

19

2 April 1294

Sophie

Sophie had been climbing since she was a young girl, but she had to admit that she'd never done anything under the pressure she was feeling now, not even in competition. She'd won many of those competitions, but she'd never before had lives on the line. Unfortunately, as soon as she thought about what was at stake, her muscles tightened, and she forced herself to breathe again and to focus on the next handhold.

The truth she kept telling herself was that under other circumstances, this climb would have been a walk in the park. As soon as the fireworks started going off, the sky had been brightly lit. At that point, they'd left their resting place halfway up the mountain. If the watchers on the walls were looking at the sky, which they had to have been, their night vision would be completely shot. She hadn't known what had possessed Chad to include fireworks in the airplane's cargo, but when they'd done an inventory, and she'd showed David the packages, she'd seen his mind begin to work. David took no credit for the idea, nor did Chad, but he and Chad apparently had read the same books, since David had instantly understood the reference on the note Chad had left him.

Sophie herself avoided military fiction like the plague, but if a fictional story had inspired David to concoct their current scenario, she was all for it. The original intent had been to use the fireworks and the climbing gear only if Roger Mortimer's total surrender or the sensible mutiny of Mortimer's men failed to transpire. That neither of those things had happened, despite knowing David was alive, was befuddling to Sophie. To her, there was a significant difference between honor and pride, and what was happening here surely looked like Roger was throwing away the lives of men because he had too much of the latter.

Beeston Castle was built on a rock three hundred and fifty feet above the valley floor. The highest point, upon which the keep itself was built, was on the northwesternmost end, and the plateau, upon which the whole castle sat, sloped steadily downwards all the way from the keep to the main gate two football fields away.

The inner ward was surrounded by a stone wall, which topped an almost vertical rocky descent on the north side. This was the face the Royalists appeared to have conquered four hundred years from now to get into the rock-cut ditch that curved around the inner ward and separated it from the outer ward. Sophie and George had decided to attack the west face, however, and with hardly any ado, they arrived in the ditch at the western end. In a group, they crouched in the bit of vegetation that had been allowed to grow underneath the wall.

She had chosen the west side for two reasons: first, the climbers she was bringing with her were less experienced than Sophie would like them to be, and the slightly less steep ascent had been a less risky one for them; second, her people had modern gear. While the gear would have made mincemeat of whichever side she chose to climb, no matter how steep, it had allowed them to get this far with minimal fuss; and finally, although by 1643 the entire curtain wall had been completed, in 1294, a gap had been left in the inner curtain wall to allow access to a natural balcony.

Apparently, the defenders thought their keep was unassailable, and the lady of the castle wanted a place to sit where she could take in the view.

No kidding.

Sophie supposed she could understand the impulse. At the time Beeston was built, the castle was in the middle of Cheshire. Its closest enemy was Wales, and according to Meg, the castle had been a jumping off point for attacks on Wales. But nobody had actually thought that an army from Wales would ever reach this far into England. Thus, the castle was a home as well as a fortress and that meant it was trying to be too many things to too many people. At a minimum, it was just too big to defend from any kind of concerted attack—a fact Callum was counting on. And, undeniably, the nine people who settled into the ditch tonight had the ability to go over both the inner curtain wall and the outer one to reach the outer bailey without being detected.

"Is everyone ready?" Sophie looked into George's face. Everyone but Andre, who didn't need to, had put charcoal on their faces to darken their skin. However, the whites of their eyes gleamed at Sophie.

"We're doing fine. Keep going," Ieuan whispered. "I've let Mark know we've made it this far and that the drawbridge is up." He tipped his head to indicate the bridge that should have spanned the ditch.

In the face of the assault, the men in the keep had chosen to barricade themselves inside. Callum had assumed that would happen, and it meant that reinforcements would not be coming to their aid from the outer ward. The defenders had assumed they wouldn't need them.

Heh.

Men shouted from somewhere in the outer bailey. Another firework burst above their heads, and it was accompanied this time not by Callum asking for the castle's surrender, but flaming arrows. The arrows arced, reached their peak, and then descended into the outer ward. Three hundred yards was a doable shot for the elite archers in David's army, especially when all the arrows were required to do was arc over the outer wall and land inside it. Child's play, as evidenced by the accompanying screams.

"Don't think about them," Andre said, low in her ear. "Lead on."

Sophie nodded and reached up for the first handhold.

The defenders would have assumed when they sited the castle here that the reverse pyramid shape of the wall would make this last stretch from the ditch to the balcony an impossible face to climb, but five minutes later Sophie's climbing hook caught on the corner of the curtain wall, and she hauled herself over the edge and onto the grassy balcony.

George and Andre were beside her within the space of a minute. Every time another fire arrow went up, the sky became brightly lit, and she feared they would be seen, but all eyes were on the sky and the havoc currently being wreaked in the outer ward.

She couldn't expect the novices with her to scale the wall as she had, so while George moved into the relative darkness of the inner ward to make sure they hadn't been detected, she and Andre anchored the ropes that would allow the rest of their companions to climb up to the balcony.

Constance and Ieuan were the last to reach her, and they panted a bit as they crouched beside her in the shadow of the wall. Their climb had been made more awkward because of the quivers and bows on their backs. Like a footballer who could play multiple positions, Ieuan could do everything required by a medieval warrior—wrestling, swordplay, and archery. Though his sister was recognized as an expert shot, Ieuan had taught Lili, and Sophie had seen him shoot. He, like Constance, was better than good, and an arrow was quieter than Andre's rifle, which would be used only as a last resort.

While Constance took a drink of water and some deep breaths to settle herself, Ieuan moved towards Samuel to confer. These two would be leading the two teams of men around the bailey to free the captives while Constance and Andre kept any attackers at bay from above.

"Are you ready for this?" Constance asked Sophie, who had her scope to her eye, tracing the tops of the battlements all around the inner ward.

"I'm not going to be the one shooting," Sophie said without looking at her. "Are *you* ready?"

"Within the hour, I will know what has become of my husband. No matter for good or ill, the wait will be over."

Sophie reached out a hand and squeezed Constance's arm, but she didn't say that Cador was alive or any other platitude. Constance was right that knowing was better than not knowing, and regardless of the outcome, one way or the other, before dawn it would be over. Growing up, Sophie's mother had talked her through many girlhood stresses, all of which seemed quaint and meaningless now, with just that thought: *in an hour, it will be over, and life will go on.*

Ieuan looked back at the two women. "How many men do you see, Sophie?"

Sophie put the scope back to her eye. "There are two guards at the top of the tower overlooking the ditch." She gave a low laugh she couldn't help. "You had only one job ..."

A second later George returned. "The main door is closed, and the portcullis is down."

"Nothing has changed since we were in the ditch." Samuel looked at Ieuan. "This is just what we wanted, isn't it?"

"I don't like how deserted this place is," Ieuan said. "If Roger Mortimer is here, he's being quiet about it."

Samuel shook his head. "I don't think he's here."

"You don't think he's here at all?" Sophie asked. "Or you think he's in the outer bailey?"

"Oh, he's definitely not in here with us, but I'm wondering if he's out there either. Now that I've had a look at the place, it isn't really a great spot to hole up in, is it? Roger Mortimer isn't stupid. Let's get the captives, get out, and regroup with Lord Callum."

With a gesture from Ieuan, the remaining climbers gathered around, including the three men whose names were something like Tom, Dick, and Harry. He gave them each a last chance to express their thoughts and then said, "Quick and quiet, just like we planned."

Constance nodded. "We have your backs."

"Go, you three," Ieuan said, referring to Sophie, Constance, and Andre. "We'll wait until you're on the battlement before we move."

Her heart in her throat, Sophie followed Andre up the steps up to the wall-walk. The curtain wall was only two stories high here—maybe twenty feet above the inner ward, though it was obviously far higher than that above the valley floor.

Meanwhile, Ieuan led three of the medieval men towards the main gate, in the opposite direction from Samuel and George, who were starting at one of the far towers.

"They'll be okay. You need to focus, Sophie." Andre sidled along the wall-walk, his feet making no noise on the stones, towards the southwest tower, tracking the movements of Ieuan and his men on the ground below them.

Constance stayed at Sophie's side. "Call 'em out as you see 'em," she said in perfect American. Who knew where Constance had learned that particular phrase, but she had her bow up and an arrow at the ready.

If any of Mortimer's men had been looking, Constance would have been unmistakably silhouetted against the sky, but just then another hail of fire arrows arced in the air. Sophie hadn't been able to see the last few flights because of where they'd been crouched against the curtain wall. Now, however, a hundred arrows lit the sky and descended into the outer ward, where many of the buildings were already on fire, along with many tents. From her current position on the battlement, Sophie could see a chain of men hauling buckets from the well to the various buildings set along the western curtain wall. Her view of the eastern gate was blocked by the inner ward's gatehouse towers.

Then Sophie turned away from the carnage and put her scope to her eye. "Your first target is at the top of the closest gatehouse tower, Constance. Take him out."

20

2 April 1294

Samuel

Samuel and the young fellow from Avalon, George, moved at a crouching run around the inside of the curtain wall that circled the edge of the escarpment, avoiding the shadows cast by the torches in their sconces on either side of the main gate. Last Humphrey de Bohun had known, William Venables and his father were being held on the top floor of the tower on the northeast side of the inner ward, which was where Samuel and George were headed.

Ieuan led the others south, towards the gatehouse. He had more men with him because it was his job to canvas the entire inner ward in case the prisoners had been moved from their original location or, if they were extremely lucky, Roger Mortimer had chosen to hide himself in one of the gatehouse towers. Unlike the orders given to the men assaulting Beeston's main entrance, theirs were to kill everyone they saw, no questions asked.

Samuel had seen the weapon that Andre handled so easily. Black on black, long and sleek, it was clearly deadly. If the weapons from Avalon did everything Callum said they would—and Samuel had no reason not to believe him—he would have thrown everything they had at Beeston from the start. Mortimer had set out to wrest England from David's control, and he needed to be punished accordingly for his overreaching. Samuel himself didn't care one whit for these traitors and didn't see the point in coddling them.

David did see it, however, and really, his opinion was the one that mattered. That was why he'd authorized the use of the Avalonian weapons only as a last resort, and again, Samuel wasn't in a position to argue. David's rule of Britain was predicated on the fact that the people themselves had begged him to lead them, and that was all the justification Samuel needed tonight. He trusted because to do otherwise would be willful stupidity. It was David who had first welcomed the Jews into Britain. He was among the *khasidei,* the Righteous, never mind that David would be the first to admit he hadn't done enough. He'd done what he could at a time when nobody else was doing anything.

"This is only going to find us Venny, right? Mathew, Cador, and Rhys are being kept in the outer ward—or they've already been killed," George said in an undertone. "Nobody seemed willing to talk about that."

Samuel glanced towards the younger man, thinking the words came from trepidation, but George appeared very focused and genuinely curious. "One step at a time. We deal with this, and then we deal with that. Truthfully, we know nothing for certain."

An arrow whispered through the air, and a moment later, Samuel thought he heard a breathy cry, instantly cut off. No body fell from the wall-walk, however, and he decided that Constance knew what she was doing, and they were to keep going. They were a dozen feet from the tower door now, and a single torch shone from a sconce fastened to the stones. The handle of the knife he held felt slick against his skin. It was a cool night, but he was sweating. He took in a breath, motioned for George to move to the other side of the door, and knocked, returning to his position before an answer came.

The door opened, revealing a man silhouetted against the lantern light behind him, and hardly a single breath later, an arrow hit him in the center of his mass. Knives at the ready, Samuel and George were through the door immediately afterwards. Samuel caught the man by the shoulders and laid him on the ground before he could fall on his own, thinking to mitigate the noise. The man was sputtering, trying to breathe through the blood in his mouth. George slid his knife between two ribs into his heart to put him out of his misery. It was exactly the kind of compassion and ruthlessness Samuel had grown to expect from these Avalonians.

If there had been anyone else in the room, they wouldn't have taken the time to be quiet. It was too much to expect that the guard was on duty alone, however, so Samuel wasn't surprised when a second guard, perhaps summoned by whatever noise they had made or simply because he had been returning to the guardroom at his appointed time, appeared through a narrow doorway at the back of the room.

That moment of hesitation where he gaped at the scene before him allowed Samuel time to throw his knife. It tumbled end over end, its aim true, but the distance was great enough that the man dodged, and the knife clattered harmlessly against the wall behind him.

But the distraction gave George time enough to bound forward and tackle the man before the guard's sword could clear its sheath.

Samuel was larger than George, and he followed immediately after in order to put his knee to the man's chest. "How many men guard the inner ward?"

Blood dripped from the guard's lips where George had punched him. Samuel took the man's head in both hands, prepared to pound the back of his head into the floorboards. "How many!"

"Two of us here. Four in the gatehouse. Two on the wall-walk."

"Where are the prisoners?" George asked.

The guard motioned vaguely with his head towards the floor above. Samuel sensed his eyes darkening. He hadn't thought George had hit him that hard, but then he saw blood seeping from the back of the man's head into the floorboards. He'd cracked his skull in the fall.

Samuel cursed under his breath, but they would get no more from him. With George on his heels, he raced upstairs. The second level proved to be empty, but the top floor opened onto a single room with a locked door. He turned to George. "We need a key."

"I'll get it."

As George disappeared back down the stairwell, Samuel knocked on the door. "Who's in there?"

A moment later, the frightened face of a young man of twenty appeared in the little window. It wasn't Venny, nor another man Samuel recognized. "What's happening? They won't tell me anything. It's been days!"

"Who are you?"

"Henry Percy." He backed off the threshold, fear evident in his face. "Who are you?"

"Samuel ben Aaron."

"The-the Jew?" Henry stuttered, hope filling his face. "Companion to Earl Callum?"

"The same."

George was back, a large iron key in his hand. "Try this."

Samuel shoved the key into the lock. It turned, and the door opened. "We're getting you out of here. Where's Venny?"

"I don't know what's happened to him. They've kept me here alone, questioning me." His voice faded away, causing Samuel to look at him more closely.

"They tortured you? Why? What could you tell them?"

"Nothing!" The word carried a full measure of pain. "Somehow they knew I was working with Humphrey de Bohun, but where he'd gone or what he planned after he left Beeston, I couldn't tell them even if I wanted to."

"He's out there waiting for us." Samuel took Henry's arm, more gently than he might have thought to do a few moments ago. "Come on." The three men hastened down the stairs.

Once back in the guardroom, Henry went straight for the jug on the table and took a long swig. The remains of a simple meal sat on a tray, and he snatched up the bit of bread and cheese and stuffed both into his mouth. He spoke around the food. "In between beatings, they barely fed me."

Samuel didn't begrudge him the time. "We have food at the camp, but you'll need your strength for what's to come. Take a sword too."

With fingers that trembled, Henry unbuckled the sword belt belonging to the guard Constance had killed with an arrow, deeming the sword attached to it of better quality than the other dead man's. "I was to have been knighted last week."

"If we get out of here in one piece, it can still happen." Samuel went to the door and peered out.

"Not with how I behaved," Henry said. "I should have fought."

"More experienced men than you couldn't have done more. Don't take too much on yourself. You are alive to fight another day, and that is what matters to the king—and your grandfather."

Henry looked up, his eyes questioning. "What do you know of him? He is well?"

"The king forgave him his treason, if that's what you're asking. He's here too."

Henry swallowed hard. "And the king?"

"He's alive."

"Keep up, why don't you," George added, though somewhat under his breath. And then to Samuel he said, "We should go."

The balcony by which they'd entered the inner ward was directly opposite, thus the reason for Constance's impressive shot. At first, Samuel was hesitant to fill the doorway, fearing she would mistake him for one of Beeston's defenders. He doused the lantern, leaving the room in total darkness, but allowing a greater contrast to the sky outside.

Then someone—by size and shape it was Sophie—stepped away from the curtain wall and waved an arm. "All clear."

Henry had recovered enough to frown. "Is that a girl?"

George grinned. "She's the one who got us up here."

Samuel smirked at the surprise in Henry's face. He decided he wouldn't befuddle him further by mentioning that the two-foot arrow sticking out of the guard's chest had been shot by Constance. Samuel hadn't always been what Callum called *enlightened*, but his first real encounter with a woman from Avalon had been Cassie, now Callum's wife and the mother of his son. These days it was either learn and adapt or get run over.

They loped across the courtyard, swords out this time, though as Sophie had promised, they encountered no resistance. All of their companions were already at the balcony.

"Henry Percy." Ieuan looked him up and down. "You don't look well." Then he turned to Samuel. "You found nobody else?"

"Nobody that mattered. We have two dead guards, one thanks to Constance." Samuel nodded at the archer, who was staring at the ground with her arms folded across her chest. She might have been thinking about the men she'd killed, but Samuel thought it more likely that she was angry they hadn't found her husband.

"She downed two more on the wall-walk," Ieuan said, "and we encountered four in the gatehouse."

"According to the man I questioned, that's the total number that guarded the inner ward," Samuel said.

Sophie let out a breath. "What do we do now? It's good we have Henry, but since we found only him, that means we're not done."

"Not even by half." Andre's weapon rested on his shoulder. As far as Samuel knew, he hadn't fired it, which was good because Callum had told him it would be loud, even with something called a *silencer* on the end that was supposed to muffle the sound. Samuel hadn't asked how the others had died, but he assumed they'd been put to the sword.

"Do we lower the drawbridge?" George said. "If we don't, we can't get back in."

"Well, we can, thanks to Sophie," Ieuan said. "I'm more concerned about Roger Mortimer retreating inside the inner ward with a hundred men and holding us off for longer than we care to besiege him. There's a well here. We could spend months trying to get him out."

"If we go out the way we came in, though, then what?" Sophie asked. "I can get us into the outer ward, but—"

"But it is full of hundreds of men," George finished for her.

"Maybe that's not a bad thing," Samuel said. "With the fires, it has to be chaos over there by now. We are only nine, and all of us speak English. We can lose ourselves among the crowd."

Sophie nudged Ieuan's elbow. "Whatever we decide, Math is waiting for our signal. They need to begin the assault."

Samuel had used the walkie-talkies himself, so he had no problem with Ieuan handing the one he carried to him. "I've been trying to get through, but it's hard to hear anything, and I didn't want to turn the volume up any louder. Now we can. Do your best to raise him. We can always send up a fire arrow of our own as a signal if we need to." Then to Sophie, he said, "You can get everyone from the ditch into the outer ward?"

She nodded. "Piece of cake."

It was a phrase Samuel had heard the Avalonians use a time or two. He knew what it meant, even if he had no idea why it meant that. "Good. I'll stay here. That way when they take the outer ward, it will be a simple matter for me to lower the drawbridge."

Ieuan nodded, gesturing to the three men who'd taken the gatehouse with him but knew nothing of climbing. "You stay too."

Tom, the closest man to him, looked comically relieved that he wouldn't be scaling the cliff again.

Then Ieuan gestured to the Avalonians and Constance. "Let's go get our friends."

21

2 April 1294

Venny

Venny didn't know what was happening. But at this point, as far as he was concerned, the specifics were immaterial. After two weeks of silence and fear that they'd been abandoned, his king had come.

That this was his king he had no doubt. Nothing else would have excited his captors this much, and the whistles and explosions above his head were like nothing he'd ever heard or seen before. The room in the barracks in which he and his companions were being held captive had a tiny window, and he could see many-colored sparks showering Beeston from above. He had no idea what these meant, since they didn't appear to be doing any damage to the castle, but if David had come for them, then it was time they did something for themselves. Long past time.

He turned to Rhys, Cador, and Mathew—and his father, Hugh, who sat in the only chair. The room consisted of one bed, which naturally had also gone to Venny's father, and four thin pallets on the floor with thin blankets to match. They'd been lucky to have had those. "It's time to go."

"Where?" As usual, his father was the man who sought to question Venny's authority. The last two weeks had been a trial for that reason, far more than the simple fact of their captivity. Though truthfully, as time had gone on, he'd come to see that Hugh's disparagement of Venny had far more to do with his father's own frustration and ill-humor at his relative impotence than because of anything Venny had done or said.

Which is why he could answer with a measure of equanimity, "Out of here."

Hugh Venables pointed towards the door. "How? Last I checked, it was locked."

Venny mimicked his father's gesture. "King David is out there and has brought an army to free us. I, for one, am not going to sit idly by and wait for Roger Mortimer to decide to use us against him rather than surrender. He kept us alive because it was all that was keeping the king from attacking. Now he is attacking anyway, as he should be. Perhaps as he should have done days ago."

Hugh sniffed. "Your precious king is dead. Whoever this is, he cares nothing for you."

Mathew had risen to his feet after Hugh's first comment, but now he strode the three paces that was the entire width of the room towards Venny's father, getting right in his face. Yesterday, Venny might have stopped him, knowing that appeasement was the only way they were going to survive their captivity. Not tonight.

"I have listened to your snarking and sniping for two solid weeks, and I'm not going to listen anymore. Your son is going to lead us out of here, and I am going to follow. You are welcome to stay behind, but if you come with us, you will keep your mouth shut, or we really will leave you behind."

For once, Hugh actually looked somewhat cowed, whether because of Mathew's words or because of his size. Mathew's hands were also clenched into fists, and Hugh might have finally realized that he'd pushed the Londoner too far. "It hardly matters, since there's no way out." He straightened his tunic with a jerk.

"There's always been a way out," Cador said.

At his father's surprised look, Venny chose to enlighten him. "We believed the odds of escaping the barracks—and Beeston afterwards—were slim to none, so we didn't choose to attempt it. They're in our favor now." Venny nodded at Rhys and Mathew. "Take off the hinges."

Hugh gaped, but Venny didn't bother to explain because the men were already at work. Mortimer's men had never allowed them any iron. The room had been built without a fireplace, and they'd been given no brazier to keep them warm. But necessity bred invention, as Venny had heard King David say more than once. It was a matter of moments for Mathew to detach two of the bedposts to use as hammer and chisel, and then some tapping and prying to remove the pegs that allowed the hinges on the door to work. The gap created between the frame and the door was narrow, but all Mathew had to do was get his fingers around the edge, and with a satisfied grunt, he pulled the door wide.

He and Venny poked their heads into the corridor and looked left and right. Nobody was guarding the corridor.

Moving on quiet feet, they left the room in single file, Venny in the lead and Cador bringing up the rear, as was his custom, even though he had no bow and arrow tonight. As Venny had said to his father, the initial escape was the easy part, but now they didn't want to alert anyone to the fact that they were free before they reached the ground floor.

Nobody came up the stairs, however, and, a moment later, Venny passed through the doorway into the guardroom. It looked like nothing out of the ordinary—a table, benches, a few trunks—and only a single guard, who stood with his back to them, facing out the open doorway. Freedom was so close, Venny could taste it.

The guard's shoulders were tensed and his hands braced against the frame of the door. His desire to be out in the bailey defending the castle with his fellows, instead of guarding useless prisoners, was palpable.

Venny himself was the slightest of his companions, barring Hugh, so he stepped aside and let Mathew rush the man. He hit him in the back, though at an angle, so his head hit the edge of the frame of the door. He went down and didn't get back up again.

Mathew loomed over him, fire in his eyes. After two weeks in prison, he was ready to kill anything that moved, but Venny made an impatient gesture. "Get his weapons."

Cador was already pawing through a trunk at the far end of the room. "Venny!" He tossed Venny a knife in a sheath, and then he cheered as he came up with his quiver. His bow stood upright in one corner. Probably none of the defenders of Beeston could use it, so they didn't recognize it for the masterpiece of craftsmanship that it was.

By now, Rhys had moved the motionless guard out of the doorway and closed the door so they could work without being observed. Hastily buckling on sword belts and adjusting their weaponry, the four of them huddled together to confer. And then to Venny's surprise, his father joined them. "Well done."

None of them responded to the accolade, though Venny wasn't displeased to have it. Then he quickly suppressed the feeling of pleasure. It did him no good to want to please his father. Even when the approval was sincere, it never lasted.

"Too many men stand between us and the main gatehouse. We'll never get out that way," Cador said.

"It's the curtain wall for us. Once over it, we can make our way down Beeston's backside," Mathew said, "steep as it may be."

Venny nodded. "Most of the buildings are on fire. Nobody is going to be minding us."

Hugh sneered, though for once not at Venny. "Some may be escaping with us."

"I have something that should help." Cador went back to the trunk and came up with two tunics with the FitzWalter crest. He gave one to Rhys and put the second one on himself, since they were too small for Mathew and too big for Venny, but just having two among them dressed appropriately might be sufficient to deflect anyone's interest.

"To the wall-walk, then." Venny moved to the door, and the others followed, to find the outer ward was in chaos. Perhaps when the barrage had first started, there had been some order to the men. But now, while many fought the fires with buckets of water, others appeared to be fleeing over the walls as Venny's father had predicted, even as their commanders shouted at them not to leave. Dozens more *were* continuing the defense, having lined the wall-walk around the main gatehouse. They had to keep their heads down to avoid the arrows, and while Venny saw crossbows in several hands, they didn't have anywhere close to enough of them.

Venny's father came abreast. "I can't drop myself off a curtain wall." He stated this as a certainty, without complaint.

Venny didn't think it was the time for talking, but the noise around them was so great, he didn't have to worry about being overheard. "We'll figure something out."

"Perhaps I *should* stay behind. I can cover your retreat. After all, I'm only going to my death."

Venny glanced at his father. "What? Why would this be your death?"

"I doubt King David, if this really is he, is going to be forgiving of a man who conspired against him."

By now they were within twenty feet of the stairs that would take them up to the western curtain wall-walk, halfway between the main gate and the inner ward. They'd been heading this way because of the lack of activity in the area, since most of Mortimer's force was centered near the main gate over a hundred yards away. The wooden roofs on both gatehouse towers were on fire, as was the healer's hut, which they'd visited two weeks and a lifetime ago.

"Do you want the king to forgive you?" And when his father had no quick answer, Venny added, "Perhaps between now and when you meet the king, you can decide how you want your life to go. FitzWalter and Mortimer haven't surrendered because of their pride. Is that your sin as well?"

Venny had never spoken so forthrightly to his father, but instead of fear, he felt a bit of pride himself at no longer hiding his thoughts.

"They're over there!" A woman's voice called from farther up the ward. "Cador!"

Cador turned at his name, and a moment later Constance appeared out of the darkness. He had time to spread his arms wide before she barreled into him. He caught her, and their arms wrapped tightly around each other.

"I was so scared for you," she said.

His face was in her hair. "I know. I didn't know what had happened to you either."

Constance took a breath and pulled back. "Humphrey de Bohun got me out with his men."

Cador's eyes widened. "He didn't betray the king?"

Ieuan came up behind Constance. "You are behind the times, my friend." But even as he spoke, his eyes strayed towards the nearest building, which was on fire. "Come. Questions and answers are for after we escape."

But Venny couldn't swallow down the only question he had. It had been banging around in his brain for the entirety of their fortnight of captivity. "Is King David—"

A woman Venny didn't recognize, who was dressed all in black like the others, tugged on his arm to get him moving and said in a strange accent, "Don't worry. He's the one who sent us."

She had a wool hat pulled down low over her ears, but her heart-shaped face and wisps of blonde hair were visible beneath it—providing a stark contrast to her black male clothing and armor.

He was about to reply when an ear-shattering sound came from behind them, so loud Venny felt the earth shake from it. As one, they spun towards the gatehouse, which was downhill from their position. Or rather, it had been.

It was gone, and both towers that had supported it were completely destroyed, replaced by rubble and flames. Not only had the gate been blown apart, but all the men on it too. They lay on the ground, moaning and dying, some with arms or legs missing.

No weapon that Venny knew of could cause that kind of damage, with the possible exception of black powder. But when he'd glanced at the wall-walk earlier, before they'd started running, the men at the top had given no indication that David had sent a siege engine to the gate. The threat had been arrows only.

"That's our distraction." The woman pulled on Venny's arm again. "Come on. We're getting out this way."

"What do you mean we're getting out this way?" Again, it was Venny's father who chose to argue, though Venny noted that he kept pace anyway, putting as much distance as possible between himself and the awful destruction they'd just witnessed.

Ieuan took in his appearance with a sweeping glance. "If you'd rather stick with the main gate, be my guest. Hopefully what we have in mind won't be too bad, even for you."

Side-by-side with the woman, Venny ran up the slope towards the ditch that protected the inner ward, and then they skidded to a halt on the edge. "Who are you?"

"I'm Sophie, and you're Venny. I recognized you through my scope." Venny didn't know what a scope was, and his confusion must have showed on his face, because she added, "It's like binoculars."

He nodded but was still puzzled. "We have never met. How could you recognize me?"

Sophie gestured to Rhys, who pulled up too, breathing hard. "I had a look at your sketchbook. You're incredibly good."

Rhys smiled at the compliment. How could he not, even in the middle of a burning castle? Venny had just met the woman, but jealousy curled in his belly.

"So the king really is alive?" Hugh asked, and for once Venny was grateful to his father for talking, since it covered Venny's own uncertainty.

"Yes." Ieuan was all confidence. "King David didn't want to leave you in the hands of Roger Mortimer any longer than he had to, and he was sorry to leave you this long."

It wasn't as if Venny hadn't believed the girl, but he'd needed to hear it again. The news had him feeling somewhat light-headed, while at the same time it was as if he was able to breathe for the first time since he'd sworn his allegiance to Roger Mortimer in Beeston's chapel. The king was alive, and what's more, had sent men to rescue them. They hadn't been forgotten. He glanced at his father, who was chewing on his lower lip, surveying the ditch, and Venny decided not to interrupt his thoughts with gloating.

"So now what are we doing?" Hugh said. "I see no way out."

"Don't worry," Sophie said. "We have that covered."

Venny didn't see how either. The bridge across the ditch extended towards the inner gatehouse but didn't connect to it because the drawbridge was up. There was no escape that way unless Ieuan had somebody inside prepared to lower the drawbridge and raise the portcullis.

Ieuan led them onto the bridge anyway, and then a light flashed in the ditch below them. Henry Percy's white face looked up from the bottom of a rope ladder. Standing beside him was a dark-skinned man Venny could barely make out but for the whites of his eyes and teeth.

"We're going down?" Venny looked at Sophie.

"Better than the keep," she said.

"Is it?"

She tsked. "The keep isn't going to do us any good. We'd still have an army between us and our men. If we were going to stay, we should have waited until our men defeated the garrison and gone out the main gate."

"We didn't want to risk losing any of you, however. Lord Callum gave us the job of getting you out of Beeston, and we're doing it." This came from another man Venny didn't recognize, one Sophie had referred to as George.

Venny peered into the darkness below them, fearful his skepticism was showing and glad that it was dark.

Sophie probably sensed it anyway, and she nudged his elbow with hers to get his attention. "Don't worry. We know what we're doing." She indicated that he needed to climb down the ladder. George had already gone down it, and having edged Henry Percy out of the way, was holding the bottom of the ladder with the black man.

"Down. Now." Ieuan waved a hand. "Before anyone sees us, though I suspect nobody has eyes for anything but the gate."

Venny shook his head, even as he obeyed, throwing caution to the winds along with his dismay, though it had been his idea to leave via the curtain wall. He turned around so he could descend the ladder, but was forced to sprawl ignominiously on his stomach on the bridge before he could get his feet on the rungs. Nobody laughed, and Ieuan even crouched to grasp his arm until he could get himself set. Venny supposed there were worse things than looking like a fool in front of a pretty girl, especially for a man who'd spent two weeks as a captive. But after two weeks of inactivity, he was weaker than he'd hoped to be.

He worked his way down the ladder until he was standing in the ditch. Henry Percy was there to greet him, looking much the worse for wear. He had been taken from them early on and appeared not to have been as well fed. Then the rest of their companions descended, Mathew coming at the last. Venny reached up to steady him when one of his feet slipped off a rung.

As Mathew dropped to the ground, Cador asked, "Why is nobody in the keep shooting at us?" He'd been standing side-by-side with his wife, both with bows in hand and trained upwards. Truthfully, it was a little late for that question, seeing as how they'd spent the last quarter of an hour descending into the ditch right in front of the towers.

"They're all dead," Ieuan said matter-of-factly. "We took care of them first. That's where we found Henry."

That was a daunting answer, but not an unwelcome one, so Venny tried another question. "What kind of weapon could take down the gate with one blow?"

"You wouldn't believe us if we told you," Sophie said.

"Please try."

George shrugged. "We call it the Goose. It came from Avalon with us."

22

2 April 1294

Sophie

Without needing to discuss the decision, the former captives brought their platters of food into the makeshift infirmary and pulled up stools to sit around the beds belonging to Hugh Venables and Henry Percy. Once they'd navigated the mountain, the captives had been given the once-over by both Aaron, Samuel's father and Dr. Abraham. Henry Percy and Hugh Venables were the only ones who hadn't been released. Henry was malnourished and weak, but Hugh had been complaining of pain in his side.

As promised, once the fighting in the bailey was over, Samuel had lowered the drawbridge, allowing proper access into the keep, which included extensive food storage areas. Mortimer had been well-prepared for his war, and there was plenty to feed the men, even after a two-week siege. Meanwhile, the doctors in attendance had chosen the large hall in the outer ward as the most comfortable and convenient place for the wounded and injured to rest, and they were moving among them solicitously.

Venny took a goblet from the table where they'd laid the provisions and poured Sophie a cup of wine while she loaded a trencher with meat, potatoes, and onions. He'd stuck close to her from the moment they'd landed in the ditch, only leaving her side to see to his father. Venny had been solicitous of him too, though his eyes had maintained a wary look that was matched only by the one in Hugh's own.

"Thank you," he said as he sat beside her.

Sophie looked over at him. "What for?"

Venny gestured generally to their companions, who included Cador, Rhys, Mathew, and Constance. Andre and George planned to join them shortly, but they were putting away the climbing gear. "Without you, we might have perished in the bailey."

"You were getting yourselves out just fine without us," Sophie said.

"Just say *you're welcome,* my dear," Hugh Venables said. "Allow us to be grateful."

Sophie blushed. She'd always had a hard time accepting compliments. "King David wanted to give you every chance to survive, and I was the one who gave you the best chance of that." She swallowed. "But you're welcome. Truly."

"Few women—" Venny paused, "—few *people* would be so capable."

He wasn't letting it go, and Sophie genuinely didn't know how to respond, so she opted to divert him. "I've been climbing since I was a little girl. My father taught me."

Venny's eyes narrowed for a moment as he glanced at her. "Is your father here? Tell me you didn't come from Avalon alone."

Sophie opened her mouth to speak, her first thought to say *of course she had and why did it matter anyway?* But then she stopped herself. Venny's concerned expression told her that he wasn't questioning her ability to manage her own life. He was concerned about her well-being. She was a single woman in a place where such a thing barely existed. Every woman had a father, husband, son, or barring that, a guardian, in whose charge she ostensibly remained from birth to death.

"I am a ward of the king," she said, finally settling on something she thought they both could appreciate and accept.

Venny's expression cleared. "I am relieved to hear it."

Hugh, who'd been listening throughout, canted his head. "In a way, we all are."

Sophie took a tentative sip of wine, her eyes flicking from father to son. Something was going on between them that she knew wasn't quite right, but couldn't pinpoint. "I miss my father very much. You two are lucky to have each other."

Beside her, Venny went very still, wary again, as he'd been off and on since she'd met him.

Hugh, however, popped a piece of potato into his mouth. "Fathers aren't always good at telling their children how they feel about them." He continued to chew with equanimity, though his eyes were on his food instead of his son.

Venny appeared to swallow down a laugh. "You have always been very good at it."

Sophie froze, realizing her mistake. The tension in the air was so thick she could have cut it with a knife. Mathew made to rise, but Cador put out hand to him and shook his head.

"Clearly, I have not, and I apologize for that." Hugh's eyes came up. "It was you who held everyone together during a very difficult two weeks. I couldn't be more proud of you."

Venny's jaw actually dropped. Sophie had never seen a person really do that before.

Hugh continued: "I'll have you know that I said as much to Lord Ieuan. The word is that he is considering you for the position of captain of the king's guard."

"Is he?" Mathew grinned and lifted his cup in a toast to Venny.

But Venny's eyes remained on his father's face. Then he gave him a slight nod. "Thank you."

As Aaron bustled over again to check on his patients, distracting Hugh, Sophie smiled and said gently, in a whisper for Venny's ears alone, "Maybe Beeston's walls aren't the only ones to come down today."

Then they heard a commotion at the entrance to the hall. Several guardsmen entered, carrying a man on a board between them. They placed him on a pallet close to the fire, only a few paces away from where Sophie sat.

At the sight of his bruised and battered face, filthy clothes, and stringy hair, she rose to her feet. "What happened to him?"

"We found him in the dungeon." Callum strode across the hall. "So far he hasn't had the wherewithal to speak."

Venny, who'd fetched up beside her, gave a grunt of surprise.

Callum looked over at him. "You know who this is?"

"Of course, though he's looking much the worse for wear. It's Robert FitzWalter."

"I didn't recognize him." Callum guffawed. "And here I was starting to feel sorry for him." Still, he allowed one of the physicians to give FitzWalter sips of wine from a cup. He managed to swallow, and she heard him take an audible trembling breath.

Venny was much less forgiving. "Your men turned on you, did they?"

The wine in the flask had warmed FitzWalter's complexion enough to speak. "It was Mortimer." Sophie had the sense that he would have preferred to spit on the ground rather than say the name.

Callum grunted. "You two had a falling out, did you?"

"I argued that our only logical choice was to surrender, and he didn't take kindly to the notion." FitzWalter was coming more to himself.

"We noticed that too." Callum stood with one arm across his chest and a finger to his lips, studying the treasonous baron. "I don't suppose you know where he's gone?"

FitzWalter managed a wry look. "Where do you think?"

Hugh spoke from behind them. "Balliol."

FitzWalter shrugged. "Where else?"

"How did he get past your men?" Venny was skeptical.

"I know nothing about anything. The day after Bohun left, a pigeon flew in from Ireland, telling us that the revolt there had failed and that David lived. I told Mortimer we needed to rethink our strategy, and the next thing I knew, I was imprisoned."

Sophie knew that FitzWalter was partly to blame for the war, but even so, she was horrified by his appearance. He'd been brutally beaten and starved. "You've been in that hole for two weeks? What happened to your men?"

FitzWalter gave a helpless shake of his head. "I don't know. Mortimer's men are loyal to him, and he swore he would return in force. Perhaps he told them I tried to betray him." He managed to raise one shoulder. "I suppose, from his perspective, I did."

"Who has been in command?" Math said.

"The only man I've seen recently is Roger Lestrange." FitzWalter paused. "You know of him, of course."

"We do." Callum said.

Venny leaned into Sophie. "Do you?"

Sophie nodded, understanding instantly why Beeston hadn't surrendered even after Roger Mortimer had left. Lestrange was what, in Avalon, would be called *a true believer*. In Avalon's history, he'd been at the forefront of the conquest of Wales and had even controlled Dinas Bran for a time after Llywelyn's death. He had served at King Edward's pleasure, but had never been granted extensive lands of his own. David had not taken to him, for good reason, and so in his discontent with the new order of things he'd taken up with Roger Mortimer.

Callum turned to Venny. "When did you last see Lestrange?"

"Yesterday," Venny said, "though only from the window of our room. His quarters were in the gatehouse, so perhaps he was there when it blew."

Callum pursed his lips. "Once daylight comes, we'll start to clear the rubble and try to find him."

"I see the prisoners weren't killed." FitzWalter's voice held genuine hope, knowing that his fate depended on whether or not they lived. "Those were my instructions, but ..." He couldn't have looked more miserable.

Venny took in a breath. "We're alive and, for the most part, we were treated well."

Sophie turned away, unable to bear looking at FitzWalter's battered face for another second. Then she found herself meeting Hugh Venables' eyes. He said gently, correctly reading her discomfort, "War is no place for a woman."

She gave him a rueful smile. "Really, it isn't a place for men either."

23

2 April 2022

David

By the clock, it was six in the morning. David lay with his eyes open, staring at the ceiling above his head. He had managed to find his bed before midnight, so six hours of sleep was pretty good, considering the events of yesterday. On one hand, there was so much he wanted to do, but on the other, none of it rose to a level of urgency that he wanted to waste the short amount of time he had in Avalon with it.

He could take a movie home with him, as it turned out. What he couldn't package up was what being in Avalon felt like.

Which was why he rolled out of bed and reached for his shoes. He knew one of the triplets, or another clone, would be standing in the hallway beyond his door. Probably more were patrolling outside. He wondered at the cost of all this, and if he should feel guilt about Chad Treadman spending it. Would either of them regret the debt in the end?

He opened the door.

Sure enough, a man stood outside it, but it wasn't one of the triplets or any of Treadman's other security people. Michael leaned against the wall opposite, his arms folded across his chest and his feet crossed at the ankles.

"Hi," David said. "Tell me you slept."

Michael gave a single bob of his head. "I did. I just got up."

David wanted to believe him. "Okay. What do you think about going for a walk?"

Michael pushed off the wall. "Do you think that's a good idea?"

"Five knows where I am. If I hadn't invited Livia, they would have followed me. I'm not exactly hiding."

"I believe Mr. Treadman is more worried about reporters."

"Are there any at the gate?"

"Not as far as I know."

"I need to breathe."

"I'll see what I can do." Michael headed down the stairs, and David followed, though instead of turning into the kitchen as Michael did, he moved towards the rear of the house. The farmstead, of which the house was a part, was located some five miles from Bangor. It was farther from the hospital than David might ideally have liked to be, but it had the benefit of being isolated.

It had terrible sightlines, however. French doors opened onto a garden and woods. There could be any number of reporters hiding amongst the trees, but David clicked the lock and went to stand on the flagstone patio anyway. Slate had been mined in North Wales for a thousand years—as he himself could personally attest—and the rock had been used throughout the house.

The sun had just risen, and a mist lay over the grass. A wooden split-rail fence separated the back of the yard from the trees beyond. He was cold without his cloak. He'd collected it from William's room before he'd left the hospital, but if he was going to wander, he needed a modern coat.

"Are you thinking to walk to the Middle Ages?"

It was a voice David didn't recognize, and he turned to see Chad Treadman himself standing in the doorway. He hadn't met him yet, but he recognized him from his picture.

David canted his head. "I wouldn't leave William."

Chad walked towards him and then circled all the way around him, as if inspecting a car on the way to purchasing it. David held out both arms expansively, humoring him—and himself, since he found himself amused. They ended up with Chad standing with his back to the garden and David facing him.

"What do you see?"

Chad shook his head. "This was all so theoretical before Anna arrived, and now with you here ..." His voice trailed off.

David studied him, seeing a brown-haired man in his late thirties, with a thin build as befitting a geek. He wore a black down jacket and black workman's boots.

"Would you like to walk with me?" David asked.

"Walk and talk? Sure." Chad lifted his chin in a gesture to someone behind David, and David turned to accept the coat and hat

Michael offered. A man in a black trench coat stood behind Michael, and he put a hand to his ear, perhaps summoning more help.

Chad gestured south. "We can follow the farm track." He set off towards the side of the house, and David followed, having shrugged into his coat and pulled the wool hat down low over his ears. He was nice and anonymous, just the way he liked it.

Or did he? The thought was enough to give him pause. He wasn't anonymous in Earth Two anymore, though less because so many people knew what he looked like than because of the entourage he traveled with. He'd journeyed all over England and Wales in the twelve years he'd lived there, but most people wouldn't know him from Adam. If he was alone, despite being the King of England, he could walk into almost any castle, and nobody would look at him twice. Here, nobody but a very small handful of people had ever spoken to him, but everybody knew what he looked like.

At first the two men strode along without speaking, and then they found themselves walking side-by-side, each following a rut in the road. "Other than the barbed wire on top of the fence posts, we could be in the Middle Ages," David said, deciding he could be the one to come up with the conversation opener.

"I hear you're facing a war."

David let out a laugh at the dispensing of small talk. "Yes." And he laid out for him how everything had been when he'd left.

They chugged up a fairly steep, wooded slope and then stopped, and David realized they were amidst the ringworks of an old hill fort. To the north, they could see the Menai Strait and Anglesey beyond it. To the south were the mountains of Snowdonia, though as was often the case, their peaks were hidden by clouds. "William will be released from the hospital this morning. He'll be tired still, but his wound isn't life-threatening."

David folded his arms across his chest. "That's what the doctor implied to me. He said William was lucky it was a through and through in that particular spot. Any other location and there could have been heavier bleeding and nerve damage."

Chad laughed. "You have the term *through and through* in Earth Two, do you?"

"We certainly have through and throughs there. The crossbow was shot in Earth Two, remember? But no, those were the doctor's words, not mine."

Chad sobered, and his eyes scanned the landscape instead of looking at David. "Do you know why only you and your family have the ability to travel?"

"No."

Chad turned to look at him, skepticism on his face.

David spread his hands wide. "Really, I have no idea. We have guesses, that's all. Even when the Time Travel Initiative was up and running, we had only guesses. I'm not a god, nor a savior. The best suggestion I heard was that my family is like the X-Men: mutants with the ability to shift between worlds and shape that reality around us."

"Is that what MI-5 thinks now?"

"I have no idea what MI-5 thinks," David said. "Their chasing of Anna feels like a knee-jerk reaction to me. Livia and the D-G implied as much. Like the saying, *when all you have is a hammer, everything starts to look like a nail.*"

"You may be right about MI-5, but I know what the CIA want," Chad said. "They never gave up on the time travel project. Did you know?"

"Suspected, more like. And again, Livia said as much to me. What do they want?"

"They want Earth Two to be their emergency bunker."

"Excuse me?"

Chad shook his head, not so much because he was saying no but to sweep away David's question. "Just like in the movies. Somebody got the idea that if things go too much to hell here, the greatest minds—or rather the ones that can pay for it—can hide out in Earth Two and start over. With their weapons and technology, they could carve out a nice piece of the planet for themselves."

David stared at Chad as the implications hit him like a punch to the gut. "Like a Mars colony except in the past?"

Chad nodded.

"That can't happen." David didn't even voice the far worse thought of what might happen if another member of his family came here, and how much more vulnerable they would be. Arthur's sweet face rose before his eyes, and he almost choked on a sudden rage.

"It can if they keep you locked up and then force you to travel, say, on a giant bus."

David turned away to look at the woods, not wanting Chad to see the struggle to control his horror. "Earth Two can't be accessible to this world. I don't care what plans the CIA think they have. I would rather be dead than help them." He turned back to Chad. "I need to go."

"I can protect you."

"For how long?"

"For now. On Monday, we'll find a way to send you home, if that's what you want." Then he dropped his chin and said softly. "What *do* you want, David?"

David gave a tsk. "To go home."

Chad pressed his lips together and didn't immediately reply.

David raised his eyebrows. "You think I should want more?"

"I'm hoping for it."

"I'm not the King of England here. It isn't my place to want anything—other than to be treated like a human being instead of a pawn."

Now it was Chad's turn to scoff. "In this world, that *is* asking for a lot."

David didn't know how to answer that. He'd been pretty powerless in 2010 as a fourteen-year-old kid, but he'd had every expectation of eventually having the autonomy to choose the life he was going to live. Maybe that was teenage arrogance, but anything else was just despair.

It turned out that Chad was thinking along those same lines. "You are a beacon of hope to this world. We have screwed it up badly.

To know that there's another world out there, and that we're not alone ..." his voice trailed off for a moment in an unusual degree of uncertainty. But then he squared his shoulders and added, "And though you haven't said it outright, you don't want me having access to that world either. I've talked enough with Ted—and with Anna when she came—to see how protective you all are of Earth Two. It kind of proves my point, actually, since you think that if just anybody could come to Earth Two—or heaven forbid, a government could somehow have access to it—they would screw it up."

"Yes. I think that."

"So do I. That's my point."

David looked at him warily. "What point?"

"Things are worse here than you know."

"I've done some reading and some talking to others. Sadly, most of your wounds seem to be self-inflicted, so I don't see how I can help, the CIA's plans aside."

"Would you help us if you could?"

The question brought David up short. His impulse was to say, *of course*, but really, "It depends on what kind of help you're asking for."

Chad nodded. "I'm not asking for what the CIA wants."

David snorted. "You wouldn't get it."

"I know." Chad sounded almost sad. "In the short term, if you could bring back a few things with you next time you come, I—and the whole planet—would be grateful."

David's interest was actually piqued. "What could I possibly have on Earth Two that would help you here?"

"It gets very little press, deliberately, but have you heard of the Global Seed Vault?"

"The one in Norway?"

Chad cackled. "Silly of me to think you didn't know of it. Yes, that one. Its purpose is to preserve the world's seeds, before modification and after. What you probably don't know—and few people do because it might cause a global panic—was that the block containing the bulk of our pre-industrial seeds was flooded by a sudden incursion of rising sea water. All the heirloom seeds were destroyed."

David's eyes narrowed, waiting for the punchline. "That isn't good, I presume, but there are other storage sites."

"The U. S. government stopped funding theirs three years ago. Other countries have done even less well."

"But ... you still have strawberries, right?"

"We do, but they're genetically modified, either directly or with breeding over time. A modern strawberry has one-third of the nutritional value of a strawberry grown a hundred years ago. Not only has our soil been leached of nutrients, but we've bred for beauty, not taste or nutrition."

"You do realize I live in Britain, right? It isn't exactly a haven for fruits and vegetables."

"I know that, but I also know that you are resourceful, and you are the King of England. You can get what you want if you want it badly enough. When you come back next, if at all possible, please bring seeds."

David was taken aback by his earnestness, but he understood too. Potatoes were transforming the medieval food system in Earth Two, but he wasn't pleased to learn that their nutritional value might be less than it should be. At the same time, he was grateful to have them at all. 1293 had been a bumper crop; potatoes lasted forever; if that was all they had to eat, he could keep his people alive.

His mother and Bronwen had been speed reading the (digital) history books Mark had brought back and had told him that 1294 was a year of famine in Britain, brought on by unending rain from mid-summer to Christmas. They were late planning for it, but there were still some things they could do to prepare.

"What seeds do you need?"

Chad pulled a piece of paper from his shirt pocket. "Will you do it?"

David took the list. "I will. If at all possible, I will."

Chad heaved a sigh of relief.

"Wow. This really is important to you." Both the fact that Chad had the list at the ready and the sigh told David that.

"Oh yeah, David." Chad started walking back the way they'd come. "You have no idea."

And when they arrived back at the house a short while later, David realized Chad hadn't even mentioned the interview tomorrow night.

24

2 April 1294

Bronwen

"Thank you for coming." Bronwen stood as Bevyn ushered Margaret, Thomas's sister, into the solar. Having left immediately after Bronwen's discussion with Lili and Bevyn, the rider had made good time to the holy well—and clearly Margaret had accepted the urgency of their request since she'd traveled the same distance in time for breakfast today.

"I'm sorry for the circumstances." Margaret caught Bronwen's hands and looked her up and down. "You look well."

"Well enough for a woman whose king has been betrayed again."

Margaret took in a breath. "I can only apologize, over and over if I must. I'm sorry for the role my family has played in these troubles."

Bronwen let out a quick breath of her own. "It is hardly your fault that your brothers chose the paths they did. Have. Did the messenger tell you why I asked you to come?"

"Thomas attempted to assassinate the king." Margaret's expression was genuinely horrified, and her eyes swam with tears for a moment before she blinked them back. "Is it—" she swallowed hard before continuing, "—does the king blame my husband somehow?"

"No." Bronwen kicked herself for not realizing that Margaret would immediately make that leap. Kings had been known to condemn an entire family because one of its members was a traitor, and here the Clares had produced two in as many years. "David didn't punish you or your husband for what Gilbert did. He isn't going to blame you for Thomas's actions either."

A lone tear streaked down Margaret's cheek. "We will never recover from what they've wrought, however."

Bronwen squeezed her hand. "You never know. Just look at the Bohuns."

"I try not to," Margaret said, recovering something of her normally dry wit.

Bronwen grinned for a second and then sobered. "David *is* alive, so the attempt failed."

"And my brother?"

"He is well too, relatively speaking. In his attempt to escape the castle, he was shot in the backside and leg, but we patched him up." She looked at Margaret a bit harder. "He *is* in a cell. That won't be easy to see."

Margaret nodded. "It is no more or less than I expected."

"Would you be willing to talk to him?"

"Of course. I would have come at your summons regardless, but I assumed that's what you wanted. I don't know what good it will do, though. You already know he is allied with Balliol, and I don't know that he will be willing to tell me anything more."

"We thought it worth asking, since he won't speak to us. Worst case, he tells us nothing more. But the way this plot fell out makes us feel as if there's still another shoe to drop. Roger Mortimer remains defiant, despite David's successful return from Ireland, not to mention his crowning as High King there. Balliol too. They've been far more confident, in fact, than it feels they have any right to be, considering who they're going up against and how their plans have so far gone awry."

"It is true that the king has proved himself time and again against what appeared at the outset to be incredible odds. He is blessed by God, as Gilbert—and now Thomas—learned too late." Margaret sighed. "I am ready. Please take me to him, and I will see what I can do."

Lili and Bevyn had agreed to allow Bronwen to handle Margaret, since she was Bronwen's friend, and Bronwen was sorry she couldn't watch the subsequent proceedings through two-way glass like in a police station, but it was worth the possibility of Thomas confiding in his sister to leave the two of them alone together. Bronwen didn't have much in the way of experience with interrogation either—beyond scolding her children—but she hoped that even if Thomas started out antagonistic towards his sister, their familiarity with each other would eventually devolve into a genuine exchange.

Thus, when they reached the cell, the guard ushered only Margaret inside. But he didn't close the door behind her all the way, and Bronwen pulled up a stool and sat near the gap between the frame and the door to listen. Bevyn had followed them into the prison, and he leaned against the wall beside Bronwen, his shoulder to the stones.

"So they dragged you into this too?" Thomas was all disdain. It wasn't exactly the loving greeting Bronwen—or Margaret—might have hoped for.

But Margaret scoffed and her words dripped acid. "I've been *in it*, as you say, a long time. I'm lucky to have survived what Gilbert did. Now I have to negotiate your treachery too? It's incredibly selfish of you to put me in this position."

Bronwen looked up at Bevyn, whose eyes were wide. They had assumed Margaret would be the comforting sister. Instead she'd gone on the attack.

And put Thomas on the defensive. "It should have worked." He sounded like a sulky six-year-old, defending his actions to a wiser sibling.

"You mean you should have killed the king? How did you think that was going to end?"

"With my death," Thomas said. "I knew it, and it would have been worth it."

"Thomas ... why?" Now Margaret's tone changed to one that was both loving and despairing. "You think you owe Roger Mortimer—or John Balliol—that much?"

"You don't understand."

"Obviously." The starch had returned.

Thomas sighed loudly enough for Bronwen to hear through the doorway. "When I lost Thomond ten years ago, it became clear to me that the only way to get it back was to enlist the aid of someone more powerful than myself. It was a humbling realization, as you can probably imagine, but I felt I needed to be realistic. Gilbert, of course, turned me down."

Margaret gave a mocking laugh. "As he would."

Thomas actually laughed too. "Indeed."

Though she wouldn't have gone about it the way Margaret had, and Bronwen herself had no siblings, she recognized the familiar banter as one rooted in family.

Thomas continued, "Then Gilbert made his ill-advised bid for the throne, and I knew that if I was ever going to achieve my aims, I needed to find help sooner rather than later, before David gave away Ireland entirely. John Balliol gave me that chance." He cursed under his breath. "My mistake was in relying on others instead of finding a way to do the job myself."

"You mean murder the king? You tried yesterday and failed."

He made a derisive tsk. "My mistake. I didn't know he couldn't be killed."

"If you had bothered to consult with me, I would have told you to capture him instead. You could have held him for ransom."

At that, Bevyn's head jerked a little, and his and Bronwen's eyes met again. She held up her hand to stop him from saying anything. Margaret was playing along—or so she hoped.

"Don't I know it! He's gone to Avalon, hasn't he?"

"So I understand."

Thomas cursed again, and he began to pace. Or at least, Bronwen could hear boots thudding on the stones.

"You know why I'm here?" Margaret asked after a moment.

"To get me to talk." The thudding stopped. "I wasn't going to, but now—" Thomas raised his voice. "I'm ready to bargain!"

Bevyn straightened, stepped around Bronwen, and opened the door. Bronwen stood too, though she made sure to keep well back. She wasn't afraid of Thomas attacking her, but he might find off-putting the fact that she was the one who'd orchestrated this meeting. Some men had a problem with a woman who knew her own mind. Though, of course, his sister certainly had no trouble managing hers.

Bevyn came to a halt beside Margaret. "I'm listening."

"My wife and children are not to suffer for my crimes."

"Done."

"They must be allowed to stay with her parents and my son allowed to inherit the lands his grandfather designated for him before he died."

Thomas and Gilbert's father had been Richard de Clare. The vast majority of his holdings and titles had gone to Gilbert, as the firstborn son, but he'd had some discretion in distributing a handful of his minor estates. David had decided he wouldn't punish Gilbert's two daughters for their father's sins, and they each had inherited a few of the over two hundred estates Gilbert had forfeited when he died. The earldom of Gloucester remained vacant, having been returned to the crown upon Gilbert's death.

"Is that why you agreed to try to murder David, despite the poor odds?" This time there was pity in Margaret's voice. "Balliol promised to safeguard your family?"

Thomas gave her a single nod. "With the failure in Ireland, I lost everything I had to lose except my life."

"So you thought to throw that away too?" Margaret said.

For the first time, Thomas's voice held a measure of humbleness. "For my son, I would do anything."

Bevyn wasn't interested in Thomas's regrets. "What do you have for me in return?"

"The threat you don't know about."

"From where?" Bronwen took another step into the room, unable to remain silent.

"Norway."

"Erik invades again?" Bevyn was disbelieving.

Thomas shook his head. "The threat comes from Hakkon, Erik's younger brother. He has promised Balliol an army equal to the one his brother brought to Scotland four years ago."

"Does Erik know?" Bronwen knew all about Erik from Callum and Cassie. Like Philip of France, he was the same age as David and very ambitious, as well as protective of his rights as King of Norway. She knew nothing, by comparison, about Hakkon.

Thomas laughed derisively. "No. He wouldn't be supportive, seeing as how he married the Bruce girl last year."

Thomas meant Isabel Bruce, sister to Robbie.

Then he shrugged. "By the time Erik finds out what his brother has done, it will be too late." He eyed Bevyn and then Bronwen. "If you don't move quickly, it will soon be too late for you as well."

25

2 April 1294

Christopher

They'd spent the night in an inn in Heptonstall, northeast of Manchester, having come well over sixty miles the day before—miles that would have taken a few hours at most to drive in Avalon. They'd arrived after sunset and slept eight hours in relatively clean conditions. Then they pushed on, spurred by a comment from the innkeeper that *foreigners* had been seen in these parts.

"Foreigners as in Scots?" Christopher asked.

"Or Welsh?" Huw said.

"Ach, the Welsh are a strange breed, but they're not so different from us, are they, my lords?"

Huw had insisted on introducing Christopher as the *Hero of Westminster*, so everybody knew he was the king's cousin. "Not so different, no."

"What about Irish?" Matha suggested.

The innkeeper looked him up and down. She was well into middle age, but her eyes flashed a little—not with disapproval at

Matha's accent but with approval at his appearance. Unlike his sister Aine, Matha's hair was dark, almost black, though he still had that pale Celtic skin that would burn in the sun if it ever shone in Ireland. He was tall and well-built, and he carried himself in a manner befitting someone who knew his own worth. Christopher knew him to be arrogant, but that arrogance had been tempered by pain and loss and a measure of fear. Christopher wasn't the only one who'd grown up in the last month.

But still, the innkeeper shook her head. "I didn't see any of these men myself, you understand, but I heard of 'em. And they weren't Irish nor Scots neither."

Christopher decided to defer any judgement about the foreigners' nationality until he met them. According to Robbie Bruce, Highlanders could seem foreign to a man from Lancashire, but so would a Spaniard or an Italian, not that he was worried about a company of Italians roaming northern England.

"Where were they?" Huw asked.

"North of here."

Matha shrugged. "We were going north anyway, so that works out."

Thus, by noon, they'd gone another twenty miles, reaching Yorkshire and the Southern Pennines, taking it a little slower and searching all the while for any trace of the foreigners about whom the innkeeper had spoken. Having learned *something* from being captured in Ireland, every time they rested the horses, Christopher had taken the binoculars and found the nearest high ground. Not alone, of course, since that was another thing he'd learned in Ireland.

But this time, Christopher didn't need to put the binoculars to his eyes to understand that they'd stumbled upon something Callum needed to know about. Before him lay a plain, cut by a winding river. A castle was perched on a cliff above the river, and an army was camped before it. He took one look, and then a second longer one, cataloging the various banners, only some of which he recognized.

For confirmation, he handed the binoculars to Huw, who'd accompanied him up the slope. "This is Skipton, right?"

"It is." Huw's expression was stony. "I'm guessing there are at least five thousand men down there."

Christopher scanned the plain, trying to count tents and fire circles, but there were so many, he kept losing track. "There are a hundred fires in the bottom left quadrant alone."

Giving up, together they slid from their perch and hastened back to where their companions waited.

"The news isn't good." Christopher took in the faces of the men before him.

"What does that mean?" Jacob said.

Last time, in Ireland, Christopher had been with his best friends. Callum had chosen these men, and while Christopher didn't know them as well, he knew them better after spending thirty straight hours with them, and all of them had fought in battle before. They had all lost friends among David's guard when they'd been murdered in France on Gilbert de Clare's orders. None of them would be taking an army at Skipton as a good sign.

"Balliol is here, instead of at Barnard," Christopher said. "Or at least his banners are here, and there are thousands of men in the fields before a castle just north of our position."

"They've come fifty miles south without us knowing?" Though his words were ones of surprise, Jacob wasn't aghast so much as grim.

"There's more," Christopher said, feeling grim himself. "Balliol has allied with someone else. There are banners in that field that Huw and I don't recognize."

Huw handed the binoculars to Jacob. "Everyone should take a look."

There were only six of them, which had seemed like plenty when they'd set out from Chester. They'd been scouts only. Because they intended to ride fast and change horses multiple times, they'd needed to keep the company small so the strongholds they stopped in would have enough fresh horses to give them. Now, Christopher was longing to be part of a company, though he supposed he would have been more conspicuous and equally unable to do any damage against the army before them.

At the top of the hill again, Jacob shook his head, but Matha looked long and hard before saying, "Norway."

"What?" Christopher took the binoculars back. "Are you sure?"

Matha pointed. "See the red banner that shows a gold lion with an axe? That's the flag of Norway." At the others' skeptical looks, he added, "I know this because the King of Norway, not the current one but his father, met with us when I was a child, and I remember his banner."

Us being the Irish clans, and Christopher was pretty sure he didn't want to know what intrigue they'd been planning with Norway, even twenty years ago. "Anybody speak Norwegian?"

Nobody raised his hand.

"Why is Skipton being held against us?" Jacob said with clear frustration. "I thought it was a royal castle? We were supposed to change horses here."

And get a hot meal, Christopher thought, but didn't add. David might well lose other castles before this war was over, but the loss of this one was definitely not a good start.

Huw chewed on his lower lip. "Skipton belonged to Prince Edmund, King Edward's brother, which he inherited from his first wife. He's dead, of course, but his second wife has two infant sons. I don't know why she would ally with Balliol, but it's more likely she isn't here, and her castellan gave up the castle uncontested."

This was the moment for which, as Christopher's mom would say, they paid Christopher the big bucks. He gritted his teeth. "Two of you need to ride right now, first to find our army and tell them to march here instead of to Barnard, and then to Callum at Beeston, though if all went well yesterday he might be heading north as we speak."

Jacob took in a deep breath. "I should be the one to go, but I'm supposed to be watching your back."

"I'll be fine here. Watching King David's back is far more important," Christopher said. "The Stewarts and the Bruces are marching to Barnard Castle, which is no good now, and this army is large enough to flank both his and Callum's. We need to flank this one instead. They need to know about the strategic value of this hill, for starters."

Flanking was a basic military tactic, which, thanks to computer games, Christopher had known about before he came to Earth Two. Those were something he thought he ought not to mention either.

Jacob nodded and then gestured to John that he should come with him. The two men slid down the hill to their horses, and by the time Christopher and the others followed, they were mounted.

"What are we going to do in the meantime?" Huw said. "Watch and wait?"

"Not hardly," Christopher said. "Someone else needs to ride to James Stewart, wherever he may be."

Huw and Matha looked at each other, and Christopher could see them weighing the pros and cons of which one of them should go. Finally, they both said at exactly the same moment, "It should be me."

"No." Huw shook his head. "James knows you, but he knows me better. More to the point, I know him better. I can find him." He wasn't taking no for an answer, and within five minutes, he and Cedric were mounted too.

Christopher caught Jacob's bridle before he could leave. "You must raise the countryside on the way. The general alarm has gone out, but the people have to know that this isn't just Scotland we're dealing with. Find the headman of every village and town you pass through on the way and make sure the people are preparing for war and ready to march this way when the army comes through. We really are going to need them."

"Yes, my lord." He spurred his horse away.

Huw and Cedric headed in the opposite direction. They'd have to go some miles to the west in order to avoid being spotted by the army in front of Skipton Castle.

"That's smart," Matha said as he watched their companions go. "Some might not see a difference between one lord and the next. Norway, however, is another matter entirely. If they hadn't already, men will respond to your summons now."

Christopher had been thinking specifically of Paul Revere's ride at the start of the American Revolution, but he didn't mention that to Matha. Everyone knew that Avalon was a strange and wonderful land, but very, very few knew about the time travel part of it. He decided he didn't feel guilty about taking credit for an idea that wasn't his.

Still, he was a little shocked at what he'd just done. "I'm not sure what just happened."

"You did what had to be done," Matha said matter-of-factly.

"I suppose so." Then Christopher looked hard at Matha. "Are you ready for the rest of the plan?"

Matha looked at him warily. "I assumed we were going to watch and wait. That's partly why I volunteered to ride to the Stewarts."

"Not exactly." And Christopher told Matha what his real plan was.

"You want to volunteer? Are you completely out of your mind!"

"Am I? If that's Erik of Norway down there, he has allied himself with Englishmen and Scotsmen. We will simply be two more who see the way the wind is blowing and go with it."

"I'm Irish!"

"We are both former servants of Gilbert de Clare," Christopher said. "He drew men from estates all across Britain, and that can explain our accents. But I don't think we're going to have to explain much. You and I were part of an army two weeks ago that was way smaller than this one. Even well-organized armies are chaotic. We just have to find someone who speaks English or French."

"Or Gaelic, I suppose. I understand these Scots well enough." Matha was still staring at him, and though Christopher feared he was going to point-blank refuse, all of a sudden, Matha's mind began to work. "I can't decide if this idea is brilliant or completely mad."

"But you'll do it?"

Matha was still shaking his head as he walked to his horse. "The king sent you north for a reason. If I learned anything from how things fell out in Ireland, it's that he, of all people, knows what he is doing."

26

2 April 2022

William

"I have to tell you the truth, William. I have no idea what I'm doing." David stood looking down at William, blocking his view of the television set. William clicked it off, pleased to already be proficient at the use of that particular technology. "It's utterly terrifying."

"Why are you telling me this?"

"Because you deserve to know the truth. Back home, I speak it only to my closest family. But we aren't there, and here in Avalon, you and I are technically equals. The more I think about my conversation with Chad, the more I've come to understand that there is a lot going on under the surface that I don't know anything about, and nobody is willing to tell me."

William studied his lord, feeling in that moment as if something again had changed inside him. In defiance of everything he'd ever been raised to do or believe, he and the King of England *were* equals here. It gave him the confidence to ask, "What do you fear most?"

David pressed his lips together for so long that William thought he wasn't going to answer, but it was only that he was thinking. "Every day, a thousand worries cross my desk, but I have learned that if you make a list, and stick to it, you can tick off what needs to be done one item at a time. Often it's better not to look at the big picture. But I can't do that with what is happening here, and you need to know that every second we remain in Avalon, I am in genuine danger, far more than I've ever been in before." He then explained about the men from 'America' who wanted to ride David back and forth from Avalon like a horse.

Using his good hand, William adjusted his position in his chair, mostly to give himself time to think. He was glad David trusted him enough to tell him of his fears. William had found that speaking them out loud sometimes made them more real, but it also made them something that could be tackled. "We should just go home."

David sighed. "Believe me, I want to. But I've been convinced that it isn't that simple."

"Tell me why not. We can climb to the roof of this hospital and jump off."

"Regardless of the intrigue that is swirling around us, I have a duty at a minimum to see this interview through tomorrow. I want to be able to come back to Avalon in the future without being put in prison, and for that to happen, I feel like I have to generate some goodwill—not only on the part of Chad Treadman's organization or MI-5, but from the people of Britain."

William grunted. That was something he understood. “Just like at home.”

“I don’t rule anyone here, and I have no intention of doing so. But yes, just like at home.” David pulled a low table closer to William and sat on it. “I know I talk a lot, and over the years I’ve lectured you about all sorts of things, but this lesson is one that I really want you to learn. Someday, God willing, you’ll be the Earl of Hereford, and things go better when the people you’re ruling have bought into being ruled by you.”

“My ancestors conquered England just fine.” William didn’t mean to argue necessarily. He was just pointing out an obvious counterpoint.

“Yeah, they did. And they eliminated virtually the entire Saxon ruling class in order to do so. That’s certainly one way to go about conquest.” He canted his head. “That isn’t what happened in Wales, however. Instead, the English nobility—and royalty—married into Welsh noble and royal families.”

“That’s how we won Ireland too.”

“That’s right. It’s a tried and true way to co-opt the native establishment and make them think your priorities are their priorities. Blood relationships are a good start.” At the sound of heels tapping in the hospital corridor, David looked towards the door to the lounge, which remained open. “I can’t do that here, obviously. So I have to use words instead.”

“All the more reason to get me out of here. I can’t help you if I’m stuck in a flimsy gown.” William pointed towards the door, through which they could see Michael, propped as usual against the far wall. Then Livia stopped in front of him.

"You won't be here for much longer. They're letting you leave."

William's eyes widened. "Really?"

David laughed. "Don't tell me you've changed your mind and want to stay?"

"Of course not. Didn't I just say so?" Then William bit his lip, finding himself fearful again. He fought down the urge to stand and pace, not wanting to open up his wound. "Where are we going? Is Alex going to be there?"

David's brow furrowed.

"She's the girl who stayed with me last night."

"I know who she is. *Fickle, thy name is William*, is it?"

William didn't even feel abashed. "I liked her."

"You like all girls," David said.

"That's true. I do." He paused. David's voice had been matter-of-fact and without criticism. "You don't mind?"

"Just because I myself fell in love with Lili at sixteen and married her three years later doesn't mean something similar is the right course for you. I like Aine fine, but love born out of crisis doesn't necessarily last, and it's better to find that out sooner rather than later."

"I still want to see Aine again." William answered without thinking, but as he said the words, he realized he spoke the truth. It would be all right if he didn't marry Aine, or if she didn't want to marry him, but he was learning that the type of girl he wanted to be with for the rest of his life needed to be along her lines.

David leaned forward, his elbows on his knees. "We need to talk."

"Haven't we just been doing that?" Then, noticing David's intensity, William put on his studious face. "What about?"

"About what you did on the battlement that got you here."

William tried not to look mutinous. "I'm not going to apologize for attempting to save your life. Turnabout's fair play and all that."

David's eyes narrowed. "What do you mean?"

"Didn't you take an arrow for me five years ago at my non-wedding?"

David leaned back a little. "Oh, that."

"Yes, *that*. You could perhaps be forgiven since you weren't king at the time, but you were the Prince of Wales and your father's heir."

"Like you are now. *You* at that time were destined for the throne."

"See." William rested his shoulders more comfortably against the cushion. "Exactly my point."

"Okay, okay." David laughed. "It seems to me I got the better end of the deal. The arrow only grazed my ribs. You got punctured." He paused and studied William somewhat pensively. It seemed that what he wanted to talk about next needed to be broached carefully.

William had known David for a long time, however, and his eyes narrowed. "What?"

"What I'm about to say, you need to take in the best possible way. This isn't about me. It's about you."

"O-kay." William drew out the syllables.

"Now that I know you're not only going to live but heal, and can heal with the medical care back home, I've started thinking about how to get there. But I need to ask you first ... are you certain that you want to come?"

"Of course I want to c—"

David held up a hand, cutting him off. "This question isn't just a formality. You have a genuine choice before you. You could stay here. Learn. Grow. Work for Chad Treadman. Attend university. Do whatever you please, really."

"You have that choice too."

"No, I don't." David shook his head. "I might have had it once, but I travel when my life is in danger, whether or not I want to. You, however, do not have to go." He gave a little laugh. "This is all predicated on the assumption that I *will* have a choice this time, because if I don't, I might well be forced to leave you behind. Has that yet occurred to you?"

"I-I hadn't considered that." Then William cursed inwardly. When he started to stutter, like when he was fifteen, it gave away the fact that he was unhappy.

"And before you decide, there is something about Avalon that I have never told you, something that might either make everything make sense or make you hate me."

"Never, my lord."

"Yeah, well—" David looked down at his hands. "It is time to tell you the truth, and it's astounding to me that I have never done so. The myth of Avalon is just so easy to perpetuate." He took in a breath, his eyes back on William's face. "Avalon is just a word we use to describe this place. I am not King Arthur, returned or otherwise. *This* is the future, though I'm going to confuse you further by adding that it isn't *your* future world so much as *a* future world."

William was staring at him. "You sound so serious, but I have no notion as to what you just confessed, my lord."

"I will tell you what I once told Ieuan, when I took him to Avalon for the first time. I was born in the year of our Lord, one thousand, nine hundred, and ninety-six."

William pinched his lips together and didn't speak, trying to make sense of what David had just told him. "That isn't possible. Your father is King Llywelyn."

"It is possible because my mother traveled from this world, what we call Avalon, to him, in January of 1268. Then, on the day of my birth, she traveled back here, just as we did, so that I was born in Avalon. When Anna and I saved my father's life at Cilmeri, we drove the vehicle that you've seen in the bus barn from the year 2010 to 1282."

William found that he couldn't look at David. What he was saying was completely absurd. And yet, it had to be true. "Why are you telling me this?"

"Because you were going to start asking questions soon, and I wasn't going to have answers to give you that were truthful. For example, have you noticed that Wales, the country, has no king?"

William licked his lips. "I guess I did. It was just one more thing I didn't understand."

David nodded. "In this world, my father died at Cilmeri, and I was never there. Edward lived."

"So—" William hitched himself in the chair again, "—if I understand you correctly, someone with my name and my father's name are part of this world's past?"

"You have always been a quick study. Yes, that's exactly right. You see the implications."

"I want to know everything about him. About who he was and what happened to him."

"Of course, with the caveat that you remember that your life has followed a very different trajectory."

"Thanks to you." William knew he sounded almost hostile.

David didn't take offense. "Yes. Thanks to me. We'll see which version of yourself you like better, but I've told you all this in part because I like my odds." He tipped his head towards the door. "Come in, Alex."

The girl entered carrying an electronic tablet.

"I've told her to read you everything and anything you want to know about." Then, at a signal from Michael, he got to his feet and strode to the door where Livia was waiting for him. The action spared William having to answer. "What's up?"

William couldn't make heads or tails of the subsequent conversation, but afterwards, David returned. "The director of MI-5 has arrived in Gwynedd, and he is willing to meet me."

Earlier, David had told William something of MI-5. While David hadn't really believed the Director-General would deign to travel to Wales to see him, to William's mind, if he really was in league with these *Americans*—or being used by them—he would want to put his best foot forward.

"Alone?"

"We are meeting at six this evening in a local market next to the vegetables."

William knew something about markets. "It will be impossible for either you or MI-5 to control the space. At that hour, there might be a hundred witnesses."

"Exactly."

"Are you sure about that?"

"Yup."

William looked down at his lap to hide his grin. Whatever craziness was going on here—whether in 'Avalon' or this apparent alternate future world—David was still his liege lord, and he had to admire his confidence.

Behind David, Livia said, "Whatever you want," into her phone, and then her heels clicked as she walked away, the device still pressed to her ear.

Now David grinned at William and answered a question William hadn't known enough to ask. "MI-5 will know that Treadman set up security at the market—it's called the Tesco—hours ago and will be scrambling now. At the start of this, all I wanted was not to end up in a cell. Now, I want more than that, and Philips is either going to give it to me, or I'm going to walk away."

27

2 April 1294

Christopher

Because they were trying to appear as normal as possible, the best plan that Christopher could see was to ride right up to the pickets and ask for entry. As the younger of the two of them, Christopher was going to act as Matha's squire.

Christopher was worried that Matha would need to brazen out whatever lack of confidence in the plan he had, and as they approached the first guard along the main road to Skipton, he urged his horse just a little ahead of Matha's before coming to a halt. They'd waited until later in the afternoon to move in the hope that the guards would be thinking more of dinner than of them.

The guard stepped into the road, backed up by two others with pikes. Christopher had a flashback to the battle at Tara but managed to shake it off.

"We are here to join Balliol." Christopher started off with English, thinking that, whoever these men were, they were low enough in the hierarchy that French wouldn't be their language of choice.

Luck was with them, and the man answered, albeit with a Scottish accent. “My lord.” He gave a quick bow in Matha’s direction and then turned back to Christopher. He’d guessed right that a lord might not necessarily condescend to speak to lowly soldiers, and it was acceptable that he’d taken on the task. “I must ask your names.”

“I am Edward, squire to my lord Matha of Breifne.”

“Irish, eh?” One of the guards to the rear looked them up and down with suspicion.

“Indeed.” Christopher tried to maintain an air of earnest intent, but Matha simply looked bored, which on the whole was exactly the right approach to take.

The guard didn’t ask for more information, and it wouldn’t have been his place to question a knight. He tipped his head to indicate the road behind him. “You’ll be stopped again a quarter-mile down the road where you’ll be asked your credentials by someone with higher rank than I.”

“As I would expect.” Christopher urged his horse forward, and they clip-clopped down the road another quarter of a mile.

“This was a mistake. We should have done this surreptitiously,” Matha said in an undertone. “We could have waited until nightfall and simply joined one of the companies.”

“No.” Christopher shook his head. “For starters, we would have had to leave the horses and our gear behind, including our swords.”

“We could have hidden them.”

"You can't just join a group—especially the two of us, who stand out in this crowd. Sneaking around would have drawn more questions than we're going to get by being upfront."

"I don't know." Matha looked genuinely worried.

"If you were so concerned, why didn't you say something sooner?"

"It's different now that we're here."

"You did great back there." Christopher bit his lip as they approached the next layer of security. He was trying to project confidence, but Matha's doubts had him wavering too. "Just do it again."

"Gilbert de Clare, eh?"

"He's dead. He can hardly argue."

"I suppose if anyone has a right to claim ownership of Clare it's the man who killed him." Matha straightened his shoulders and affected a haughty look. This time the man who stepped out to bar their way wore a sword.

"We're here to join Balliol," Matha said, now in excellent French. "I'm Matha ap Gilla of Breifne."

It was only now that it occurred to Christopher that they should not be using Matha's real name. Hopefully, nobody here would know the details of anything that had happened in Ireland, and certainly not the name of the son of a man who had been a minor lord of Breifne. In retrospect, it was also far better that Huw had gone to James Stewart. He had been David's companion far longer than Christopher and might be more recognizable, especially with his great bow on his back.

The man's eyes narrowed, but he responded in the same language, indicating Matha had guessed right. "Where are your men?"

"Since Clare was killed, I have none. I lost everything."

The man's lip curled briefly, a reflection of an internal sneer at Matha's obvious mercenary tendencies. But as Christopher had hoped, he didn't hold them against him, simply lifted his chin in acknowledgment. "We can use your sword, my lord." His eyes went to Christopher.

Matha saw it and added, "My squire, Edward."

The man nodded. "Does King Balliol know you're coming?"

"No. We have never met."

"You can probably find billet in the town. The captains are meeting tonight at the castle to discuss the battle plan. We won't be privy to that, but at least we can eat. Give the man at the castle gate my name, John Bulmer, and he'll admit you."

Matha bent his head. "Thank you."

Christopher bowed his head too, and they rode into the camp. Again, Christopher had to blink away thoughts of Tara, and although he managed to clear his vision, sweat beaded on his forehead.

"Are you okay?" Matha said.

Christopher closed his eyes, breathing in and out until the anxiety passed. Callum had suggested some techniques for getting past the immediacy of post-traumatic reactions, and he'd been working on them. After Tara, he'd been fine initially, but it felt as if the more time passed the worse things got. When he'd confessed this to Callum, he'd laughed, though not in a mocking way, but with understanding. Christopher still thought one of the real reasons Callum had agreed to send him on this expedition was to give him something to do and take his mind off himself.

"I'm okay." He opened his eyes and forced his vision to clear.

"We all have bad memories," Matha said. "Some men have been known to drink too much because of them."

"I'm not doing that," Christopher said. "I know better than to do that."

"If you ever start not knowing, tell someone. Tell me."

Christopher nodded, though inside he wondered if the point at which he drank himself to sleep would be past the point where he would be able to ask for help.

The ride through the camp was uneventful, considering the fact that they were enemy soldiers, and every second Christopher was sure that someone would recognize them. He wasn't wearing his helmet, which on second thought might have been a good idea. As it was, they reached the entrance to the town, which was being guarded on the road by two men. It wasn't much of a defense, really—literally no more than two sawhorses and two men with pikes barring access to the main street through the town.

A newly dug or re-dug ditch on both sides of the road was the only other barrier of any kind between the army and the town. To the left, the ditch ended at the river, and the water level was such that a moat had formed for a hundred feet. To the right, the ditch looped east and north until it stopped at a stone wall demarcating a farmer's field.

If someone had a mind to, they could leap the ditch and cut through the yards behind the houses and workshops to the left and right.

Christopher and Matha, however, were waved through the barrier. They both knew enough about how these things worked to realize that before entering the castle on foot they had to find housing for their horses, if not themselves. Neither of them was high-ranking enough—nor did they want to be viewed as such—to justify staying in the castle itself.

So Christopher leaned down to speak to a guard, who appeared to be coming off his shift. He didn't wear a sword, and his tunic indicated he belonged to the town's garrison, not to Balliol specifically. Christopher said in his best medieval English, "Do you know where we could find lodging for us and our horses?"

The man stopped. Knights, whatever their nationality, were to be respected. "We have only one inn, and I know it's full, but my aunt and uncle decided this noon that they'd do their part and take in lodgers. No point in passing up the opportunity for coin." He hesitated, seeming to have more to say, but he swallowed it down. Christopher could only hope that his hesitation was because he wasn't thrilled about hosting a rebellion against the king. "Tell them Alvin sent you."

The name wasn't one Christopher had ever heard in medieval England before. It wasn't Saxon or Norman. Christopher might have thought the man was Norwegian except for his perfect English. He didn't feel he could explore any of that, however, at least not at this time, so he and Matha accepted the directions and made their way to their possible lodging.

Skipton was a small town, really a village, that had suddenly turned into an armed camp. The streets were packed with soldiers. Unlike in Shrewsbury or London, the houses had been built a good twenty feet apart, with yards and gardens, many of which were fenced. The house to which they'd been directed was slightly larger than most, two full stories, and Christopher wondered if Alvin's uncle was the village headman—or rather, since this was England, the town's mayor.

The front door was right on the street, and as Christopher and Matha arrived, the door opened, and a woman came out with a broom to sweep the dirt as if the road was her porch.

It was a lost cause to Christopher's mind, but it saved him the need to knock. He dismounted and approached her. "Excuse me. Your nephew Alvin sent us. We are looking for lodging for the night."

At first, the look the woman gave him was startlingly fierce, and he felt taken aback, but then her expression smoothed into something entirely noncommittal. "It isn't much for great lords like you."

"We would be grateful for any bed you could offer us, and even more, a safe place to leave our horses."

The woman paused again, clearly hesitating to commit. Then her husband appeared around the side of the house and intervened. "Alvin sent them. Of course we have room for you and your horses. I am Gunnar, and this is my wife, Inge. Please come with me, my lords."

As they followed him around to the back of the house, Matha, who'd dismounted by now too, leaned into Christopher. "They're Danish."

Being from Ireland, Matha knew Danes when he saw them, and Christopher vaguely remembered that the Danes had once been big in the north of England, so their descendants would still be here. At one of the crossroads that morning, before they'd discovered this mess, they'd passed someone heading to Thorlby, an adjacent town, named (obviously) after Thor, the god of thunder and a personal favorite of Christopher. If he'd known then what he knew now, he would have told the man to turn around.

Gunnar led them into a largish yard, thirty feet square, that included a couple of outbuildings. One was the kitchen, set apart from the house because of the danger of fire, and another was a barn. Chickens strutted across the dirt, and a boy of seven ran after a pig that weighed twice what he did.

The house butted up against the river, so they didn't have any neighbors on that side. From the bank, Christopher could see the raised drawbridge, protected by a wooden gate on the town side, and the road heading north out of town.

He turned to look at Gunnar. "We appreciate this."

"Certainly, my lord." Gunnar stood in front of them, looking from Matha to Christopher with an expectant expression.

"Payment. Of course." Christopher dug into his purse for a few coins, the same amount he'd paid the innkeeper for a room and food last night.

From Gunnar's wide-eyed look, it was something of an overpayment, but Christopher was happy to have a place to stay at all. It was late afternoon by now. He hoped that Huw and the others were well on their way to completing their tasks too.

Gunnar pocketed the coins. "Bread is just out of the oven, and the beer is fresh if you'd like to take your rest."

Christopher looked at Matha, who nodded. "Thank you. We aren't due at the castle for another hour. It would be good to settle in first."

A large table took up one side of the central room, necessary for the numerous children Gunnar and Inge had, but only Matha and Christopher were eating now. Inge seemed to want nothing to do with them, because it was Gunnar who served them. The walls were decorated with various weapons, many of them ancient. He even had a bow, though it was half the size of Huw's great weapon.

At the sight of it, Matha got to his feet to inspect it, and when Gunnar reentered the room with a small plate of cheese, he said, "This is of Irish make."

Gunnar set down the plate. "I have relatives in ... Ireland."

He turned to leave, but Matha put out a hand and spoke in a foreign language.

Gunnar stopped, his eyes narrowing as he listened. Then, he answered in English, “My ancestors came to these parts hundreds of years ago.”

“I’m surprised, then, that your loyalties lie with Balliol,” Matha said. “Or that you support his alliance with Norway.”

Gunnar’s feet appeared frozen to the ground, but he had something of his wife’s ability to remain expressionless, because his face gave nothing away. “I try to stay outside of the affairs of kings.”

“That’s probably wise,” Matha said.

To hide his discomfort, Christopher took a big bite of his buttered bread. After Gunnar hastened away, relief he couldn’t hide on his face, Christopher spoke around the food, which was delicious, “Why’d you ask him that? He can’t tell us the truth.”

“But we know it now, don’t we?”

“I suppose we do.” Christopher sat back in his chair.

“It could be that most of Skipton feels as he does.”

Christopher nodded thoughtfully. “And before we’re through here, we might need them.”

28

2 April 2022

Livia

MI-5 had pulled out all the stops for this one—as had Chad, Livia was sure, though little of what he was doing had been shared with her. She'd known something was afoot from the moment she'd woken that morning, but nobody wanted to talk to her about it, for obvious reasons. They treated her like a mole in their organization. And of course, that's exactly what she was.

"I would ask you to tell me the truth, but I'm not going to bother." David gazed out the car window as they left the rental house in one of Chad's vehicles.

The roads were congested, and it was a good thing the windows in the vehicle were tinted black, because otherwise people might have been able to see David's face. She knew without asking that the vehicle was armor-plated, just as Five's would be. The sun was near to setting as well, which she assumed was why David had chosen this hour to meet.

"I am telling you the truth."

He looked at her. “As you know it. Maybe.”

“Mark trusted me,” she said as mildly as she could manage.

“I’m not going to be taken in again. For the thousandth time, I have absolutely no reason to trust them.”

“Then why are we even doing this?”

David tsked. “Because I am just like you and Mark. I want to believe. I want to trust them, and somehow I can’t help giving them a chance.”

“So this is a test?”

He laughed. “Yeah, it’s a test. Didn’t you know that?”

Livia hadn’t thought about the meeting that way, and it was too late to mention David’s thoughts to the D-G without everybody overhearing. To her, this meeting was intended as a meet-and-greet, a chance for them to get to know each other after several bad years of estrangement. To her—and she was pretty sure to the D-G—David’s relationship with MI-5 was the one that really counted, while his current arrangement with Chad Treadman should be viewed as a temporary aberration.

In other words, MI-5 was family; they were the known quantity and who David would want to work with once he got over these current difficulties. For David to include Chad Treadman was like a cousin bringing the boyfriend nobody liked to Christmas dinner. Livia had been thinking—and she was pretty sure that Philips had been thinking it too—that David just needed to be coddled a bit, and he would come around.

It hadn’t occurred to her that some things couldn’t be fixed.

They arrived at the Tesco, which was packed, as David had assumed it would be on a Saturday afternoon. There could even have been more tourists present than usual, either hiking up Snowdon to see where the plane didn't crash or over to Beaumaris, which might well end up as some kind of shrine. The driver parked in the middle of the parking lot, while the two other cars that had driven in with them found spaces nearby.

"How are you going to do this?" Livia turned to look at David. "You may be the most recognizable person in Britain right now, and that includes the current royal family."

"Nobody is going to expect to see me here." David pulled a black wool hat with a Welsh dragon emblem on it down low over his ears. The emblem came to rest off-center between David's forehead and ear. He looked foolish, and he appeared to know it, because he grinned at her. "It's raining, so we'll carry an umbrella. Just you and me."

"You are out of your mind. What if someone does recognize you? You'll be mobbed."

"That's why Tesco's staff has been augmented by a dozen of Chad Treadman's men. I bet half the shoppers in there are MI-5 anyway. We'll be fine." Having accepted the umbrella Michael offered, David got out of the car and came around to her side to open her door. It was a chivalrous move she hadn't expected, augmented by the umbrella he held open over the top of the car to prevent a drop of rain from touching her head.

Thankfully, she'd had the foresight to pack trousers and sensible leather shoes instead of the heels she normally wore. From the look of it, David was already getting wardrobe advice from Amelia, since he was in black jeans, shoes, and leather jacket. And then, of course, there was the hat. The rain was coming down hard enough now that she planned to keep her hood up too.

With Livia's hand tucked into David's elbow, they hustled through the rain to the front doors. On the way, they passed twenty people coming and going, and nobody looked at them twice. David picked up a basket and wended his way through the shoppers towards the produce section, which was somewhat in the center and to the back of the store. He stopped in front of a bank of squashes. "Zucchini was never my favorite, even when I could get it."

"We call them courgettes," Livia said. "You don't have them in the Middle Ages?"

"Most squashes are New World." He poked at a fat yellow squash. "I could see bringing back pumpkin seeds. Did you know the Celts invented Halloween, but they carved turnips, not pumpkins?"

"I didn't," she said flatly.

Her eyes continuously scanned the store for threats. At the opposite end of the aisle they were in, someone dropped a container of chocolate milk, and it exploded. Instantly, service workers were there with a yellow warning sign and mops, and it was only then that she realized the entire scene had been orchestrated to close off that end.

David was watching too, and a smile played around his lips. Then he turned and looked behind Livia. "Director Philips, I presume."

It was. In his suit and tie, he was more out of place than David in his funny hat—but the D-G stuck out his hand as if meeting a time traveler in the produce section of a Tesco was utterly normal. His hair, streaked with gray at the temples, was wet, as were the shoulders of his raincoat.

David shook. "Thanks for coming."

"I was in the neighborhood." The statement came out something like a drawl.

David laughed. "As was I."

This was going better than Livia had hoped—feared—it might.

"We would like to put our relationship back on what we consider to be a proper footing," the D-G said.

"As in, not hostile? I wouldn't be opposed to that."

"Let me begin by apologizing again for what happened with your sister. It was a mistake."

"I still have questions about that. Which part, exactly, are you referring to as a mistake?" David said. "The part where you hunted her across England, or the part where you sent fighter jets to drive her plane into Snowdon?"

Philips took in a breath through his nose. Livia knew he hated apologizing, for all that he'd done it a half-dozen times so far to David. He wanted things to go well, but he was loath to grovel. He did it anyway. "I know that Livia has expressed Five's regrets in that regard. I would like to assure you of mine as well. I am truly sorry."

David nodded, his eyes never leaving Philips' face. "You do realize where the problem lies, don't you?"

A gesture from the D-G encompassed their surroundings. "Meeting in a Tesco is all very well and good, but walking into Thames House and walking out again? We have never allowed you to do that."

"You have not."

There was a pause, and then Philips said, "What about Chad Treadman? What makes you trust him?"

"For now, he has given me no reason not to."

"He broadcast your face across the planet."

"Yeah, I didn't like it, but I can see why he did it."

"So you're going to give him what he wants?"

David's eyes narrowed. "I am not for sale."

The D-G put up a hand. "I would never dream of suggesting it."

"He told me what the CIA hopes to gain from me, which is more than you have done, though you have to know." David paused. "And if you don't, that's far worse."

The D-G's benign expression wavered for a second. "What did he tell you?"

"That they want to ride me back and forth from Earth Two to Avalon. They want to make me their slave."

Livia could feel the rage in David at the thought, though he mostly kept it out of his voice.

"That is not my doing," the D-G said, "and I would never help them achieve it."

"I would hope not."

Philips' jaw clenched for a moment. "I know you agreed to allow Treadman and his people to help you when you are in this world." He took a card from his breast pocket and held it out to David. "I would hope that next time you, or whoever returns here, would extend us the same courtesy."

David took the card. "Next time?"

"There will be one, surely." Philips paused. "That's what you fear, isn't it?"

David looked down at the card for a count of five. "That's it? You're willing to wait?"

"We are not fickle. Nor are we subject to the same rules and laws that govern the rest of the world, including your new friend Chad. The Security Service have been defending Britain for over a hundred years. We'll be here after a hundred more." Philips canted his head. "Can you say the same about Treadman Global?"

29

2 April 1294

Ieaun

Ieuan stepped out of the pavilion that had been set up at the center of the camp they'd established near the village of Bury, roughly fifty miles from both Chester and Beeston, having reunited with the bulk of the army that had set out from Chester yesterday morning.

With no guilt whatsoever, he'd left Beeston in the hands of lesser captains, who were perfectly capable of cleaning up the mess he'd made, and taken only mounted men north. He, Math, and Callum had bigger fish to fry. Except for Mark and Cador, the twenty-firsters and former captives had been left behind as well. Mark had learned horsemanship in the time he'd lived among them, but the others could not have kept up today.

The sun had set two hours ago, but men were continuing to trickle into camp. Hundreds more had joined the army as it marched across England. They would need to get settled quickly and on their way to resting, because they would be asked to move again at dawn.

The barons had dined, and now were meeting about their plan of action for the coming days, most of which didn't require a great deal of discussion, since it primarily involved a slogging march north towards Barnard Castle. The victory at Beeston had been gratifyingly quick. Without Sophie and the rocket launcher, they would still be camped around the fortress, trying to figure out a way to get in.

As they'd arrived in Bury, storm clouds had threatened, and Ieuan had been called from the tent by what he thought was thunder. He saw now that what had drawn him was the sound of thundering hooves.

A company of thirty riders stopped at the far pickets and then were waved through quickly, which meant they were known to the guards and possibly had an urgent message. Ieuan braced himself for bad news.

But then, as they trotted down the pathway towards the main tent, a groundswell of cheering began among the soldiers on either side. Hats were being thrown into the air, and the noise became a roar.

Ieuan had a flash of hope that it was David, coming to lead them.

It wasn't. Lili, not David, dismounted in front of the pavilion. She had her bow and quiver strapped to her back, and she was wearing that newfangled dress she and Sophie had invented. Ieuan liked the style, actually. It was both feminine and eminently practical, just like Lili herself.

That admiration didn't stop him from cursing under his breath, however, even as he stepped forward to greet her with a smile plastered on his face. He wasn't going to undermine the men's joy by baring his own disapproval. They had to think she was expected and that their leaders were united.

"What are you doing here?"

Lili wrapped her arms around his neck. "I had to come."

He embraced her, careful to avoid being whacked on the forehead by her bow. "What about Alexander?"

"He's loves his auntie Bronwen. Don't be angry, brother."

And all of a sudden, he wasn't. He had been the one who taught her to shoot, after all. He could hardly blame her for wanting to fight when she and everyone else knew she was perfectly capable of it. It wasn't as if she was asking to be put on the front lines with a sword.

And besides, the men loved her. David inspired hatred or jealousy at times (obviously), but Lili was beloved. And fast becoming a legend in her own right.

Now, releasing Ieuan, she turned and waved to the hundreds of soldiers before her, all of whom continued cheering, though those at the front of the lines bowed respectfully.

Then she grabbed Ieuan's arm and pulled him towards the entrance of the pavilion. "I didn't come for this. We have some bad news."

"I would expect nothing less."

The men in the tent had noticed the uproar outside, and several had left their seats and started towards the entrance, to be halted by Lili and Ieuan's sudden appearance through the tent flap.

"My lady!" Humphrey de Bohun was the first to gasp, and he went down on one knee an instant later.

Several of the barons in the tent were from the north and would not know Lili to look at, but everyone bowed anyway. Ieuan had never been to this region of England, but within a half-hour of the army's arrival, various nearby lords had come to do them homage. Math had very generously granted Roger Pilkington, the preeminent baron of this region of Lancashire, the dubious honor of putting up the army on his land for the night.

Lili, typically, smiled and motioned that the men facing her rise. "Up, up. We have work to do." She strode towards the table, which had been cleared of dishes and upon which several maps lay spread.

Mark had been standing at the table too, but with a tablet in his hand. "What information can I get you?"

"Everything you know about Hakkon of Norway."

From behind Lili, Callum choked. "What?"

"He's Erik of Norway's younger brother," Lili said. "And he's here."

"I know who he is, my queen." Callum got control of his surprise. "He's a hotheaded fool. You're sure it isn't Erik himself who's come?

"Not according to Thomas de Clare." Lili turned to look at Callum. "Thomas is the man who tried to assassinate Dafydd."

That was a torrent of information in a few short sentences. Ieuan moved to stand beside his sister. "What exactly are you telling us?"

"Hakkon of Norway has come with an army of his own to support Balliol."

"How many men does he have?" Edmund Mortimer asked.

"I don't know. Thomas wasn't privy to that information."

"How did you get this information out of him?" Callum said.

"It was your wife, Margaret." Lili turned to look at Almain, the Earl of Cornwall. Tall and lean, with dark hair and a closely-trimmed beard, Almain was the same age as both Humphrey de Bohun and Edmund Mortimer, in his mid-forties.

In reply, Almain pressed his lips together in a partial, self-satisfied smile. He and Margaret were estranged, which didn't endear Ieuan to the man, and he was pompous and arrogant, but Ieuan also knew from Meg that Almain would be dead of cancer before the turn of the century and would leave no heirs. That, combined with the fact that he'd marched an army of a thousand men north from London, made it easy for Ieuan not to be judgmental.

"How many miles to Barnard Castle from here?" Lili asked.

Pilkington, the man with the local knowledge, answered. "Ninety, my lady, give or take, and that's marching through the mountains. It would be a hundred and ten to go around them."

Math looked at Callum. "That's four days minimum, and that's if it doesn't rain." So far, it hadn't, but this was April in England. Could they really be so lucky?

"Does anybody know how far away the Bruces are?" Callum said to the general audience.

Nobody answered in the affirmative. Pilkington cleared his throat. "We haven't heard from them, my lord. We would have said if we had."

"Excuse me, my lords and lady, but we can leave now. We're rested." Morgan, the captain of David's archers, spoke earnestly in Welsh.

He led two hundred men, all of whom were seasoned warriors, understood guerrilla warfare, and were mounted on smaller, quicker horses that could make good time. The Bruce army only had sixty miles to march from Carlisle to Barnard, and a messenger from James Stewart had arrived a week ago to say that they were leaving Carlisle. Unfortunately, there had been no news since, and none of the messengers David had sent north from Chester had returned.

"The rest of our cavalry can get some way down the road too," Callum said.

"I brought thirty more," Lili said. "We've ridden long today, just as you have, but we could start again by midnight."

Ieuan's jaw was tight, but he nodded. "Knowing those archers, they'll get there first."

"What about communication—these *walkie-talkies* I've heard so much about from Nicholas de Carew," Almain said.

Ieuan tried not to smile at hearing *walkie-talkie* come out of Almain's well-bred mouth. "We have enough to send one with the archers, another with our heavy cavalry, and keep a third with the main army. Once we begin moving, we will all be out of range of each other very quickly, but if we're anywhere close, we'll be able to find each other once we're within striking distance of Barnard."

Math and Callum exchanged a glance. Each, in his own way, was the leader of this army. Callum wouldn't want to take over if Math had a different opinion. He canted his head in approval, however, so Callum gave a sharp nod. "If nothing else, we have enough men to pen Balliol in the north until we determine how exactly to defeat him."

Ieuan was pessimistic enough to think that they'd ultimately be forced into a long slog through Scotland, like King Edward and his ilk had done in Avalon's history, but he didn't mention it. They had to deal with what was in front of them first, which was more than enough to be going on with.

Throughout the meeting, Humphrey de Bohun had been uncharacteristically silent, but as the barons dispersed, he approached Ieuan. "I'm riding with you and Queen Lili, because, of course, you both are going tonight."

"We are," Ieuan said, though he hadn't discussed it yet with Lili. She hadn't come all this way to march along with the spearmen, and they both knew it. "What about Edmund?"

"He's coming too, as you must have guessed. He and I have a hundred riders between us. We'll be four hundred strong, without the archers. We wouldn't want to ride with more anyway, nor leave the army without any cavalry at all, in case Balliol's army is doing something different from what we've been told."

Callum had spent a few moments conferring with some of the Lancashire barons outside the tent, but he now he returned, throwing back his hood as he reentered the pavilion. He was followed by two other men, their clothes mud-spattered from a long journey. Their eyes were alight, however, and Ieuan knew them. These were two of the riders whom Callum had sent with Christopher.

His heart fluttered that something could have happened to the boy *again*, but before he could ask, Callum said, "Balliol and Hakkon aren't at Barnard after all. They've marched to Skipton Castle, from which these men rode today, sent by Christopher, who remains there."

To have had two different sets of riders arrive in their camp within an hour of each other was something of a miracle, especially considering the distances and difficulty in discovering exactly where the army had ended up. And while he welcomed the news, he grimaced to think that Balliol could have come so far without any of them hearing of it.

Lili had her own perspective. "Thank goodness for that! Skipton is miles closer than Barnard."

"It means the Scots have reached farther into England," Callum said, echoing Ieuan's thoughts. "That they've put the Pennines behind them means they have the whole of England before them.

From Skipton, they can move in any direction. That said, it also means that any supply line from Scotland is stretched very thin."

Math folded his arms across his chest. "If they've come so far south, it means they're confident in their plan. I'm sure they're already probing for us, looking to engage us on ground of their choosing."

"Can they really not know the Bruces are behind them?" Ieuan asked.

"Maybe they're hoping to engage us before we can link up with them," Callum said. "Or Balliol is still assuming David is dead, and he will face less coherent opposition. That's why they've moved now. Maybe he intends to march on London. We've been a step behind him for weeks, and perhaps he thinks we still are."

"He wouldn't necessarily be wrong," Ieuan said, though under his breath so only Lili heard him.

One of the riders, the one named Jacob, put up a hand. "Christopher sent Huw and Cedric riding north, hoping to divert James Stewart towards Skipton."

Lili bit her lip. "It's a longer journey for them now."

Pilkington was still present, and he filled in the geography again. "Skirting the Pennines to the west, they have ninety miles to travel from Carlisle to Skipton." He canted his head. "But that makes fewer than forty miles for us."

"Do you know, between Balliol and Hakkon, how many men we'll be facing?" Math asked the riders.

"Five thousand at least," John said.

"We can match that with the men here," Lili said, drawing herself up to her not very tall height but every inch the queen. "With or without Dafydd, Balliol's army cannot be allowed to penetrate another mile into England."

30

2 April 1294

Christopher

Christopher ran a hand through his hair, making it stand on end. It was shorter than when he'd arrived in Earth Two nine months ago, since washing it was out of the question a lot of days. Better to keep it only an inch long because then nobody would notice if it was dirty. Short hair meant he had no floppy bangs to hide behind, however, and he didn't know that he'd ever been so nervous in his life.

He and Matha were risking their lives right here, right now. It was making Christopher's mouth dry and his hands sweaty. He felt that in Ireland, when he'd been captured and made to stand before Aine's father, he'd been almost too innocent to be nervous. Even when they'd taken Roscommon Castle from the inside, the hours of waiting had pretty much drained most of the anxiety out of him by the time they were actually able to leave their hiding place.

Since Ireland, he had a much better understanding of the badness that was possible.

But then again, maybe those experiences also made him realize that, whatever happened, he could survive it.

They approached the castle gate, and Matha stepped in front of Christopher to speak to the guard. Meanwhile, Christopher attempted to look bored, while praying that nobody at this castle had ever seen him in person.

"John Bulmer told us that we should come here tonight. I am Sir Matha of Breifne, and this is my squire." Matha didn't name Christopher, which they'd agreed might be more normal than not. Squires were unimportant in the social hierarchy, unless they were sons of famous men. Even then, they should be seen and not heard. Christopher could definitely see the benefit of keeping his mouth closed at all times.

The guard bent his head in a quick bow and waved them through, which Christopher was almost sorry about because it meant they were committed. Skipton Castle was pretty big as castles went, with a massive gatehouse that faced the town and a bailey the size of a football field. It also had a large central keep with five towers of its own. The keep itself was unevenly pentagonal, with a long side that abutted the curtain wall built on a cliff above the river below it. It was the same river that flowed past the house where Matha and Christopher were staying.

The setup looked a lot like Chepstow Castle, in fact, with the river cutting a deep channel behind the castle perched above it. Skipton was located here for a similar reason as Chepstow too, except in this case, the Eller Beck was meant to act as a barrier against marauding Scots rather than the Welsh. Unfortunately, it had done no good against Balliol, the King of Scots. Christopher had noticed as they'd left the mayor's house that the town's drawbridge remained raised. Nobody was getting across the Eller Beck without getting wet.

"Balliol had to have had someone on the inside," Christopher said to Matha in an undertone as they crossed the inner courtyard and entered the keep.

"Shush. We are not talking about this right now."

Christopher subsided, but he was still outraged on David's behalf. It was crazy the number of people who thought betraying the king was a good idea. Then again, they'd probably done it because Balliol had assured them David would be dead.

Whoops.

He and Matha followed their noses towards the great hall, which was up a flight of stairs from the keep's inner courtyard. The door was open, but nobody was really guarding it. They had plenty of guards throughout the rest of the castle, and with all the comings and goings, stopping people coming in and out of the hall would have stalled traffic too much. As it was, the great hall was packed with men, and Christopher followed Matha as they edged sideways to the right around the inner wall. They had entered the castle near the tail end of the meal, in hopes that it would make blending in easier. With the battles ahead still unfought, Balliol wouldn't allow drunkenness, but watery beer would be flowing.

Matha tipped his head towards the end of one of the tables, where two men had just risen to their feet. Christopher and Matha hastily sat themselves down. Matha had his back to the wall, which gave him a better view of the room. Christopher had to turn in his seat to take in his surroundings.

A frazzled servant plopped two cups and a trencher in front of them. He waved a hand to indicate that they should help themselves to the platters that were already on the table. A couple more seats next to theirs cleared out, and Christopher stood to fill his trencher with meat and bread.

Only high-ranking men were allowed to eat in the hall, but with five thousand soldiers in the fields, that was still a few hundred knights, squires, and higher-status men-at-arms. The food would be doled out in quantity, but it would need to be kept simple. He speared a few potatoes too, laughing mockingly to himself that Balliol might not like the changes David had brought to Britain, but he wasn't above taking advantage of the more stable food supply potatoes gave him.

Christopher sat back down and put the trencher between him and Matha.

"What are you doing here?"

The words came from behind Christopher, whispered urgently in his ear, and then Thomas Hartley stepped one foot over the bench and sat beside Christopher, facing him. His bright blue eyes glared.

Christopher had already taken a bite of bread, which he proceeded to almost choke on. Matha slowly lowered the cup back to the table, awareness in every line of his body.

Thomas eased back slightly and took a nonchalant drink from the cup he'd brought. "At least you sat in the back of the room. I think I'm the only one who has recognized you so far. You can't be here!"

"Why not? What about you? We figured nobody would recognize me out of context and this far from London." Christopher had swallowed his bread and recovered enough to defend himself.

Thomas looked daggers at Matha. "And you are?"

"I could ask the same of you."

Christopher tsked through his teeth. "Matha, Thomas. Thomas, Matha. Both of you are companions to King David. There. Is that good enough?"

The two men reached out and grasped forearms. "A pleasure," Matha said.

"Likewise," Thomas said. "I'm here with Henri."

Deciding a more detailed explanation now would save time later, Christopher leaned across the table and gave Matha a hurried summary of how he knew Henri and Thomas and what they'd done for David. He then told Thomas how he knew Matha.

"The Templars are supporting Balliol?" Matha attempted to cover up the way his face had drained of all color by taking a drink himself.

"Of course not. We're spies, like you."

"I thought Templars had to wear the cross at all times." As a devotee of medieval history, Christopher had made it his business to know about the Templars long before he'd come to Earth Two.

"We ... have learned some things since the king was almost killed in France."

"Haven't we all." Christopher ate a piece of meat. "Where is Henri right now?"

"At the high table. He's an emissary from the King of France. I'm his squire." Thomas pulled a face. "It irks me to say so."

"I'm Matha's squire for this, though I was knighted after Tara." Christopher had tried to stop himself from adding the last half of the sentence, but it came out anyway.

Thomas leaned in. "You were at Tara with the king?"

Christopher and Matha both nodded.

Thomas eased back again, casually looking around to make sure nobody was observing them. If someone was, they were far enough away that Christopher didn't think they could overhear the conversation. "We arrived yesterday, a few hours after they took the castle, so we have gathered less information than we'd like. The king really is alive?"

Christopher and Matha nodded again.

Thomas continued to look pensive, as if he didn't believe them. "Balliol has acknowledged that the king survived Ireland, but insists that another attempt on his life at Dinas Bran was successful." He paused, both fear and hope in his voice. "Do you know about that one?"

"The attempt was made at Chester, if we are talking about the same one, and we were there when it happened," Christopher said.

"The assassin injured William de Bohun, but David is well. The English army is marching here now."

Thomas let out a shuddering breath. "Praise the Lord."

Christopher felt momentary guilt at not mentioning Avalon to Thomas, but he didn't feel like he should talk about what might not matter. David could have returned by now. And the army *was* coming.

"The king will be going to Barnard, though, not Skipton." Thomas's worry face was back.

"I sent riders south. They should know soon about the change of location, if they don't already."

Thomas looked Christopher up and down. "*The Hero of Westminster*." He shook his head. "You really do live up to the name."

Christopher scoffed. "You were as much a hero that day as I was. You and Henri."

"That reminds me." Thomas turned his head with studied casualness to look towards the high table where Henri sat.

Christopher had met both Henri and Thomas at Westminster in the aftermath of Gilbert de Clare's death. With dark hair and eyes and olive skin, Henri looked Greek to Christopher, but apparently he was a younger son of a French lord, having joined the Templars because he would inherit no lands of his own.

Henri gave no indication that he'd seen Thomas's glance, but he leaned into the man next to him and said a few words, before standing and walking away from the high table. He didn't look in

Thomas's direction, but once Henri had passed through the main doors of the hall, Thomas motioned with his head for Christopher and Matha to come with him.

They left the hall, still hopefully with nobody remarking them, and found Henri in the outer courtyard, in the shadows of the northern curtain wall.

"In the name of Saint Gerard, what are you doing here?" were his first words to Christopher.

Thomas related what they'd told him, and Henri subsided. "It's still dangerous for you to be here. Christopher, at least, is a known companion to King David, and just because you don't recognize anyone doesn't mean someone doesn't recognize you."

"That's what I said," Thomas said smugly.

"I felt it was worth the risk. We need to know what the plan is."

"It appears to be evolving." Henri gestured towards the main gatehouse. "Let's find a better place to talk."

They followed him, and he was of a high enough standing that the guard bowed to him fully as they left the castle.

"Did King Philip actually send you?" Christopher hastened to come abreast so they could keep talking.

"My master spoke with him. So much of what has transpired in the last month has caught everyone by surprise." He turned his gaze on Christopher. "Your king most of all."

"He needs better spies, that's for certain," Christopher said.

"Intrigue does not come naturally to him, and what worked for him in the early years of his reign is no longer sufficient." Henri's chin wrinkled as he thought. "Perhaps he would be willing to listen to some suggestions."

"After all this, I'm sure he would." Christopher said.

"Your French has improved since last we spoke."

Christopher laughed. "Given that it was nonexistent before, that bar is pretty low."

Henri laughed too, nice and casual, and they turned onto the main village street. Like the great hall, it was full of people, though most were of a lower class. Henri stopped at some tables set up in front of a house. The owner had created a makeshift tavern, in the same way that the stalls on the street were newly erected. Food vendors were doing a brisk business, as were the stalls selling boots, clothing, sewing supplies, and other household items. Because of the army's arrival, a market had grown up in the town.

"We can talk here." Henri put up four fingers to the bartender, who came around his table with four crude clay cups, not even fired. They might have been made that day.

"War is a boon for merchants as well as kings," Henri said before taking his first drink.

Christopher drank too, pleased to find he was drinking cider, not beer. And as he set down the cup, he noticed a small dragon carved into the side, the same dragon as on David's crest. He traced it with one finger thoughtfully before being distracted by Henri, who commented, "I hate English beer. Cider is better."

Thomas clearly didn't agree, since he was sipping his drink with a curled lip. "So, what's David's plan?"

"I'm more interested in Balliol's at the moment," Christopher said, not quite ready to tell his new companions that David was in Avalon. "I get that they did all this thinking David would be dead. What I don't see is how they think they can win with him alive."

Henri grunted. "They think they have good numbers with the addition of Hakkon's army."

"They've come really far south." Matha was drinking the cider with enthusiasm. He had never taken to English beer either, though Christopher thought his dislike was more a matter of principle. "Balliol has committed everything to this fight. What's happening back in Scotland that made him think this was a good idea?"

"Balliol would take the rule of England over Scotland," Henri said. "He descends from King Henry I of England, and with the throne empty, he would have more right to it than most, including his allies in this war. Hakkon wants Scotland and thinks he deserves it for coming to fight."

"That's what Balliol has promised him?" Christopher was shocked. "Which Scottish barons support that?"

"Those who hate the Bruces. But remember, when all this started, Red Comyn was going to win Ireland, in part by the murder of not only David but also James Stewart and the Bruce heir. I understand that Robert Bruce survived an attempt on his life around the same time."

"Robert Bruce being Robbie's grandfather?"

Henri nodded. According to Bronwen's shorthand, Robbie was *Baby Bruce,* his father had been *Daddy Bruce,* and his grandfather was *Grampa Bruce.* Christopher and Matha looked at each other. They'd not heard anything about that, and they were certain David did not know of it. Christopher drew in a breath. "The Stewarts, Bruces, and their allies are marching south even now, and I sent riders to them today too."

"I want to know what the plan is *now,*" Matha said. "David is alive. Robert Bruce is alive, and five thousand men are on the verge of ravaging England."

"Balliol doesn't yet know David is alive," Henri said, "and I am not going to be the one to tell him."

"So do we let this happen?" They'd fought the battle at Tara because David had deemed it necessary. They'd won, but Christopher could do without more killing.

"Do we have a choice?" Henri said. "Balliol isn't going to back down, and King David can't."

"If it comes to open battle, both sides are going to take huge losses," Matha said matter-of-factly, "though David cannot help but win. Balliol doesn't have archers." After Tara, it was a huge sin, even to an Irishman.

"We could kill Balliol," Thomas said in a low voice.

"A king does not kill a king," Christopher said, also in an undertone, knowing David believed it.

Henri pressed his lips together. "I honor that sensibility, but it is one that Balliol clearly does not share."

31

3 April 1294

Lili

"Are you ready to admit this was a bad idea yet?" Ieuan caught the bridle of Lili's horse, holding it steady in preparation for her mounting.

The sun had finally risen after an endless night. When she had chosen to ride north with the cavalry, she'd known what it was going to feel like, but it had been a long time since she'd put herself through this kind of hardship two days in a row. That didn't mean she wasn't going to brazen it out to her brother though.

"Was it?" She stopped in front of him. "I don't think so. You saw how the men responded to my presence. If they can't have Dafydd, then I will do. For now."

Her current circumstances reminded her in many ways of what had happened when she first admitted she loved Dafydd. She'd been chased out of her brother's castle by soldiers, who had ridden right up to the front door and been admitted by the traitorous castellan. Those riders had belonged to Roger Mortimer too. The man had been quiet these last few years, but she was in no way surprised to find that he'd been merely biding his time.

"At least you have Constance back." Ieuan eyed Lili's bodyguard, who was seeing to her own horse. Beside her, Constance's husband, Cador, ate bread and cheese in preparation for the journey. Ieuan had almost not allowed him to come, since he was out of shape after two weeks of captivity. But Cador had insisted that his wife wasn't riding into battle alone, and Ieuan had given way. It would have been hypocritical not to, seeing as how Ieuan wasn't letting Lili go alone either.

"Alexander has never spent a night without me before. But that night is over, so I can breathe more easily. It passed for him, one way or another. I'm telling myself that he slept snuggled up to Bronwen or Arthur and is completely happy. How much farther do we have to ride?"

Callum was close by, and he answered instead of Ieuan. "Some twenty miles. We could do that by noon, except once we are within striking distance, we will want to go very carefully."

Lili nodded. She had come fifty miles from Chester to Bury yesterday and then twenty more overnight, so this last twenty was by comparison easier. It was going to be much more difficult on the foot soldiers they'd left behind. Math had determined to let them sleep last night, but once they started marching, he might ask them to walk all night tonight. For Lili's journey, the horses had alternated between walking and cantering, which was much faster, in order to have rest periods for riders and horses. Lili had managed a few hours of sleep during those times.

One of Humphrey de Bohun's captains put up a fist. "Hold!" The word came out a harsh whisper, but in the morning air, his voice carried well.

Everyone fell silent, listening hard. As Callum had just told them, they were twenty miles from Skipton. It was hard to believe that they faced any danger here, but Balliol could have moved again or be sending his own cavalry south, probing for resistance.

After a moment, Lili heard what had caught the captain's attention. She frowned. "Feet, not hooves, Ieuan."

Lili moved with her brother towards the opening in the stone wall bordering the field in which they'd rested during the two hours before dawn. It had dripped rain for an hour overnight, though fortunately not while they'd been sleeping, and not hard enough to slow their progress. The rain could even have been viewed as a blessing, since it meant their horses wouldn't be leaving a pall of dust in the air behind them.

Then four men came around a bend in the road, followed by four more, and more after that. They just kept coming, upwards of sixty at least, but Lili wasn't worried anymore about who they were. The great bows on their backs told her they were Welsh. She stepped into the road.

The man in the lead was muddy past his knees, but he had a grin on his face at the sight of her. "My lady." He bowed. "It is an honor."

The man behind him laughed and bowed as well, and soon all the archers had come to a halt in the road, making merry with the cavalry, who mingled with them. Though the archers had clearly run many miles, they appeared no more tired or worse for wear than Lili's companions.

Their leader, Andras, was a man from Aber's garrison.

"What are you doing here?" Ieuan asked him.

"The king sent us." *King*, in this context, meant King Llywelyn, not King Dafydd. "He felt—and *we* felt—that Gwynedd needed to be represented. Dafydd is *our* prince, after all."

They were all Welsh here, and his familiarity with both Lili and Ieuan reflected the way they were like family.

"How did you know where to go?" Humphrey said. "We didn't realize Balliol was at Skipton until yesterday."

"We were overtaken by Sir Morgan and his men in the night. He pointed us in the right direction." Andras shrugged. "He offered to share mounts, but we know our own strength. It isn't so far now."

Lili laughed, and even Ieuan's glower was less than sincere. "You can't really plan on beating us to Skipton."

Andras raised his eyebrows. "We'll let James Stewart know you're coming."

"You do that." Ieuan laughed as the archers set off again.

Humphrey de Bohun was somewhat more disbelieving and said, channeling his son, "You have got to be kidding me!"

Lili smiled at him. "They'll do it, too, and arrive with the strength to shoot. You'll see."

Humphrey growled under his breath. “I pray the Stewarts and the Bruces are as good as their word too.” He shook his head. “Those sixty archers may well make all the difference.”

32

3 April 1294

James Stewart

The late afternoon sunshine shone brightly down on the town of Skipton as James put his binoculars to his eyes again, having already surveyed the situation without them. The device had been a gift from Callum years ago, and was one of James's most prized possessions. They'd certainly come in handy in Ireland.

Robbie Bruce, who'd chosen to ride with James instead of staying with his grandfather to besiege Barnard Castle, peered south to where James pointed. "That's the ground we want to claim."

James turned to look at his former squire. Now that Robbie was a knight, he could have been forging his unique path, but he'd chosen to stay beside James, at least for now. James had stood in for Robbie's father since his death, and James was not too proud to say that he'd learned some things from Robbie too.

"I agree. It would be madness to bear down on Skipton from directly south along the road."

"So we go?" Robbie said.

"As soon as the sun sets. Two and a half miles in a straight shot."

Robbie looked relieved, which James could understand. It would feel better to be moving decisively instead of the painstaking crawl they'd kept to as they'd circled around Skipton.

Huw's arrival had not, in fact, caught James on the hop. He had known for the whole of the last week that Balliol had left Barnard. He'd sent his own messengers to David to tell him so, and he was more than a little disconcerted to learn they'd never reached him. He had to assume they were dead, possibly at Balliol's hand.

James's respect for John Balliol had grown significantly since Trim. And because he had considerable respect for him, newfound as it was, James had to assume that he knew they were coming.

Still, his forces had made no move in their direction, and over the last few days since Balliol had taken Skipton, James and his company of a hundred cavalry had been slowly working their way through the mountains to the north of the town, both aided and hindered by a covering mist that had dissipated today. Its absence was why they hadn't yet crossed the river and taken the distant high ground, unimaginatively named Black Hill, a single mile to the southeast of the castle of Skipton.

It was a mighty fortress, well-guarded on all sides and built on the English side of the Eller Beck, which is why Balliol had taken it. James was a little annoyed that he'd been clever enough to do so. Not to mention his foresight in bringing in the Norwegians.

Meanwhile, the bulk of James's army, composed primarily of pikemen and led by James's brother-in-law, William Douglas, had camped on the high ground also above the town to the north. They were prepared to stop any retreat back to Scotland on the part of Balliol's forces.

The Bruces hadn't been idle either. Furious at the attempt on his life, Robbie's grandfather was determined to take Barnard Castle, since Balliol had exposed it by advancing south. The man was eighty if he was a day, but he'd insisted on riding out on what James had to think might be his last journey. He was supported by his two younger sons, Bernard and William, and their five hundred men, which was plenty to maintain a siege. James had left them to it.

The rest of the army had been sent quick marching south into Yorkshire. A messenger had arrived an hour ago from James's cousin Alexander, Earl of Menteith, that he was in position just this side of Bolton Abbey, ready to cut off Balliol's retreat in that direction, or to advance and attack Skipton.

A great deal depended upon the location of King David's army. James could sit in these mountains a little longer and wait for him to come, but not forever. Since Huw had arrived, however, James was considerably more cheerful about his prospects, and he found himself grinning at what his young charges had become.

"My lord!" A whisper came from behind them. "A scout has returned."

This was the news James had been waiting for. He and Robbie retreated from their lookout point, heading into a fold in the landscape, and then came to an abrupt halt.

Callum stood before them grinning. “Hello, my friend.”

James gaped at him for several heartbeats, and then laughed. “You made it!” The two men embraced, pounding each other on the back. Callum had already seen Huw, who stood a few paces away, looking deservedly self-satisfied. James stepped back and went straight to the point. “How many men do you have?”

“We’re only the advance,” Callum said. “The main army is still a full march away, but they’re coming.”

James pursed his lips. “How is it that you are here at all?”

“Christopher sent us word too.”

James gestured to Huw. “I knew that, but how did you get *here*. How did you find me? We were trying to be secretive.”

“I can think like a Scotsman when I have to.” Callum grinned. “Huw says he hardly had to work to find you, since you’d already heard the news and turned south.”

James nodded. “We’ve been shadowing Balliol since he left Barnard.”

“We have four hundred mounted men.” Callum paused, allowing himself another smile. “And more than two hundred archers.”

Robbie gave a low whoop. “Morgan and his men are here?”

“Along with some who ran all the way from Gwynedd.”

"I have two thousand pikemen divided into two groups. Each is camped less than five miles from Skipton, and all are champing at the bit at the inactivity," James said.

"The plan so far is simple," Callum said. "As soon as it's dark, we need your men to take all of the ground on the other side of the river from the castle."

"To what end?" Robbie said. "They can't force the river to attack this army. There's no ford at the town, only a drawbridge."

"That's not what we intend," Callum said.

Robbie still looked confused, but James understood. "You mean to cut off Balliol's retreat." He paused. "That could cause Balliol to make a preemptive strike. He'll know his back is to the wall and that he has nowhere to go."

"Or he could surrender sooner," Callum said.

"You sound like King David."

"I will take that as a compliment," Callum said.

"Truthfully, I will do anything to nip this war in the bud." Then James lifted his chin. "What of Beeston?"

"It has fallen, but Roger Mortimer escaped."

Robbie made a sour face. "We thought we saw his banners in the field, but we didn't want to believe it."

James shook his head. "A moment ago, I thought Balliol had made a brilliant move to take Skipton, but with you here and the king's forces approaching, now I'm not so sure. He is far from Scotland."

"He has sent a stream of assassins after David. If one of them had been successful, the whole of England could have been rolled up like a rug. Now, he is caught well into England with no way back." Callum looked hard at James. "How have the alliances fallen out for you?"

James rubbed his chin. "John Balliol and his allies are on one side. Robert Bruce and I are on the other."

"Plus Erik of Norway," Robbie said helpfully. "He's not pleased."

"Erik is here?"

James grimaced. "No. Not yet. Robbie is being optimistic."

"I'm sure Hakkon is hoping that by the time his brother finds out where he is and what he has done, it will be too late to stop him becoming King of Scots," Callum said.

"God forbid. My peers chose John Balliol to rule them, in part because the Bruces can be arrogant and overbearing—" James put out a hand to Robbie, "—no disrespect intended, my friend."

"I know my grandfather," Robbie said. "You speak the truth."

"—but rule by Norway?" James continued. "We might have accepted Erik under duress, but his younger brother? Never."

"That's why this war has to end here," Callum said.

James had seen this kind of grimness in his friend before. It had never boded well for King David's enemies, and for the first time since he saw Red Comyn on the docks at Drogheda in Ireland, hope began to outpace his anger.

33

3 April 2022

David

"You nervous?" Amelia smoothed the lapels on David's suit jacket, under which he wore a very light blue shirt without a tie.

The debate about what he was going to wear tonight had exceeded all reason as far as David was concerned, but he knew the argument well too. As he'd told Amelia, he had a valet, a wife, and advisers from London to the Irish Sea. They all had argued at one time or another about the message David sent with his attire. Even the colors he wore had meaning. For some reason, he couldn't greet an Italian ambassador wearing green.

Fundamentally, he believed it shouldn't matter what he wore, but he'd learned that theory and practice were not the same thing. It was better to acquiesce gracefully and be smart about it, not only because clothing *did* matter in the real world and he wasn't stupid enough to pretend it didn't, but because he also didn't make a habit of disparaging things other people cared greatly about.

Amelia cared what he looked like. So did Chad. So did, apparently, the world, though David thought that was taking it a bit far. But he was starting to accept that everyone on the planet was going to be watching the interview, and he was hoping the studio would be kept at sixty degrees so he wouldn't sweat through his suit. In addition to his glee in general at scooping the story, Chad had also been rubbing his hands together, like a real-life scrooge, over the market share he'd be getting tonight. He claimed that people would begin by tuning into the show airing before the interview, just so they wouldn't miss anything.

Truth be told, David was surprised television still existed at all in 2022. Chad had explained that, while regular cable channels hadn't disappeared, the vast majority of the watchers would probably be seeing the broadcast on their phones, which he would be providing as a live stream for free on the internet. David hadn't had to ask him to make that happen, and he knew enough about the way the modern internet worked to understand Chad's pleasure that ad revenue would be going through the roof.

"I'm not nervous. You guys honestly have more at stake here than I do. I'm going to leave again, and if this goes badly, it will be your mess to clean up." He'd been far more nervous to make his many phone calls this afternoon: to Cassie's grandfather; to Bronwen's parents, whom Chad had tracked down in Mexico; to Mark's family; to some of the bus passengers, including Shane's family; and to Callum's money manager, who turned out to be a no-nonsense sixty-something. A five minute conversation was all it had taken for David to understand completely why Callum trusted her.

Amelia shook her head. "We talked about this. You can't be cavalier. Stay focused, and watch out for the traps I mentioned. Owain agreed to do the interview only if he could ask real questions."

"I know." David let out a breath. "You're right. I swear I'm not being cavalier. I'm just trying to stay calm." He gave her a dark look. "You realize that I have never been on television before."

"Oh, believe me, I am aware."

The interview was being filmed before a live studio audience, in what amounted to a huge warehouse, with a stage set before several hundred chairs, those in the back raised up in bleachers. Massive lights that lit the stage and the audience were suspended from big I-beams and scaffolding up in the ceiling. David could barely make out the people adjusting them manually, forty feet in the air. Other men and women manned four cameras, so the stage could be filmed from every angle. The sound board was off to one side, so as not to impede the view of the audience, and David would be wearing a wireless microphone.

Ten minutes later, David was introduced by the host, and he walked on stage. The second he appeared, everyone stood and clapped. Some seemed to be screaming, while several women in the front row were outright crying. David tried not to look at them and instead smiled and raised a hand, thanking everyone for coming—though nobody could possibly hear his words. Then he shook hands with Owain, whom he'd already met, and was gestured to a seat.

The moment he sat, he sank down so his head was a good foot lower than where Owain was sitting at his desk, and David's heart sank with it. The seating was one of the things Chad had tried to arrange in advance, not wanting David to immediately feel at a disadvantage. Owain himself was no more than five foot eight, so David could understand that he didn't want to stand during the interview and spend the whole time looking up at David, but this was going too far in the opposite direction.

For a fraction of a second, Owain's eyes crinkled in the corners while his mouth twitched wider in an extra bit of smile. It told David that he knew exactly what he'd done, and he was pleased that it had turned out the way he'd expected. It wasn't as if David could walk out in response. He was committed to go through with the interview, whatever the circumstances or the outcome. In that moment, he chose to accept that his best bet was to play along as if he hadn't noticed, and even if he had, it didn't matter.

He relaxed into the softness of the couch, crossed his legs so his left ankle rested on top of his right knee, and put out his right arm to its full length across the top of the couch. David was a big man, and the couch was pretty small as it turned out.

While waiting for the audience to calm down, he bounced up and down and shot them a grin. "This is really soft."

Owain finally managed to wave the people to silence. "Not what you're used to, is it?"

"Not exactly." David grinned again. "We have cushions, but—" he bounced a bit more dramatically, "—not like this."

The last of the crying women seemed to have gained control of herself, and Owain straightened in his office chair to face the central camera. "Welcome to the Owain Williams show. Thank you for being with us, and special thanks to David ap Llywelyn for being here tonight." He pronounced the *ll* correctly.

David bent his head, having stopped bouncing. "My pleasure. Happy to be here." Amelia had told him that his instinct to say *thank you for having me* would come off a little weird and not to say it.

"First off, how is William—that's the name of your friend, isn't it? I understand that he arrived with an injury. A crossbow bolt, was it?"

"Yes. He is healing. Thank you for asking. And thanks especially to the staff at Ysbyty Gwynedd in Bangor. Because of them, William should be fine." David lifted his chin to point to the opposite wing of the stage, effectively behind Owain as he was turned in his seat to look at David. "He was well enough to come tonight."

Owain nodded and for the audience's benefit said, "We hope to speak to him a little later. For now, how's he taking all this?"

"It's an eye-opener, that's for sure," David said. "For me, too, actually."

"Why is that?" So far Owain was leading him along gently, making small talk to put David at ease and warm up the audience.

"I am never here long enough to become adjusted. It has been less than a year and a half, and the changes in technology alone are daunting."

Owain smiled and then spent the next ten minutes asking questions about David's family. He particularly wanted to hear the story of how David and Lili had met and married. These were easy questions to answer, and David started to feel more confident that he was going to get through the interview in one piece. Then Owain said, "So if I understand correctly, you were last here during the bombing of Caernarfon Castle."

"Yes."

Owain motioned towards a large screen behind him. "We'll get to that later, since we're getting ahead of ourselves. Let me just say, for our audience, that you claim to be the King of England in an alternate universe. Do I have that right?"

David canted his head. "It isn't something I claim to be. I *am* the King of England in an alternate universe." Amelia had been firm on this point, and David had been happy not to concede it.

Owain gave him a ghost of a smile, and David had a sinking feeling that, whatever his and Amelia's intent, what he'd just said was going to trip him up later. He could see Amelia standing in the wings, her hands clasped before her lips. Livia was beside her, her arms folded across her chest. As David caught Amelia's eye, she nodded. He hoped she wasn't being encouraging only because at this stage she couldn't be anything else. David had never been interviewed before, except by Rupert Jones, the twenty-firster reporter. Being filmed was something else entirely.

"Why don't we show the clip of your most recent appearance two days ago, and you can tell me what is happening in it."

The lights came down slightly on David and Owain, and the video of his arrival at Beaumaris played. When it ended, the lights came up, and Owain looked intently at him. "You seem to appear out of nowhere."

"Yes."

Owain waited a beat, but David decided then and there that he wasn't going to be more helpful. He didn't know why any of this happened to him anymore than anyone else did. He had theories, but that's all they were. And he wasn't going to humiliate himself on worldwide TV by talking about fate or God or destiny.

Instead, he thought of facing down MI-5 interrogators or Gilbert de Clare at Westminster—and tried to look interested but unintimidated. He was beginning to realize that the dangers before him in this interview were far more diverse than he'd naively thought, despite the warnings of Amelia and Livia. He'd been dumb. And arrogant.

But he was stuck now, and he had to see this through—despite the fact that Owain's next question was deliberately antagonistic: "I'm sure our viewers are wanting to know if you and this alternate world pose a threat to those of us in this world. How do you respond to that?"

David tried to look sympathetic. "I would hope it doesn't. I have worked with scientists over the years in both the private and public sector in hopes of finding the truth. We have no evidence that it is doing damage."

"But none that it isn't."

David smiled gently. “I have been much more concerned about this world damaging that one.”

“How so?”

“That world is pristine in a way we haven’t seen on this earth since before the industrial revolution.”

“Unpolluted, you mean.”

“Yes, and by our standards, unpopulated.”

“It will become more of both, however, with or without us.”

“We don’t know that,” David said. “It is important to remember that the people there aren’t our ancestors. It’s a different world; they are their own people. They don’t *belong* to us just because they share the names and some of the history of our own ancestors. Their history is not our history, and their future is not our history either.” Without being aware of it, he’d moved from his casual sprawl on the couch to leaning forward, his elbows on his knees, looking intently at Owain.

“Especially now.” Owain gestured to him. “You, an American born at the end of the twentieth century, are the King of England.”

David didn’t react to the certainty in Owain’s voice. He didn’t want to crow. In the space of five minutes, Owain had gone from doubting to belief. “Yes, through circumstances which I still almost can’t believe myself.”

“So what’s that like, being King of England in an alternate universe?”

Before the interview, while she hadn’t hesitated to coach him, Amelia had told him that he would win over his audience when he forgot that he was in an interview and showed his real self. David glanced towards the audience. Every person he saw had a posture indicating they were intent and listening, and he eased back a little, realizing he would do well to engage them too.

"Being king is a huge responsibility. I feel it every day, perhaps more so because I wasn't born to it. Even though my father is the King of Wales, I didn't meet him until I was fourteen. I started out as a typical American kid."

"Hardly typical, according to our sources," Owain put in.

David made a *maybe* motion with his head. "I thought of myself as normal. I spoke a little Welsh, thanks to my mother, but I'd never held a sword before."

They'd strayed away from describing what it was like to be king, which on the whole David thought was good, until Owain said, "You're a soldier too, I understand."

"Yes." If he hadn't been on television, David would have eyed Owain warily.

"Have you killed people?" It seemed Owain had remembered he was supposed to ask hard-hitting questions.

In the wings, Michael started forward, though he got only a step onto the stage before Livia and Amelia together hauled him back. Chad Treadman was there a second later, whispering urgently in his ear.

David canted his head, and he made the pause long enough to let everyone know that he didn't approve of the question. "The answer, of course, is *yes,* though I wonder at your decision to ask me that. The fact that I've fought in battle puts me apart, doesn't it? I'm outside polite company. It's one of the reasons soldiers don't talk about their experiences in war except with each other."

Out of the corner of his eye, he could see Michael subsiding, though his arms were folded hard across his chest, and his chin was up. David met his eye for a heartbeat, and then looked at the audience. A few people had gasped at Owain's question, and David felt all of a sudden that they had moved firmly to his side if they hadn't been there already. Maybe he was wrong about that, but he took a chance and stood in order to walk to the edge of the dais to talk directly to them. He was tired of sitting and looking up at Owain anyway.

"I've been thinking about what I wanted to say to all of you if I got the chance. Now that I have one, I want to thank you for being who you are. I am grateful in ways I never could have imagined or anticipated for being born here and raised on this planet. I know at times it's impossible to see beyond the crime, gossip, political backstabbing, and a level of environmental degradation that may well be terminal, but I want you to know how deeply I treasure your values and ideals. They have the power to transform this world and my new one too.

"Growing up, I never thought very hard about what it meant to be raised by a single mom. She believed herself a capable and worthwhile person, equal to any other person on the planet, and she taught me to see myself that way too. In the universe I live in now, however, ideas we take for granted are centuries away from being understood, much less common. Men and women aren't equal, and science isn't a concept. Before I became king, everybody had to follow one religion, only the rich went to school, and King Edward was hell-bent on conquering most of Europe.

"You see that as your history, and not relevant to today. But you couldn't be more wrong. I could not be the king I am now if not for the boy I was then—the boy this world made." He tipped his head. "You made."

He put his heels together and bowed slightly from the waist. "So thank you for that. Thank you also for caring enough to give some of your valuable time to watching this interview, and finally, thank you—some of you—for believing, or at the very least *wanting* to believe."

Finally, David gestured towards the wings, where William now appeared on cue. He was looking dapper in a suit and tie, with a black sling holding his right arm to his chest. As it turned out, all this time he'd been a left-handed man forced to use his right, so he was actually doing pretty well with his right arm in a sling. Whether he could use a sword remained to be seen.

At the moment, all he needed to do was walk across the stage, which he did with aplomb, raising a hand to the audience and smiling as David introduced him by his full name. Having practiced with Chad's staff how to shake with a firm grip, William shook hands with Owain and then with David, though with him it was the medieval way, gripping each other's forearms and grinning.

William had wanted to come on stage. Though he thought it absurd, he understood at least in some small way that who David was in Earth Two was a far cry from who he was in Avalon. For David's part, he was more glad than ever that of all his medieval companions, it had been William who'd stepped in front of him and taken that bolt.

Both with Owain and without him, David and William posed before the audience, still shaking hands, allowing people to take picture after picture. It went on too long, but nobody appeared tired of either the pictures or the applause. David's eyes strayed towards the wings, hoping for a clue from anyone there how to end it. But while Livia and Amelia were smiling and applauding, Chad was focused on the rafters, making David glance upwards too. He didn't see anything untoward until he looked back at Chad, who'd made a slight gesture with his hand, not at David, but at someone behind the light array David couldn't see.

An instant later, a gunman opened fire with an automatic weapon, the bullets chewing up the area in front of the stage and the steps up to it. Fortunately, David was already gripping William's forearm when he felt the tug of his departure.

One, two, three ...

34

3 April 1294

David

For once, David was glad of the blackness because it gave him a moment to think. At first he hadn't known what was happening because the echo of the guns in the warehouse was so overwhelming that it drowned out every other sense. In retrospect, he thought there may have been two gunmen, one who aimed his weapon at the ground and steps in front of the stage rather than actually at David. The shot to the chest, however, had been shocking in its power, even though the bullet had hit the ceramic plate over his heart. David thought he might have heard a second shot, but he'd traveled before it hit him.

They arrived three heartbeats later in Earth Two. As before, they both staggered, but this time, David couldn't maintain his balance, and he cursed as he fell sideways onto his right hip. He'd have a bruise there tomorrow to go with the one on his chest. Kevlar spread out the energy of the bullet, but that energy still had to go somewhere, and that meant his chest had taken quite a punch. It hadn't been punched through, though, which would have left him dead. He was alive, and so was William, and that was all that mattered for now.

After a moment, during which they both fought to breathe, William rolled over until he was lying flat on his back on the stones of the battlement next to David. Stars shone above them, though the giant tower to David's left blocked some of the view.

"Mary, Mother of God, that hurts."

In an instant, David was up on one knee, hovering over his friend. He checked the wrappings on William's wound. "It isn't bleeding, or at least not much."

"Small blessings, I guess. Help me to sit up." This was a new William, one actually willing to ask for help.

David got him to a sitting position and crouched before him. "Are you really okay?"

"I think so. Are we home?"

"You tell me. What do you hear?"

They both went silent as they listened to the world around them.

After a moment, William said, "Water running. I think there's a river somewhere below us. I hear men's voices in the distance." He paused. "Birds." Then he focused on David. "No motors."

"No motors. Twenty-first century noises encroach on even the remotest places. But not here." David came up from his crouch. They were on a wall-walk behind a tower. A doorway off the curtain wall lay ten feet away. The wall-walk continued to the right and left, curving around the back of the tower, which currently hid them from the view of anyone in the castle's bailey. "My best guess is we are somewhere in England." He glanced down at William. "Sorry about that. I really meant to give you a choice."

"There was never any choice. I wouldn't have stayed. In the end, my obligations aren't dissimilar to yours, and I love my family and my people."

"It wouldn't have had to be forever."

William grunted. "I learned what I needed to from Alex. Thank you for allowing me to see what could have been possible—what *was* possible, back in Avalon. You were right to think that I would choose to make my own history, as you have done."

David gripped his friend's hand and helped him to his feet. "It was a risk telling you the truth, but even if you'd chosen differently, I wouldn't have been sorry."

"Water under the bridge." William guffawed as he peered through a nearby crenel at the river below them. "And I mean that literally as I was right about the river. We appear to be on an outer curtain wall."

David looked too. He and William could jump from here, but he'd rather not risk ending up right back in Avalon. They were both hampered physically at the moment as well, and a plunge into cold water wouldn't be good for either of them.

"Is it too much to ask for this to be a friendly castle?" William asked

"Probably. I'm glad now we went to Avalon without our swords and armor, because we would have left them there." David grunted. "At least I brought you back. That will make your father happy."

"At least it's night. The dark can hide us."

"Only up to a point. We need new clothes ASAP."

The view otherwise wasn't informative, and with no moon, David couldn't make out much beyond the lights that lit the sides of the castle. "Between the two of us, we've been to virtually every castle in England, Wales, and the March. This is none of them."

"We were being shot at with guns, weren't we?"

"Yes." Unsurprised by the change of subject, David put a fist to his chest and coughed. He was having a little trouble breathing, but he figured if he had a broken rib and a punctured lung, he would be in more pain than he was currently feeling. The who and why of it, and Chad Treadman's possibly troubling role in what had just happened, was a problem for another day. "Can you walk?"

"Of course." William grasped David's shoulder with his good left hand to steady himself. "Life is always an adventure with you, sire."

David coughed again, trying to laugh. "We'll see how happy you are about that in a minute." They moved along the wall-walk far enough to peer around the curve of the tower, and then kept going into the darkness, leaving the castle's large keep behind. The curtain wall enclosed an area a hundred yards across.

"It feels like late evening." William said with a glance at the sliver of moon that had just come out from behind a cloud.

For his part, David's attention had been drawn to the lands beyond the walls, which were dotted by hundreds of lights. Thousands.

William gave an unhappy sigh. "That looks like an army."

"To me too, and by the banners, I'm guessing it doesn't belong to me."

"Could we be in France?" William sounded almost hopeful.

"I don't relish another ride for my life across Aquitaine and Normandy." David pulled back as a man opened the door at the base of one of the towers in the curtain wall and headed across the bailey towards the massive outer gatehouse.

With the man out of sight, they hastened again along the wall-walk, pleased but anxious that they had so far encountered no other guards.

"We could go to the hall and announce you. You are the king."

"That would be a bad idea if this castle belongs to someone who's allied with Roger Mortimer," David said.

William's expression turned pensive. "How many more traitors can there be?"

"Obviously, I'm the last person to ask. All I can say is that, since we didn't appear at Dinas Bran, I have to assume that I've—we've—arrived where we were meant to arrive and that me being here is better than me not being here." He frowned. "Let's see if we can find different clothing and work up from there."

They approached the nearest tower door, halfway between the gatehouse and the keep. Before David could think too hard about it, he simply reached for the latch and pulled the door open. They found themselves in a guard room, exactly like a hundred or even a thousand such rooms he'd entered in the last twelve years. Nobody was present, and he told himself again that he'd arrived here for a reason and to accept the gift.

"Look in there." David gestured to two trunks set against a nearby wall.

While this wasn't an armory, most guard rooms stored extra weapons and clothing as a matter of course. Three cloaks hung on hooks near the exit door, and he grabbed two.

Meanwhile, William flipped open the lids and gave a satisfied grunt. "Bingo."

It was the perfect use of the idiom, and David laughed before moving to his side. "Next time, remind me to limit your television viewing."

"Next time?" William held up a mail shirt to check the size. "Do you think there will be a next time?"

David pulled out two axes, their heads in sheaths, two belts, and two knives. He left a sword where it was, deciding in a moment of clarity that they were better off looking more like common soldiers than commanders. "You never know." He glanced at his former squire. "Would it please you?"

"Ask me again after my wound heals." William handed him the mail and a tunic to go over it. "This should fit you. We can't do anything about the breeches and shoes, but it's dark enough that maybe we can get away with what we have on for now."

"A leather coat will have to do for you." David looked at William assessingly. "But the modern sling has to go. We'll rig something else—" He broke off as Christopher came through the door of the guardroom.

The cousins stared at each other through several laughing gasps, and then Christopher lifted David off his feet in a bear hug. "What are you doing here?"

"Oof! Ow! Let me go." David coughed.

Christopher set him down. "You're injured? We hoped the bolt hadn't touched you."

"It didn't. This is from the way back." David put a hand to his chest and tried to take some easy breaths. "I'll tell you later."

"Where are we?" William took a step forward. "Is my father here?"

"You're at Skipton Castle," Thomas Hartley stepped through the doorway, "and the army in the fields outside is the combined forces of John Balliol and Hakkon of Norway, who has come without his brother's blessing." He paused and then went down on one knee before David. "My king. I can't tell you how happy I am to see you alive."

"Get up. Get up." David motioned with one hand. "I can't tell you how happy I am to see you two. *I think*. Why, and God help me, *how*, are you here?" But then before they could answer, he put up a hand. "Never mind, maybe we don't have time for that right now either. Rather, tell me what you are planning that brings you to this guardroom in this moment?"

Thomas looked sideways at Christopher for a second and then said straightforwardly, "Christopher had a feeling."

David studied his cousin. "About me?"

"No." Christopher gave a little shake of his head. "I just felt that we should come to the tower to see what we could see. The army is moving tomorrow."

Thomas added, "The captains were instructed to make sure their men slept, which is why it's so quiet."

David waggled his hand to encompass both Christopher and Thomas. "How did you two get together?"

"Matha O'Reilly and I met him in the hall yesterday evening," Christopher said.

"And I'm with Henri. He and Matha went to the north side of the castle, by the keep," Thomas said as if it was the most normal thing in the world for all of them to have found each other.

David squeezed Christopher's shoulder, but he was looking at William, who said, "Right place, right time, my lord."

After putting on their medieval gear and fashioning a new sling for William out of a piece of cloth, they took the stairway to the top of the tower, upon which a guard watched. At their arrival, he startled, but Thomas said, "You are relieved for now. We'll watch a while. Get yourself warm."

"Thank you, my lords." He descended the stairs.

"The guards are used to us by now," Thomas said by way of an explanation.

"When did you arrive?" William asked.

"Two days ago, right after Balliol and Hakkon took the castle—without resistance, I might add. Christopher and Matha came yesterday."

David went to a nearby crenel and looked out. This tower stood to the east of the gatehouse, allowing him a clear view of the landscape south of the castle. So many fires and torches lit the night that it was difficult to see into the darkness of the countryside. "What do you know about this Hakkon, Thomas? I've met only Erik."

"He is a few years older than I am. He sneers at everyone."

David coughed. "I could have guessed that. Who else is here?"

"Roger Mortimer."

"Aymer de Valence?"

"No. Or at least I haven't seen him."

"You could say hi to them right now." Christopher handed David his binoculars. "They're all in the keep, planning their war."

"I'm tempted, believe me." David put the binoculars to his eyes. "What's Balliol's plan?"

"To march south," Thomas said.

"To Beeston?" David asked.

Thomas gave a vigorous headshake. "However long it takes for your army to take it, Balliol knows it's lost. But that's good news to him. While your army is busy there, he'll be slipping past to the east." He gestured to David. "He's also still hoping you're dead."

"Wouldn't he have heard by now that I'm not?"

"Who would have told him?" Christopher said.

David's gaze followed the road and then around the curve of what appeared to be a fairly steep hill to the east. He frowned and put out a hand to the others. "There! Do you see movement?" He gave Thomas the binoculars.

"Riders?" Thomas asked tentatively.

"That's what I think," David said.

"There are too many of them to be scouts." Thomas peered into the darkness. "Where are they going?"

"And look!" David pointed again. "Did you see that?"

"I did," Thomas said a little grimly. "That was light reflected off metal—but not among the horsemen. It was farther up the hill."

"Balliol must have binoculars by now," William said reasonably. "It's perfectly possible he realizes the importance of that high ground and has gone to take it."

"He hadn't placed a force there before." Thomas brought down the binoculars. "He doesn't think he needs to. Who would be mad enough to confront five thousand men head on? On top of which, why bother with the hill now when we're moving out in the morning?"

"It could be James Stewart." The binoculars were back in front of Christopher's eyes. "Matha and I came to Beeston with Huw and three other men. I sent two south to Callum and the army, and Huw and the third went north to find James Stewart. He would have known without anyone telling him that attacking this massive army is impossible with the river as the defensive line. But I specifically suggested that Huw tell him about the strategic advantage of that hill. And James would know to go around in order to come at the castle from the south."

"I wish we had a way to find out," William said.

As he stared out into the darkness beyond the fires, David wished with his whole being that his allies were on that hill. And then he reached for the torch that shone from its sconce near the steps that led down to the wall-walk. "If you can bear with me, I have a crazy idea."

35

3 April 1294

Lili

Lili left Morgan's men gathered behind the mountain, along with the archers from Gwynedd who had, in fact, arrived first. Even Humphrey's pride didn't extend so far as to countenance a journey that would end with their horses blown. They would be useless in battle for days if they'd done that. A stream ran behind the hill, and the men and horses were freely watering themselves from it. If the plan was to attack, they had some hours yet to rest.

"Has anyone seen Christopher and Matha?" Lili asked the commanders. They'd gathered in the draw on the hillside to hide their light and numbers.

Most shook their heads and looked troubled, but Huw said, "If I know anything about Christopher at all, my lady, I know he can take care of himself."

Callum stood twenty feet above her with a pair of binoculars, gazing through them towards the castle. He had been uncharacteristically silent throughout the war conference, which, with the arrival of the Scot forces, had commenced in earnest. While he could see the castle from where he stood, she could not.

Now, he put out a hand. "Give me a moment, if you will. I'm trying to count. Ieuan, get up here and tell me if I'm seeing things."

It was an odd request, but Ieuan didn't hesitate, and Lili clambered up the rise as well. At first Lili couldn't figure out what they were looking at, and then she saw the flickering torch. The wind wasn't blowing hard enough to make it go on and off like that, and then she realized what she was seeing was being done on purpose.

"Someone write down what I say," Callum said.

Robbie hastened to find paper and pen, and Callum started reciting, "Dash, dot, dot, dot, pause, dash, dot, dash, dash, dot ..." The dots and dashes went on and on, and though Lili knew their intent, she had never learned Morse Code. When the dashes and dots started repeating themselves, Callum stopped speaking and had Robbie recite exactly what he'd written.

Then Robbie scrambled up the hill to show Callum the paper. But Callum didn't need to read it, since Humphrey de Bohun had worked it out in his head: "B moving tomorrow. Attack tonight. Cavalry. Arrows. Cymerau. Rohan. KDVD." He stared at Lili.

James gave a rueful shake of his head. "Christopher really deserves the title *Hero of Westminster*."

"He does, but the message isn't from Christopher." Callum slid down the slope, hastening towards one of the lanterns that had been kept low to the ground so its light couldn't be seen beyond a short distance. He grabbed it along with a shield and took it with him up the mountain, dragging Robbie Bruce along with him. "Hold it high, son."

Robbie obeyed, and Lili found herself riveted by Callum's next antics, because he held the shield over the light, much in the same way the person on the wall-walk of Skipton must have been doing.

Dot-dot-dot-dash-dot.

Understood. Lili knew that much Morse Code. Callum quickly returned the lantern to the draw, not wanting to give away their position more than he already had. Then he put his finger on the paper at the word *Cymerau.* "What does he mean by that?" He moved his finger to *Rohan.* "Or that?"

Lili could recite that story of Cymerau in her sleep, but so it seemed could Humphrey. "Cymerau was a great victory over English forces by King Llywelyn back when I was a child. He barraged them with arrows and then defeated them on the field of battle afterwards. I don't know the other word."

"Nor I." Lili looked at her brother, who shrugged.

"It's from the Lord of the Rings, Callum. Where have you been?" Mark chuckled and turned to Lili. "The riders of Rohan are responsible for one of the most famous cavalry charges in the history of cavalry charges."

James was still stuck on who was sending them the message. "What do you mean it isn't Christopher on that battlement?"

Lili found her hands trembling slightly. "It means he made it home, doesn't it?"

Callum's face was pale in the lantern light. "I think so. But if we're right, he's fallen right in the middle of it again."

"And is William with him?" Humphrey said.

"What are you talking about? Who sent us that message?" James stepped closer.

"KDVD, James. King Dafydd. It's Dafydd on that battlement." Emotion choked Lili's throat, so her words could come out only as a whisper.

James's head swung towards the castle, though they were back in the draw, and he couldn't see it from here.

Lili put out a hand to him. "Your army started moving as soon as the sun set, yes?"

James nodded. "As Callum encouraged."

"How long until they could reach the Eller Beck?"

"Less than two hours from when they left."

Lili heart beat a little faster. "We must do this the Welsh way, then, as Dafydd just suggested."

James's eyes narrowed. "What exactly do you mean by that, and why am I thinking that it might be synonymous with something dishonorable?"

"Is winning dishonorable? Is saving the lives of thousands of men dishonorable?" Lili asked.

"No," James said shortly.

Lili nodded. "As we already planned, your men can corral Balliol's army from the north and east, while we attack from the south."

Humphrey frowned. "With only five hundred riders, our casualties will be high."

Callum gave a jerk of his head. "Even if we were to wait for the men we have coming in order to better match their five thousand, both sides would lose far too many good men, and there remains the possibility that we could be flanked. I'd rather not leave these things to chance. It is the archers who will make the difference."

Lili nodded. "Our arrows will mow down their army like a scythe through ripe hay."

James gave her a jerky nod too. "Believe me, I know. I saw it at Tara. But they shouldn't do it from any place that can be reached by Balliol's men. Since we don't have enough men here to defend them, we need to get them across the Eller Beck, to my men."

Ieuan put a hand on Lili's shoulder. "You can shoot forever with a river between you and your target."

Lili was pleased that her brother assumed she would be among the archers. She had fought before, and while she didn't like it, she was determined to help.

"My lady, are we absolutely certain that David is in that castle?" Humphrey looked intently at her, and she realized that he knew about her *sight* and wanted her to speak from it. She hadn't felt that spirit move since Dafydd had fallen from the battlement with the King of France, however, so she gave a little shake of her head. "As certain as I can be without asking him, which I dare not do. Even the short response we gave him made this spot on the hill a target for the men in the field."

Ieuan motioned with his hand above his head. “Let’s move, friends.” He took Lili’s arm. “Are you ready for this?”

“You must like asking me that. It’ll be like when we were children.”

“When we hunted Humphrey de Bohun in the woods?” He swallowed down a laugh. “You can think that if it helps.”

She glanced towards the man himself, who walked a few paces ahead on the narrow trail. “Have you ever told him about those days?”

Ieuan shook his head.

She laughed. “I think you should. All of us have come a long way since then.”

36

3 April 1294

David

"It's probably time for us to leave." David put down the binoculars. There had been no further response from the hill, and he hadn't expected any. Bad enough that they'd responded at all, but he was glad they'd done so. The future of England looked a lot rosier than it had fifteen minutes ago.

Christopher stared at David. "We can't! What's the point of you arriving *inside* Skipton Castle if we're just going to flee it an hour later?"

David narrowed his eyes at his cousin. "Are you thinking that maybe we should be opening the front gate to our men, never mind the five thousand men camped between us and them? Or even more dramatically, that I should confront Balliol in his hall?"

From the uncertain look on Christopher's face, David could tell that this was exactly what he'd thought.

He respected his cousin enough—and all of the young men with him—to explain why he couldn't do either. "Balliol wants me dead. That's all that matters to him. If I appear in his hall with the three of you, he's going to cut me down where I stand, and all of this will have been for nothing. Imagine what would have happened if I hadn't escaped from Trim Castle when I did. We would have lost everything."

"Maybe we would have at Trim," Christopher stepped closer, "but Skipton is different. You're not in Ireland anymore, and as it turns out, the only reason most of Balliol's men support him is because they believe you are dead. If you were to appear in their midst, how many of them would be willing to murder their king in cold blood?"

"All it takes is one, Christopher," William said.

"Okay, I'll give you that, but you will have more than just us behind you," Christopher said. "You'll have the garrison of Skipton, for starters."

David frowned. "What do you mean?"

"We've had a whole day to explore, and Thomas and Henri a day more than that. The members of the garrison that resisted—about twenty of them—are being held beneath our feet, in fairly awful conditions, I might add."

Thomas nodded. "The rest of the garrison chose expediency over loyalty, but it's likely they would also be glad to see you. And that's only to start."

"The town is with you too, including the mayor in whose house we're staying. But even more important than that, if there's a battle, the townspeople are completely unprotected." Christopher's voice went up an octave and a few decibels in his urgency.

Open battle was one thing, civilian casualties were quite another. David folded his arms across his chest as he studied his companions. "To stay would be insane. The expedient thing to do would be to get out now, while we can, and find our army." He sighed. "But you are right that I can't leave the people to die, and Balliol is unlikely to lift a finger to help them."

"I knew you'd say that once you understood," Christopher said.

David scoffed. "Where's my elder statesman to tell me not to listen to you three?"

Christopher pointed. "He's out there, obviously, starting a war. It has to be Callum who responded, because who else understands Morse Code?"

"My father, for one," William said.

David turned to look into the distance, making up his mind, because really there wasn't anything to decide. Things got easy really quickly when he put the people he served first. "All right. You guys know the terrain. What needs to happen next?"

"We need to find the mayor and tell him to get his people inside the castle," Christopher said.

"And we need to free the garrison and retake the castle," Thomas said. "We'll need the king for that."

Christopher frowned. "The townspeople need to see David to believe he's alive. He has to come with me."

Thomas shook his head vigorously. "We can't risk him being shut out of the castle. Besides, few here know what he looks like, especially dressed as a common soldier. You and Matha know the people. You can do this."

David watched the exchange with interest. They'd grown up while he hadn't been looking.

Then Matha appeared at the top of the stairs, and as David turned to look at him, he almost fell back down them. "Sire!" He went down on one knee. "Henri and I saw lights on this tower, and he sent me to investigate."

"He's gone back into the keep?" David asked sharply, right before dragging Matha to his feet and hugging him.

"Yes." The word came out strangled.

David had been squeezing him hard, and he stepped back and put a hand to his own chest, realizing that he'd been distracted from his pain. "I wish he hadn't done that." He looked at Thomas. "While Matha and Christopher roust the townspeople and William and I free the garrison and take the outer gatehouse, you need to get Henri out of there. He cannot be in that hall when the fighting starts."

William frowned. "He could be our spy if he stays."

David's jaw was set. "I will bring the keep down on their heads before I negotiate with Balliol. This has gone too far and cost too much." He pressed his lips together for a moment. "We need to evacuate the servants too."

"Leave that to me." Thomas sketched a bow. "It is good to see you, sire." Then he left without explaining what he was going to do, which, on the whole, David decided he didn't need him to. These boys had become grown men, and he could leave them to it.

Christopher and Matha set off at a quick walk for the town, Christopher regaling Matha as they left the events of the last hour, and David and William moved determinedly across the outer bailey to the dungeon tower. Nobody questioned them, and David hadn't expected anyone to. The main gate was open, allowing free passage in and out of the castle. There were too many men from too many different lordships to account for everyone. Their heads were already at tomorrow's march and not thinking about infiltration by a few men. As William had said back in Avalon, *turnabout's fair play.*

Once at the tower entrance, David turned to William. "Let me handle this. I believe you can fight left-handed, but we haven't tried it yet, so let's take it slow."

"What's the plan?" William said.

"Disarm, recruit, kill only if I have to. These are my subjects, even if they are on the wrong side in this war. That's why I asked Thomas to get the servants out. None of this is their doing." David took in a breath to settle himself. This exact moment was the reason he trained harder now that he was king than he ever had when he was younger.

Lili had commented that he had filled out in the last few years. He guessed some of that filler might be fat, but at twenty-five, he could run farther, hit harder, and move more agilely than at any other time in his life—even with a bruised chest.

He went through the door with his axe in his right hand and his knife in his left. When the door banged back against the inner wall, William, who was right behind him, caught it with the flat of his hand to stop it from rebounding. By then, David was already three feet into the room, and neither guard had time to pull his knife from its sheath. Both men appeared to be in their early thirties, and they wore the colors of John Hastings, whose wife was a Valence. No surprise he was here.

William closed the door, and the four of them looked at each other for a few heartbeats, David assessing and the guards gaping at him, their hands on the hilts of their swords but not pulling them out.

David decided to go straight to the point. "Your choice is simple. Put up your hands and live. Fight me and die."

"There are two of us and only one of you." The nearest guard, who was wearing leather armor, sneered in the direction of William's sling, which was more noticeable now that it was white instead of black.

David's gestured with his axe. The weapon was unfamiliar, but it was weighted well, and he resisted the arrogant temptation to flip it in the air like he might have done a tennis racket or a baseball bat. "I defeated King Edward in single combat when I was only sixteen. Are you sure you want to take me on?"

The guard's sneer didn't leave his face, but he appeared to hesitate for a moment, processing what David had just said. Then both guards moved at the same time.

But David had moved a half-second before them, slashing the axe downwards from right to left across the chest of the guard on the right. David's arm kept moving to the left, and his next blow slashed horizontal, digging into the second soldier's thighs. He'd been taught long ago that the best way to defeat an enemy was to aim for his limbs. Once he was on the ground, he was vulnerable to be finished off.

In this case, the first man fell to his knees, and William, who'd followed closely behind David as if they'd rehearsed this, kicked out with a booted foot to put him down beside his friend, who was moaning in pain on the floor. Neither was actively dying, but they were disabled. William took the key to the dungeon from the wall.

David held out a hand for it while looking down at the wounded men. "How many guards patrol this tower?"

The guard with the thigh wounds pressed his lips together, refusing to answer, but the other replied immediately. "There are two more on the wall-walk. We are due for a shift change in an hour."

David nodded at William. "Kill them if they so much as move." Grabbing a torch from a sconce, he went down the stairs himself, alone. The steps ended at a wrought iron gate, through which two dozen faces looked back at him with wide eyes. They were crammed into a space that should have been for storage only, with no ventilation or natural light, not that there would have been any at this hour of the night.

He held up the key. "My understanding is that you are here because you didn't support Balliol's takeover of the castle. Am I wrong?"

"You are correct, my lord," one of the men in the very front said. He had a full beard, and his hair was unkempt.

"Tell me your name."

The man cleared his throat. "Bernard, my lord."

"Where's your captain?"

"Here, sir." A young boy's voice piped up from near the back, and the men in front shifted so David could see to whom he was referring. "He's wounded in the leg."

David lifted his torch higher in order to see the man lying flat on the stones of the dungeon. He had a bloody bandage tied around his leg just above the knee. The man lifted his head to look at David. "Gilbert de Stanford, at your service. May I ask your name?"

David grinned. "You may ask." He thrust the key into the lock and opened the door. "Everybody out. I am reenlisting you into the service of King David."

The men accepted his offer with alacrity, filing upstairs, and even after their incarceration, many managed to take the steps two at a time. The last two made a chair with clasped fingers for their captain. The stairs were very narrow, but they managed to shuffle sideways to the top. David followed last, and by the time he arrived in the guardroom, it was clear that William had filled the garrison members in on who he was, because as he turned into the room, all but the captain, who couldn't, went down on one knee.

He was glad to see that the time had been put to good use as well, in that they had passed around a jug of beer and finished off the loaf of bread on the table. Nobody looked more worse for wear than their captain.

David gave the key to Bernard, gesturing at the same time to the wounded guards. "Stick these two in the cell." Then, as the men were dragged down the stairs none too gently, David looked at the rest. "You know this castle. We are currently outnumbered, but with twenty of you, if we plan correctly, we can take it from the inside."

"And then what?" A man with a gray beard raised a hand. "There's an army between us and freedom."

William smirked. "Two armies, and the second belongs to us."

David nodded. "The Stewarts have marched from Scotland with two thousand men, and I have five thousand more on the hill to the south. If we take the castle, we can leave the soldiers in the field to them." He didn't actually know those numbers, but he wanted to hearten them. Callum *was* here, he would swear to it, and if the whole army hadn't made it yet, they were coming.

Some of the tension in the men's faces eased at David's confidence. There were even a few grins.

"Our armor and weapons should be on the floor above us," a lanky man said, pointing with one finger towards the ceiling.

That was a bit of luck David hadn't expected. But then, he'd armed himself from a storage room in a similar location in the tower on the other side of the castle. "Go, all of you."

While they went up one more floor, David moved to crouch beside the captain, who turned his head to meet his gaze. "Can I trust all of them?"

"To a man," Gilbert said. "We are English, not Scot."

"What about the rest of the garrison, the men who turned traitor?"

Gilbert's lips twisted. "Most had families to support or decided when they saw what happened to those who resisted that their loyalties were flexible. Most, if not all, will gladly fight for you."

"Can we take the castle?"

"How many men are you willing to kill to do it?"

David didn't hesitate. "Everyone who gets in my way."

37

4 April 1294

Christopher

Once through the castle gate, Christopher and Matha pulled up. The street before them was deserted. Where last night at this hour, shops had been packed with people, now they were closed up tight. The only men in sight moved purposefully in and out of the barrier that demarcated the town or passed through it heading straight to the entrance to the castle.

"This way." Matha tugged on his arm, and they loped down the side street to the mayor's house.

But when they arrived at their lodgings, they found the house closed up as tightly as the rest of the street. Christopher had to pound on the door to be admitted by Gunnar. He was fully clothed, so hadn't gone to bed, and he held a knife in his hand, which he hastily put on the table when he realized who was at the door.

Christopher got straight to the point. "We lied to you earlier about our identities. I am Christopher—"

"—the Hero of Westminster," Matha said.

Christopher overrode him, "—the king's cousin. Allies are freeing the imprisoned garrison as we speak. King David's forces are even now prepared to attack the army in the field. Balliol has given you no thought because you are not his people, but the citizens of Skipton need to get inside the castle if they're going to survive this battle."

For two seconds, Gunnar gaped at him, and then his mouth snapped shut. It was Inge who spoke first, however, coming out of the back room with a blanket wrapped around her shoulders. "What do you want us to do?"

"Awaken the town," Christopher said, "but quietly! We don't want to call attention to what we're doing until it is too late to stop us. Everyone needs to come to the castle. At most, bring food to tide you over until the battle ends. Leave the rest of your possessions behind. The king's army is not here to plunder. The main gate is open now, and we'll make sure it stays open until everyone is inside. We also need every person prepared to fight, with whatever weapon they have to hand."

"We will do it." Inge reached for her husband, who put his arm around her shoulders.

"My nephew—Alvin—who sent you. He-he is on duty at the entrance to the town right now." Gunnar was so anxious he was stuttering. "He will help."

"Thank you." Christopher turned to go.

But Inge put out a hand to stop him. "The king. He really is alive?"

Christopher smiled. "He is not only alive, but he's here. I spoke to him just now."

Inge's eyes widened, and he sensed she remained disbelieving, interpreting Christopher's reassurance as a boast, but she didn't argue further. A few moments later, Christopher and Matha were hurrying down the street at a fast walk. It had to be past midnight by now. The deserted streets and the lack of movement in the field before them were testimony to how strictly Balliol's orders to sleep were being obeyed.

They stopped in front of Alvin, who looking at them questioningly. "My lords?"

"I don't know how to say this, so I'm just going to say it straight out. King David is here, along with his army. They are just out of sight beyond that hill." Christopher didn't point in case anyone was watching. "He has commanded us to take the castle. Your aunt and uncle said you were loyal to the king. Are you?"

Alvin's eyes were as wide as saucers. "The-the-the king is here?" He looked south as if David might materialize out of the darkness.

Christopher was impatient with his question. "Yes, but he isn't leading the army. He has personally infiltrated the castle and is taking it back. Your aunt and uncle are waking the townspeople to get them safely inside the castle, since once the king's army attacks, nobody will be safe out here."

Alvin licked his lips.

Matha nodded. "You rightly guess that if you don't help us, you know too much, so if you decide to continue as a traitor, we will kill you."

Alvin put up both hands. "No, no! You don't have to threaten me. I was on your side from the start."

He swung around to look at his partner, who was just returning from relieving himself in the ditch and had missed all but the tail end of their conversation.

Matha stepped towards him with unmistakable menace, his hand on the hilt of his sword. "Decide your loyalties right now."

The man put up his hands. "I'm with you! I'm with you!" Then his attention was caught by movement in the street behind Christopher and Matha.

Christopher glanced back and saw Inge, who seemed the more partisan between her and her husband, knocking repeatedly on the door of a house three down from the barricade.

"What's the plan?" Alvin said.

"How many soldiers are on patrol in the town?" Christopher said by way of an answer.

"Just us tonight." Alvin gestured to the yards and yards of campfires in the fields south of the town. "A larger patrol seemed unnecessary."

"Except for the man on the drawbridge, of course," his companion said.

The drawbridge. Christopher looked towards the river. He could see the drawbridge workings poking up above the level of the houses' roofs. It was still up, as it would be. Balliol meant to leave it up as a defense against Stewart's men, but David had other plans, which meant *they* needed to control it.

Alvin said in a low voice, "We rotate duty, so I could offer to relieve him. Too long at one post makes a man bored and complacent."

By now, Inge had encouraged many townspeople to move towards the castle. For forty or more people, they made very little noise. There wouldn't be so many of them in total anyway, maybe three hundred people. It shouldn't take long to get them safe.

Christopher looked between the field and the castle. "Matha should stay here. Nobody has noticed us yet, but they will if two men aren't manning this post."

Matha's eyes narrowed, but he nodded. "The moment arrows start flying, I'm coming after you."

"Feel free!" Christopher set off down the street that led to the bridge, which lay one street closer to the castle than Gunnar and Inge's house. He'd noted the drawbridge earlier, of course, but it hadn't played into his initial plans, in large part because he'd been so focused on not getting caught that he hadn't had room to think about anything else. David might not realize its importance or even that it was there.

They reached it to find two men rather than only the one standing sentry in front of it. Alvin walked straight up to them. "We will keep watch a while."

The two men didn't argue, nor question the presence of a squire not in the garrison on lowly guard duty. On his way past, one of them said to Alvin, "Only one more night, and we'll be rid of them."

"Do you mean that?" Alvin reached for the man's arm to stop him walking away.

The man paused, his eyes on his partner, who continued towards the castle. He was in for a surprise when he reached it. "You know I do."

"Then stay with us." Alvin glanced at Christopher, who nodded.

While Alvin related what they were doing at the drawbridge, Christopher turned in a circle to survey the ground they had to protect. The three of them couldn't possibly survive a concerted assault. They had a guard station the size of a phone booth to stand under when it rained. Otherwise, the space was entirely open.

Then Matha appeared in the road. He put up a hand but then disappeared down the street to their lodgings. Two minutes later, he returned with the bow and quiver they'd seen on the wall in the mayor's house.

Christopher eyed the weapon. "You don't stand out at all with that."

Matha ignored the gibe, pointing instead across the river. "Look."

With his night vision ruined by the light from the torches in the town, it was hard at first to tell what had caught Matha's attention, but then Christopher saw movement on the other side of the river. In the murky darkness, what appeared to be a colony of very large ants, so many it wasn't possible to count them, had invaded the northern bank of the Eller Beck.

"The Stewarts," Matha said for Alvin's benefit.

Alvin swung around to look at Christopher. "You told the truth!"

"Why did you follow me if you doubted?" Christopher said.

"You are the Hero of Westminster and the king's cousin. How could I not follow you?"

Christopher glared at Matha, who shrugged, "I didn't tell him. I have no idea how he knows."

"My uncle recognized you when you first arrived," Alvin said. "He's been to Westminster as a member of Parliament. He was afraid you'd betrayed the king."

A group of townspeople, possibly the last to get moving, appeared in the road, making their way up to the castle gate. But then one of them broke away from the main group and ran towards the drawbridge. "You can't stay here! You must come with us into the castle!"

Christopher waved him off. "We can't. We have to defend the drawbridge until the Stewarts are ready for us to drop it."

The man hesitated, but then he turned back to his fellows, motioning as he did so for others to come with him. Five men and a woman, ranging in age from twenty to fifty, each armed with a staff or pitchfork, responded to his summons.

"You don't have to do this," Christopher said when they reached him.

"When the Scots came we hid in our homes," the man said. "We are not soldiers, but still, it was cowardly. We didn't even send a man to warn the king of what had happened to his castle."

The woman next to him nodded. "If the Hero of Westminster, a man who owes us nothing, is willing to defend our town, then the least we can do is stand with him."

38

4 April 1294

Thomas

Thomas strode through the main entrance to the keep as if he owned the place. He'd noted over the course of the day how Christopher and Matha also were able to affect an air of confidence that he was fairly sure they didn't feel any more than he did. He was doing what had to be done, however, so he maintained an air of superiority and arrogance that was expected of a young nobleman such as he.

Very few people were awake. The call to march in the morning meant that everyone who wasn't anyone was abed. Several of the great lords, however, continued to drink and talk, and it was with real trepidation that Thomas crossed the keep's small enclosed courtyard and mounted the stairs to the great hall. At the far end sat a half-dozen lords, and Balliol and Hakkon were involved in a discussion that had turned heated.

"You told me David would be dead!" Hakkon slammed his fist onto the table. "You promised it!"

Thomas hesitated on the threshold, scanning the hall for servants. Tonight, there were no female servants at Skipton at all, barring two middle-aged women in the kitchen. All sensible fathers and husbands had fled the castle with their daughters and wives the moment the army arrived. A single manservant remained, wiping down the tables nearby, and Thomas sidled closer. "You must gather any other of your fellow workers who are still in the keep and leave it. Immediately."

The man gave him a startled look, but then he pulled on his forelock. "There's only me, Nob, and Charlie left, my lord. It's an early day tomorrow."

"Good. Go to the main gate. All will be explained once you reach it."

The man bobbed with his whole body, but unfortunately, their conversation had been noted at the high table.

"You there! Thomas, is it? What do you want?" It was the castellan of Skipton, the one who'd let Balliol take the castle, a man named Hugo Renard.

Thomas dismissed the servant with a wave of his hand, hoping he had said all he needed to, and strode up the hall towards the high table. "I was merely asking for some wine, my lord." He paused to look around the room. "I was also looking for Sir Henri."

Renard left his position at the table and came towards Thomas. "He excused himself a moment ago." He looked Thomas up and down. "I swear again that you look familiar to me."

"Leave the boy alone, Renard." The King of Scots himself leaned to one side to see past the bulk of his castellan and gestured towards Thomas. "Get *me* some wine while you're at it." He was in his middle forties, with a full brown beard and brown eyes. Without a crown on his head, he looked no more royal than the other men at his table, and Thomas wouldn't have marked him either as the King of Scots or the author of such an intricate plot against England.

"Yes, my lord. Immediately." Thomas was off like a shot to the kitchen door, located near the main entrance to the hall. The kitchen had its own access to the inner courtyard, so he could leave the keep without Balliol knowing it.

Before he could reach the doorway, however, Henri appeared through the hall's main entrance. Thomas dragged him out the door again and down the stairs before anyone at the high table could notice anything amiss. "Where have you been?"

"Taking some air." Henri frowned. "What are you doing?"

"Getting you out of here. King David has come." Thomas whispered the last words.

"What did you say?" Unfortunately, Hugo Renard had followed him out of the hall and now gaped at them from the top step.

Thomas motioned with a hand that Renard should come to him. "Hurry."

Obeying because he was curious, Renard trotted down the steps to stop in front of Thomas and Henri. "Did you say—"

Thomas cut him off. "Why did you have to follow me?" As he spoke, he grabbed the collar of the Renard's tunic and, in the same breath, drove his belt knife into Renard's chest.

Henri gasped his surprise but, despite his shock, grasped Renard's upper arm to keep him from falling to the floor. "I hate to ask what you're doing."

"I have followed you for months," Thomas said. "I hope you can follow me in this."

"I'm here, aren't I?"

Together, Thomas and Henri dragged the body towards the wine cellar and dumped it behind a barrel, grateful yet again that Balliol had ordered most everyone to quarters.

They returned to the central courtyard, and neither broke stride as they passed through it and out the inner gatehouse.

Henri continued to keep pace across the outer ward. "Tell me what is happening."

"We are retaking the castle." King David stepped out from the shadows of the curtain wall. "The phrase *Join us or die* does have a habit of focusing the mind."

Henri sucked in a breath before bowing before David. "Sire."

The king stepped closer and embraced him. "I am really glad to see you."

"Not, perhaps, as happy as I am to see you." Henri lifted his chin to point to the gate. Upwards of ten men were moving in and around it. Beyond, townspeople hastened through the barbican. "Balliol and Hakkon remain in the keep."

"And Roger Mortimer?" David said.

Henri frowned. "I haven't seen him in at least an hour."

David grimaced and related the state of their insurrection.

"We'll get him, my lord," Thomas said bracingly.

"We will if I have to hunt him to the ends of the earth," the king said.

In addition to the main gate, King David had already conquered the keep's gatehouse and its tower entrances on the wall-walks, and now shouts came from the barracks, implying that it soon would be in his hands too.

Thomas glanced up to see a guard on the top of one of the keep's towers peering down at them through a crenel. "He's really beginning to wonder what's happening," he said in an undertone, "but he's afraid to leave his post."

David grunted. "Everyone was thinking of the march tomorrow, not of the danger tonight."

"Your arrival from Avalon was hardly predictable, sire," William pointed out.

"Wasn't it?" David said musingly. "Balliol has been listening to the wrong people."

"They'll have crossbows inside the keep," Henri said. "We could be pinned down any moment."

David turned on his heel as people from the town started moving into the outer bailey of the castle. "That is not going to happen."

One of the younger members of the garrison ran towards them. "The barracks are ours!" He was breathless with excitement, in part because he'd probably never been in any kind of fight before.

"What's the toll?" David asked.

"We lost one and killed two who resisted."

David nodded. "And our gains?"

"Fifteen more."

"Better," David said.

"The castellan is dead," Henri said softly.

Thomas swallowed as he looked at the king, but David merely nodded. "I'm sure you did what you had to."

Another member of the garrison huffed up. "My lord."

"Bernard," David said.

"What of the keep, sire?"

"While the gatehouse is ours, I'm none too keen on trying to take it room by room just yet." As Thomas had just done, King David glanced up at the guard on top of the tower. "We will make them sweat a little while longer."

Thomas hadn't ever heard that phrase before, but he understood immediately what it meant.

Their small group was drawing attention from the increasing number of people in the bailey, but few approached closer than thirty feet. Thomas attributed that fact to the growing understanding of David's identity. To see the king in person, to have him standing in the middle of the castle right in front of you, was not something to be taken lightly.

A burly man with a tall pike in one hand called down to the king from the top of the outer gatehouse tower, "My king, the Stewarts have come!"

"It's about time." David moved towards the steps up to the wall-walk, and Thomas was grateful to be able to climb them in his wake, rather than have to stay on the ground with the rest of the garrison and townsfolk.

From the battlement, they gazed out at a changed landscape. Torches blazing, because it appeared they wanted Balliol's army to know they had arrived, Stewart's soldiers had filled in the ground on the other side of the river to the north and east of the castle.

Then, between one heartbeat and the next, the field before them erupted into chaos. At first Thomas couldn't make sense of what was happening because the Stewarts themselves hadn't moved. Heart racing, he trained the binoculars Christopher had left with the king on the field before him, so he saw the moment the first fire arrow was launched into the air, coming from the west. Archers had positioned themselves on the other side of the river, but behind the initial lines of Stewart's troops.

"They really did make it." From beside Thomas, William grunted with satisfaction.

"Arrows aren't actually going to win us the war," David said. "We need more men."

Though he would never contradict his king, Thomas didn't know that he was right. He watched, riveted, as volley after volley ripped through the ranks of the army before him. The first thousand arrows came within a single minute, hardly time for those asleep to wake and those awake to react. And with that barrage, all that could be done was cower behind a shield or retreat inside the castle. The latter thought occurred belatedly to the troops, and almost as one, they surged down the main village street.

David had ordered the castle gate closed, however, and while men could cower in the now-empty houses, the castle was no longer a place to which they could retreat. Nor could lowering the drawbridge and escaping across the river be an option, not with Stewart's men waiting for them on the other side. Meeting them was the last thing they wanted.

Thomas turned back to the bailey to find that all of the wall-walks and the tops of the towers were lined with people.

The barrage of arrows continued, and it was clear to Thomas that the archers were keeping themselves to a specific rhythm. He guessed they were short on arrows, and if he was right that these were David's personal archers, each man carried twenty-four in his quiver. At six arrows a minute, an accomplished Welsh archer could shoot that many in five minutes. That wasn't the approach it appeared they were looking for tonight, wanting to instill fear as well as death. Maybe the archers were even aiming.

Regardless of their intent, after only two rounds of fire arrows, every tent in the field was on fire. The only saving grace for Balliol's and Hakkon's men was that it had rained yesterday so the grass was wet.

"They're sitting ducks out there," William said. "I almost feel sorry for them."

"I do feel sorry for them," David said.

"Is that why you insisted that the defenders at Beeston be given a chance to surrender?" William asked.

"Were they?" David looked at his former squire. "Given a chance, I mean?"

"Callum said they would be. They were intending to follow your plan."

David shook his head like he was dismissing a fly. "I wasn't there, so Callum would have done what he must. As he should."

"How about these men?" Thomas said. "Should they be given a chance to surrender?"

"Perhaps they should," Henri said, "but there can be no mercy for Balliol."

David turned to look at him, seemingly about to speak—but an odd crackle resounded in the air, followed by a hum, and then David's own voice rang out across the field. "My friends! You may have been told I was dead, but I stand before you now, alive and well. Lay down your weapons and surrender, and we can end this war tonight!" The voice projected louder than it had any right to do, and it was obviously not the voice of David himself, since he was standing at Thomas's side.

"How-how is it possible that you are speaking from over there when you are here?" Thomas said.

"I recorded those words a week ago to broadcast over Beeston. Mark wanted the recording so the enemy couldn't use my voice to zero in on my location." David let out a laugh. "I guess it came in handy after all."

Thomas wasn't laughing. Nor were the men on the field, though nobody seemed to be putting down their arms or up their hands to surrender. Maybe it was because these men were Scots or Norwegian, and David had spoken in English.

David cursed. "Surrender, you fools!"

"It's always the common man who pays for his lord's hubris," Henri intoned.

"They're about to pay even more." William pointed directly south.

It could have been thunder they were hearing, but Thomas knew enough of battle to understand that he was hearing cavalry. And they were riding hard. Then a roar came from the east, and another from the men across the river.

"What's happening?" David leaned through a crenel. "I wish I could see!"

"It's the Stewarts!" Somebody, Thomas didn't know who, was shouting and gesticulating on the western wall-walk. They couldn't see all sides of the castle from their position on the gatehouse tower, but a few moments later, they couldn't miss the men pouring past the castle into the town, coming from the river. Ten heartbeats later, the Stewarts were paces away from the barricade and meeting their first resistance, fighting hand-to-hand in the streets of Skipton.

"The drawbridge must have been lowered, but who—" Thomas's voice broke off.

"Christopher." David's face paled too. "He and Matha never returned to the castle?"

"No, my lord."

David pressed his lips together in a tight line, knowing as everyone did that nothing could be done about Christopher's welfare now. James Stewart's men wouldn't have harmed them if they knew who they were, but there was no denying that they were out there in the middle of it.

Face ashen but posture resolute, King David watched the unfolding of the victory, and Thomas stood beside him on the battlement until the glorious and bitter end.

39

4 April 1294

Lili

When the Normans first came to Britain, they viewed the arrow as a coward's weapon. No man of honor would use them, which is why they were left to the peasantry and common soldiers. Even so, William the Bastard hadn't been a fool, and he did have archers in his army that day at Hastings when he began his conquest of the Saxons.

Tonight, Lili herself had been charged with shooting fire arrows, aiming specifically for anything that could burn. That amounted primarily to tents, which was good policy anyway since these were the purview of commanders.

Her army of archers shot for three hours and used all but the last handful of missiles. It wasn't quite the story of Cymerau, but in the process, they laid waste to Balliol's army.

To Callum's frustration, which was evident through the walkie-talkie, Balliol's captains didn't sue for peace. It didn't seem to matter that they were caught between the cavalry to the south and the Stewart army on every other side. They fought on rather than surrender. Though the blood lust of the men around her was up, and they were ready to hunt, she knew that this fact would cause Dafydd dismay too.

It was only when the rising sun showed men covering the hills to the south of Skipton as far as the eye could see that they finally were willing to surrender. The bulk of Dafydd's army, led by Math, had arrived, having marched the forty miles from Bury in a day and a night.

To those who knew him, Dafydd's victory had been as inevitable as the rising of the sun. As it should have seemed from the start to these rebellious barons.

When the castle gates finally opened and Dafydd himself rode out, Lili was well in the back of the crowd of onlookers. She'd crossed the drawbridge in the wake of Stewart's pikemen and been hugged by Christopher, who was bleeding from a wound in his upper arm. He, along with Matha and a dozen townspeople, had defended the drawbridge until the time came to drop it so Stewart's men could cross the river.

She followed in Dafydd's wake towards the southern end of the town. She hadn't wanted to call attention to herself, but he further confirmed her belief that he had a bit of the *sight* because he spied her anyway, with Christopher mounted behind her. He put his hand on his heart, and she nodded. That was all that needed to be said for now, until they could really be together.

In the last few minutes, Dafydd had been joined by Math, Callum, Edmund Mortimer, and Humphrey de Bohun. The latter three had been part of the cavalry charge. Humphrey was nursing a head wound, but that didn't stop him from reaching for William, who himself had an arm in a sling.

"Where's Balliol, Christopher?" Lili asked over her shoulder.

"Locked in the keep still, presumably."

Lili glanced towards the castle gate. Now that the battle was over and many arrows had been salvaged, Morgan's men lined the top of the curtain wall. They seemed to have taken it upon themselves to prevent anyone in the keep from getting away. As she watched, one of the archers launched an arrow at one of the towers.

"Who's that?" Christopher nudged her and indicated that she should face forward again. He pointed to a man who'd risen to his feet out of the cluster of prisoners just beyond the borders of the town. The man spread his arms wide and took several steps forward.

"That's Roger Mortimer," she said, and then put a hand out to hush Christopher since Roger was speaking.

"I demand to be heard! It is my right as a member of the House of Lords!"

Dafydd stopped twenty paces away and then dismounted. He indicated that the other men should stay back, and all obeyed except for Edmund, Roger's brother. Dafydd didn't protest, and they walked forward alone, stopping ten feet away from Roger, to the undoubted relief of everyone who cared about their safety.

"You forfeited that right, brother, when you rebelled against the king," Edmund said.

Lili and Christopher were still mounted, so she urged the horse along the outside edge of the crowd that was gathering, wanting to be able to see everyone's faces.

Roger clenched both hands into fists. "By my blood, then! I have a right to trial by combat! Fight me, and we will see upon which of us God smiles and gives the right to rule."

Dafydd's shoulders tensed, but before he could step forward, Edmund pulled his own sword from its sheath. "I will fight him, my king! He is my brother and my responsibility."

"No." The word resonated all the way to where Lili and Christopher waited.

Dafydd looked at Edmund, and the fierceness in his expression had even Lili shrinking back slightly. Gilbert de Clare had tried to provoke Dafydd in much the same way in the courtyard of Westminster Palace, so it was no surprise that Dafydd's response was the same—though with Christopher behind her, as far as she knew nobody was going to save Dafydd the trouble of a trial by killing Roger with a car.

"Sire?" Edmund licked his lips.

"Are the two of you fourteen and twelve again that he retains the ability to make you furious in a way only little brothers can do?" Dafydd shook his head. "There are enough fools on this field without you joining their ranks. You will not fight him. Enough men have died at his behest for two lifetimes."

Then Dafydd flicked out his fingers in Callum's direction. "Tie the traitor up and put him under guard. If he so much as looks sideways at you, feel free to shoot him."

"With pleasure, my king." Callum, as had Edmund, recognized a time for formality.

But Dafydd put out a hand before he could take a step away. "I hear you used the rocket launcher at Beeston."

Callum nodded.

"You have it with you?"

"Yes, my lord, now that Lord Mathonwy has arrived with the army. We also brought the C-4 and other explosives."

"Good. Balliol is surrendering immediately, or we are bringing down that keep with him in it."

40

4 April 1294

David

"Callum didn't actually need to shoot Roger Mortimer," Math said.

"Pity." David knew before Math turned to look at him that he would see questions in his eyes. "Are you asking where my mercy has gone?"

"No." Math barked a humorless laugh. "I'm marveling at how patient you've been up until now. How was Avalon?"

"Interesting." David attempted a grin, but his eyes were on Callum and Mark, who were setting C-4 charges around the base of Skipton's keep. "I'll tell you about it later."

Then, almost to his regret, a white flag appeared at the top of the keep, and a man David didn't recognize showed his face.

Thomas leaned in. "That's Hakkon of Norway, my lord. We can be grateful he speaks French, for my Norwegian is poor at best."

Now David genuinely smiled. "I will never regret being captured by your uncle."

"Nor I in setting you free."

Given the archers present in the bailey, it was remarkably brave of Hakkon to stand alone on the wall-walk, but he must have realized how dire things had become for him and decided to take the bull by the horns, so to speak. David could admire him for that, even as he cut him off at the knees.

Hakkon put up a hand. “I am the Duke of Norway.”

David lifted his chin so his voice would carry. Standing awkwardly in the bailey while Hakkon looked down at him from above reminded him of his interview with Owain Williams. David was at no disadvantage this time, however. His was the greater power no matter where he stood. “I am David, King of England, whose kingdom you invaded.”

Christopher was standing a little behind and to the right of David and had his binoculars to his eyes. “He looks disconcerted.”

“Good,” Math said. “He should be.”

“I demand free passage to the sea,” Hakkon said. “If you do not grant me this, my brother will come and free me by force.”

“You still don’t understand to whom you are speaking, do you?” James Stewart separated himself from the cluster of men around David. “You think you have something to bargain with, here? You do not. Your brother has already sent word that he never countenanced your invasion and for us to do with you as we please. It would save him the trouble.”

“He did, did he?” David said in an undertone. James was lying through his teeth, but it served David’s purposes for now, and he lifted his chin so his voice would carry. “Erik asked me to spare your life, if I could, so here's the deal: I am not accepting your surrender without Balliol's. Everybody in that keep is coming out without weapons and with their hands on top of their heads to surrender to me, or you will come out on a pallbearer's stretcher."

"What will happen to us if we surrender?" Hakkon asked.

Beside David, Math scoffed. "He's a child to ask that question."

"But he should know the truth." David raised his voice again. "If you surrender, then you, Roger Mortimer, and John Balliol will be carted to the Tower of London in a cage, to be mocked and abused by citizens along the way, as an example of what happens to traitors to the crown." He gestured to the charges being laid around the keep's base. "Alternatively, I will bring down the keep and send my regrets to your brother that I could not save you from your stupidity. You have one hour to think about it. If you cannot convince Balliol to surrender, then you have one hour to live."

He turned on his heel and stalked towards the outer gatehouse, where Lili was waiting with Ieuan. He hadn't even hugged her yet, which he remedied the moment he saw her.

"All of you must be utterly exhausted," he said to Ieuan, his arms still around Lili. "We should get some food while we wait—"

"They're coming out, sire!"

David turned to look, almost sorry Balliol was surrendering so soon. He'd had a long night too and had been looking forward to sharing a meal with his wife.

"Eat with Lili." Ieuan tipped his head to indicate the castellan's quarters, located in the gatehouse, which had been appropriated for royal use. "Let me handle this. Balliol was once a king, but now he is beneath your notice."

David licked his lips. "You know I don't like what I have to do to them."

Ieuan shrugged. "You're meting out humiliation, not death. And it must be clear to everyone that your authority cannot be challenged ever again."

* * * * *

The next morning, James Stewart and Robbie Bruce settled themselves at the table across from David. He'd just said goodbye to Lili, who was heading back to Chester with an escort. She had nearly ninety miles to travel, but knowing her, that would be two days of riding at most. She loved David, but her boys called to her.

"What now for Scotland?" James said.

David eyed him, feeling that this was Robbie's question more than James's. James had a wife and son in Ireland, which had become a second homeland to him. He saw himself as straddling the Irish Sea, an adviser to kings, but he wasn't asking to rule himself. It made him incredibly qualified for the job, but David actually had something else in mind.

"You do intend to take the throne, do you not?" Robbie said.

"How much would you resent me if I did?" David asked.

For a moment, Robbie looked taken aback. Then he relaxed, his elbows on the table. "I wouldn't. You deserve the crown."

"Would your grandfather agree?"

"If my father were still alive, it might be different, but my grandfather knows better than to fight you on this, and I am too young to claim the throne myself. Besides, your great-grandfather was King Alexander. How can he object to your claim knowing that? How can anyone?"

David gave a short laugh. "Then it will perhaps come as a relief to you to learn that I have no intention of becoming King of Scots."

Both James and Robbie blinked and then said in unison. "You don't?"

"No. My plans are bigger than that—and possibly an even harder sell."

Robbie narrowed his eyes. "Christopher has used that phrase before. Are you saying we won't like what you intend? What are you planning if not to take the throne?"

"Oh, I intend to take the throne, just not *that* one."

James sat back in his chair. "You mean to become High King of all Britain."

Callum pulled out a chair and sat. "He does."

"This dream of yours will never work." James shook his head. "All these diverse peoples will never be united."

"They are already united," David said.

James sniffed. "What do you mean?"

It was Callum who answered. "Who came at David's call? Do you realize how many different peoples are present in Skipton Castle right now in alliance with the king and each other? Englishmen, Welshmen, Scots, Irish, Danes, even a Frenchman ... all working together, united in one cause: to keep David on the throne." He turned to look at David. "I don't think we've given enough consideration to the future of Aquitaine, by the way."

David opened his mouth to reply, but Robbie, brow still furrowed, spoke first, "So if you do not become King of Scots, I repeat James's question. *What now for Scotland?*"

Callum laughed, and David was pleased to find him as excited about the future as he was. "You tried your hand at democracy four years ago and ended up with Balliol. He's proposing that you try again."

"You want us to vote for a new king?" Robbie's lip curled.

"Not a new king." David dampened down his enthusiasm and looked intently at the two Scotsmen. If he could make them understand, then others might too. "I want the people of Scotland to vote themselves a Parliament, which will then choose a Prime Minister, with a five year term." It was the British system, and David could see enough issues with the American one to accept giving it a try. "You'll need a constitution and probably a Bill of Rights too."

"You can't be serious." James laughed, apparently genuinely surprised and amused.

David fixed his eyes on his friend. "I am completely serious. And you'll be happy to know that this plan is not just for Scotland. I want the people of Ireland to vote too." He tipped his head. "And I'm really hoping that one of those prime ministers will be you."

"Democracy, my friend." Callum grinned at James's shocked look and buffeted him on the shoulder. "Welcome to Avalon."

The End

Acknowledgments

First and foremost, I'd like to thank my lovely readers for encouraging me to continue the *After Cilmeri* Series. I have always been passionate about these books, and it's wonderful to be able to share my stories with readers who love them too.

Thank you to my husband, without whose love and support I would never have tried to make a living as a writer. Thank to my family who has been nothing but encouraging of my writing, despite the fact that I spend half my life in medieval Wales. And thank you to my posse of readers: Lily, Anna, Jolie, Claudia, Melissa, Cassandra, Linda, Brynne, Carew. Gareth, Taran, Dan, Yvonne, Olivia, Mark, and Venkata. I couldn't do this without you.

About the Author

With two historian parents, Sarah couldn't help but develop an interest in the past. She went on to get more than enough education herself (in anthropology) and began writing fiction when the stories in her head overflowed and demanded she let them out. While her ancestry is Welsh, she only visited Wales for the first time while in college. She has been in love with the country, language, and people ever since. She even convinced her husband to give all four of their children Welsh names.

She makes her home in Oregon.

www.sarahwoodbury.com

Printed in Poland
by Amazon Fulfillment
Poland Sp. z o.o., Wrocław
22 November 2020

25710e78-c349-480f-aff3-77b76d45d28aR01